Crowns
of
Gold

Eileen,

Enjoy the adventure!

Abbot Granoff

Crowns
of
Gold

Abbot Lee Granoff, MD

Crowns of Gold

Copyright © 2019 by Abbot Granoff

Publishing History
First Edition, 2019
HARDCOVER ISBN: 978-1-7335073-0-1
PAPERBACK ISBN: 978-1-7335073-1-8
EBOOK ISBN: 978-1-7335073-2-5

Contact Information:
scythian1@cox.net
www.abbotgranoff.com

Published in the United States of America

CONTENTS

BOOK IV: THE TAKEDOWN 223

ACKNOWLEDGEMENTS

This book has been in the works for the past 4 years. Lots of research went into it for all the history it contains. There were people who helped me along the way without whom it would never have been written, let alone published.

I am ever grateful to Paul Evancoe, retired SEAL and author, who helped me from the beginning with the take over of Prax. I have never been in combat and didn't know its subtleties. Most of all he also helped me begin to hone my writing skills giving life to the characters and their surroundings.

All of the characters in the book are fictional and are from my imagination. However, I must thank Michael Teller and his staff at TK Asian Antiquities in Williamsburg, VA. I have known and dealt with him for over 30 years. He introduced me to Asian arts and recently the Scythians. He is loosely described in the book as Stephen Holder with his permission and has indeed perfected the nuclear physics to authenticate ancient gold.

Mike Kennedy, former Special Agent in Charge of the DEA in the Hampton Roads area educated me about illicit drugs, especially heroin and how it is smuggled, cut and distributed. Without his help, I would have been flying blind. Thanks.

Thanks to Missie Smith who lives in Nags Head and began my education about the area. She is loosely described as Missie, the waitress at Pirate's Cove Marina in Nags Head with her permission. I appreciate her introducing me to Marty Brill. His radio fishing show in Nags Head is an institution. His knowledge of the area and its history was an invaluable resource. He took the time to show me around the area and explain the complex interaction of its residents along with the fishing and boat building industry, along with smuggling. Marty you are one of the living treasures of the Outer Banks.

I also have to thank my friends David Gladstone and Bruce Forrest for reading through the first several drafts of the manuscript and gave me honest feedback which wasn't always pleasant to hear. Their brutal critiques were necessary to move me forward, making a better product.

Thanks to my German friends Peter and Margie Richter for their heroic edit. They had to muddle their way through the first draft to make valuable corrections.

I also have to give recognition and thanks to the James River Writers organization. Attending one of their seminars opened my eyes to how much I didn't know about writing and publishing. The information and freely offered help from their members brought me to the next level and gave me the direction and next steps to take to move forward.

Many times along the way, I thought my book was finished only to find out it was still considered a draft that needed more work. I needed an editor to help me to polish it up. After a long search I was lucky enough to find Laurie Chittenden living in New York by the way of Gloucester, VA who had just left the mainstream publishing and editing business after many years. Her experience at the big publishing houses gave her the experience, knowledge and compassion to help a new green author with the right amount of push and pull to refine my draft. Her sensitivity to my frustration during this process was a key to continue to move me forward without just giving up. The book now flows smoothly, the characters are more well-rounded. She went to William and Mary and even though she was well-schooled in the history of the area she had fun learning new facts about it.

Most of all I have to thank my wife, Ann, for tolerating the many hours watching me work on the book. Her solid support and love are a treasure I cherish.

PROLOGUE

Humanity is on the path of self-destruction. Greed has become the modern god. We are no longer a collective trying to live in harmony and balance with ourselves or our environment. Striving for individual power has outweighed the need to seek the best for humanity.

With the focus off our collective best interest, greed has seduced the few to speak for the many to the detriment of all.

The masses have always been lulled into believing that their leadership looks out for them. When they become abused beyond the point of tolerance they finally revolt.

BOOK I

GUN RUNNING

CHAPTER 1

A light chop added to the night chill coming off the water. Brad feathered back the throttles to slow the boat a bit. His twin 150hp Mercury engines purred like kittens. Fort Monroe, the largest stone fort built in America, was off their starboard side. Started in 1819 and not completed until 1834 a large moat circled the fortress. They continued to motor quietly through the water passing over the Hampton Roads Bridge Tunnel near where the battle of the Monitor and Merrimac took place during the Civil War. Brad turned to TJ, "I hope our prey shows up tonight. That take down would make a perfect ending to the trail we've been following."

TJ answered, "I don't like it when the bad guys have the same top of the line equipment we do. That break-in at the Naval Weapons Station Yorktown three weeks ago was a masterful job. Taking twenty 50 cal armor piercing sniper rifles with 1,000 rounds of ammo was as professional as it gets. Eight minutes in and out before anyone could react! No wonder ATF and the Navy had trouble trying to piece together how they did it. It was obviously an inside job." TJ's voice contained both anger and marvel. "I'm still amazed that all four were from Gloucester, just across the York River from the Weapons Station. It's clear the two in the Navy stationed at the Weapons Station were the masterminds and tapped their two old buddies who all grew up together. Quite a feat for small-town guys. By the way did you know that Gloucester was near Chief Powhatan's capital Werowocomoco at Purtan Bay just west of Gloucester and Gloucester was considered to be the first English capital in the Virginia Colony? That was turned down by England and Jamestown remained the capital.

Brad answered, "Interesting stuff. I admire Powhatan. He was one powerful chief with a long reach. His interaction with the first English colonists made him famous along with his daughter, Pocahontas."

Getting back to the current situation Brad went on, "Luckily ATF got word from their informants the guns were on the black market." He continued, praising TJ for posing as a Nigerian weapons buyer with ISIS. "They really believed you wanted to buy the rifles and ship them through Newport News Marine Terminal on the *Delara* to Lagos, Nigeria, then on to Niger, Chad and Sudan. We've already lost some good men in that area of the world. The ambush of the four Army Rangers in Niger was a tragedy. These specialized rifles would up the ante and we could lose a lot more."

TJ and Brad loved the action their new job gave them. It wasn't quite the same as the adrenalin rush being SEALs provided them before retirement, but they weren't as young as they once were. There was still enough of a rush and the job fit them well.

They were good at being players involved in illegal activities that required them to mingle in the murky world of drugs, prostitution, gambling and gun running and they enjoyed working for the various government agencies that called upon them. Having grown up in Hampton Roads, playing football on the same college team and later stationed together in Virginia Beach as SEALs they trusted each other with the strength this role required.

"I hope Ryan and his boys at ATF have everything set up on their end. I don't want to get in a firefight without backup. We'll be sitting ducks on the water." TJ replied, more than a little concerned looking across the water and considering the danger.

Brad wanted to reassure his partner and friend along with himself. "Ryan was a Marine for sixteen years. He saw action in Afghanistan and Iraq before he became the ATF liaison to the DEA. He knows what he's doing. He'll have our backs."

"Yeah, I know. I just want to make sure we didn't overlook anything." TJ felt more settled as they rounded the tip of the peninsula and entered the James River. He could feel his adrenalin begin to pump getting him ready for what was to come.

He wanted to distract himself, so he wouldn't peak too soon. As they motored past Hampton University he thought about its history with some pride.

Fort Monroe remained in Union hands during the Civil War. The South wanted the runaway slaves flocking to it returned as contraband policies dictated. General Benjamin Butler refused. The first class of African Americans was held near there in 1861. Today it is one of the top African American schools in the country.

Soon both men began to tense as they approached Newport News Marine Facility. Brad went past the facility and circled back after reaching Newport News Shipbuilding. He felt some degree of relief now that they were among the buildings where they built aircraft carriers and submarines. It gave them better cover to reconnoiter the area instead of the open water.

TJ poked him on the arm with his elbow. "There's the *Delara*. Check in with Ryan."

"Raptor 1 calling Raptor 2. Come in Raptor 2."

"Raptor 2 here. Go ahead." Ryan replied with a hint of excitement.

"We've passed the Marine Terminal and now we're heading back slowly. No sign of the pigeon yet. Are you in position?"

"Affirmative. We have two men amid ship on the port side of the *Delara* waiting for the pick-up. Three other teams are strategically placed around the docks with full view of the River. I'm in a Boston Whaler tucked in at the end of the adjacent wharf. Our drone is monitoring up and down the River. We have visual on you. We're awaiting your signal."

"Roger that, Raptor 2. They are either late or hiding along the waterfront."

Minutes seemed to pass slowly like watching a pot of water waiting for it to boil.

"Raptor 1 we have visual. They're in a 26-foot open Carolina Skiff coming out slowly from under the I-664 bridge and heading for you."

"Got'em. We'll wait here for their approach. We don't want to seem too anxious." Brad's tone was calm and focused, like a predator ready to pounce on its prey.

"TJ you're up."

As the craft approached, TJ flashed his light twice. He immediately got a return signal and the boat pulled alongside.

"Nice night to do business." TJ said nonchalantly.

"Sure is. Do you have the cash?" The leader was quick to get to the point.

"Of course, we do but we need to verify that the goods are as described." TJ didn't want to move too fast. He wanted to be sure they had the guns.

"Right." Two men in the boat opened each box with the rifles and shined a light inside. They then opened the four ammo boxes and did the same. "Now show me the money."

Brad opened the suitcase stuffed with stacks of banded one hundred-dollar bills, but in reality, there were only hundreds on the top and bottom. The rest of the stack consisted of ones.

TJ directed, "Pull alongside the *Delara* so our men can hoist up the goods. Once aboard we'll give you the money."

"No funny business. My men have itchy trigger fingers. If you try to leave without the money transfer it will be your last act."

"Understood." TJ replied flatly.

The men on the *Delara* lowered a net several times to hoist up the guns and ammo. Once aboard Brad threw the suitcase with the money into the waiting boat. This distracted the men long enough for he and TJ to turn tail and run. They didn't want to blow their cover if any of the gun runners survived.

That was the signal for Ryan and his team to close in. "POLICE! Drop your weapons. You're surrounded." The leader lifted his gun to fire but before he could get a round off Ryan's team took him out. The other three were stunned and dropped their weapons.

BOOK II

GETTING THE CROWNS
AND
MEETING THE SCYTHIANS

CHAPTER 1

Arthur Alain tolerated having to travel but he was never as comfortable as when he was at home. He had spared no expense building the home he considered a fortress.

The house looked like a castle on a hill. The walls were 5 feet thick surrounded by a 20-foot-wide 10-foot-deep moat which held lotus, water lily and koi. There were parapets along the roof and protected turrets manned by guards with machine guns, sniper rifles, and RPGs. Phalanx Gatling guns were strategically placed in sunken housings around the roof line. These, along with short range surface to air missiles, would automatically raise and fire with impeccable precision, should the need arise. The highest point of the roof held what appeared to be an astronomical observatory but was actually a radar dome. Various satellite dishes were scattered around the grounds and on the roof. The large glass windows were bullet proof.

Arthur had carefully selected Loudoun County, Virginia as the location for his home, since his family already obtained 1,000 acres there during reconstruction.. He liked the county's long history and it's convenience to Washington, DC. Established in 1757 and named after John Campbell, 4th Earl of Loudoun and governor of Virginia 1756-59, it was nicknamed the "breadbasket of the revolution" after supplying grain to George Washington's Continental Army during the Revolutionary War.

Arthur sat at the head of the table in his drawing room. His presence was imposing, 6'2 and 220 pounds. His steel blue eyes complimented his light brown hair that with time had become peppered with gray. His friend and long-time antique dealer sat opposite him. Stephen Holder brought with him two wooden boxes covered with red silk. His company logo on top. He knew Arthur would be interested in what they contained. He'd been anticipating Arthur's reaction the entire ride over and was now pushing them slowly toward Arthur in an attempt to build suspense. He stopped the boxes inches from Arthur's hands.

Arthur carefully watched as Stephen pushed the boxes toward him. In all the time they'd known each other Arthur had never seen Stephen seem so serious. As Arthur opened the boxes it was as if sunlight blasted into the otherwise darkened room.

The contents were exquisite. A soft aromatic incense floated up from them and filled the room as if to take over.

Arthur couldn't believe what was inside and his eyes opened wide in amazement. He was mesmerized by the blinding light emanating from the two gold crowns sitting before him. They were beyond his wildest imagination. *The legend is true!* Not accustomed to being off-balance his breath became shallow and short.

"Where did you get these, Stephen?" Arthur's normally deep commanding voice was soft with astonishment and he hoped Stephen couldn't detect the slight tremble it contained. He still had to negotiate a price for the crowns and he didn't want to give his excitement away.

"I've been trying to get them for 20 years." Stephen's tone belied his feeling of triumph. "They were found in a tomb in western China in 1904 during an excavation. This find was their crowning achievement, no pun intended," he chuckled. "After the Communists took control of China in 1949, the wealthy family who funded the excavation moved to the Philippines. They took the crowns and other objects from the tomb with them, but now the family is selling them off gradually in order to support themselves."

"I have worked with the family exclusively for 40 years and they trust me to be discreet about their identity." His voice was firm and proud.

Stephen Holder had been in the Asian antique business in

Williamsburg, Virginia for 40 years. Five-foot-seven and medium build, he always dressed impeccably. This made his presence appear larger than it was. His highly tailored deep blue silk suit with its dark red pin stripes concealed a light blue pima cotton shirt. His signature French cuffs peeked out of the sleeves. Dark black hair and thick eyebrows with a touch of silver in both added to his aristocratic flair. His deep set brown eyes always contained a flash of humor softening his otherwise serious look.

Stephen hailed from a family of diplomats, bankers and Admirals who had been stationed in Asia since the early part of the 20th century. His grandfather had been the US diplomat to China during the Boxer Rebellion. And later his father became the diplomatic envoy to Hong Kong and subsequently US ambassador to China before WWII.

Schooled at Oxford and in Switzerland, Stephen ran in the finest circles. His love of Asian art and history along with his families' connections dropped the Asian antique businesses into his lap when he was a teen. Over time he'd become known as THE expert able to identify real versus fake Asian antiques.

Not an easy skill to attain since the Chinese had become adept at creating forgeries throughout the centuries from porcelain to jade to bronze. Stephen had been able to set himself apart because of this and because the big auction houses didn't care if the lots they sold were fake or not. They had a list of caveats in their auction catalogs to prevent them from being sued.

Stephen opened his antique business in Williamsburg, not only because of its proximity to William and Mary established in 1693 as the second oldest college in America, but also because restored Williamsburg was a jewel of American history as the former Colonial Capital of Virginia starting in 1699 to its becoming the first Capital of Virginia as a state in 1776.

"Are you sure these are genuine?" Arthur questioned.

"Along with the help of several nuclear physicists I have developed scientific techniques to determine the age of antiques, especially ancient gold. Museum curators aren't interested in learning about this. They have little scientific training and don't want anymore. They don't want to take the time to study or make the effort to learn new material. The techniques are expensive to do and some of the objects in their museums might turn out to be fakes. The curators don't want to be embarrassed by their oversights and lack of competence."

Stephen finished by saying, "These crowns are genuine." He added, "These are the only Scythian crowns with garnets known to be in existence. My experts have confirmed they are circa 200 BCE to 200 CE."

Arthur was dazed and couldn't tear his eyes away from the crowns. He remembered the legend passed down to him as a child.

His father had told him that he came from a long line of Scythian royalty. Thinking back to his father's stories, *"Our family descended from the first Scythian leader, Theocraxis, who had gold crowns made for himself and his son. They wore these into battle to show their power and wealth. The original crowns were later lost during the battle with Rome in 168 CE, but duplicates were made immediately. Theirs were the only gold crowns with garnets in their design and they were the most highly treasured Scythian crowns ever produced. Passed down through the generations, they were ultimately lost toward the end of the Scythian Empire somewhere in western China, but the legend said the crowns would one day be found and returned to their rightful heirs who would rebuild the Scythian Empire and take over the world."*

All who are of Scythian descent will be waiting for the crowns to reappear and again be forged into the world's most lethal fighting force. Arthur could not believe the crowns were sitting in front of him now.

Stephen continued his scholarly dissertation unaware of Arthur's far off look. "The Scythian's ancestors were the first to domesticate the horse about 5,000 years ago. With the horse they developed the first and foremost cavalry battle tactics, allowing them to conquer and rule this vast land mass."

"Ruthless as warriors their reputation of fierceness in battle was well known. The Greek historian Herodotus described the Scythian warrior's custom of drinking the blood of the first man he kills. The heads of all slain were brought before them so they could use their scalps as handkerchiefs or as a decoration on their horse's bridle or fashioned into cloaks. Skin from the conquered's hands were made into quivers. Skull caps were sometimes adorned with gold and used as wine cups.

Exceptional warriors sometimes had two cups and drank from them at the same time."

Arthur suddenly realized Stephen was talking, but he'd been so lost in his own thoughts he'd not heard a word.

"The Greek historian Herodotus wrote of Scythian's obtaining mare's milk from their udder by placing a hollow bone into a mare's vagina and blowing so the udder could be easily reached. They then fermented the milk."

Stephen's odd mention of mares brought Arthur back to the present.

Arthur interrupted, "I've had the pleasure of tasting it from my steppe horses I raise here. Actually, it is very tasty and possesses a powerful kick, just like the mare the milk comes from."

Stephen smiled broadly. "I've never had the pleasure of drinking fermented mare's milk, but I've heard it's potent." Stephen chuckled.

Arthur wanted to take a break to regain his composure. He got up and pulled a braided golden rope hanging on wall. The door opened almost instantly, and a pretty young maid dressed in a short black skirt and matching shirt and white apron entered "Yes Sir, what can I get you?"

Arthur looked at Stephen with a questioning expression. He turned away and then said without waiting for an answer, "Make us a cheese plate with charcuterie and bring a bottle of 1996 Pichon Lalande."

He was still weak-kneed from seeing the crowns, but with the order he felt in control again. He realized he'd been abrupt, but he didn't consider the tone of his request rude. He was privileged, and the crowns reminded him of that fact. He returned to his seat still considering what their reappearance meant.

Stephen recognized the distraction on Arthur's face and paused. He knew the crowns were very special and unique, but Arthur had bought other unique antiquities from him before. Why was he reacting like this? Why did these crowns have such a deep impact on him? He wondered and waited for the food and drink to arrive before going on.

After a few minutes, there was a soft knock on the door and it opened slowly. Leysa, whose name in Scythian meant defender of men, brought the wine and cheese into the room on a sterling silver tray. She, like all the women and men in the compound, was from Eastern Ukraine. She put a place setting in front of each of the two men then placed the cheese and charcuterie plate between them. She then proceeded to open the wine with a loud pop as the cork was removed. With a small white linen towel on her left arm she expertly poured a three-ounce serving to each with a twist of the bottle at the end to prevent dripping.

She looked at Arthur and asked, "Is there anything else I can get for you?" Her gentle accent and soft voice made her words dance.

"No, thank you Leysa this will be fine," Arthur replied in a firm voice dismissing her. Stephan had been meeting with Arthur at his home for years. He always liked any interaction with Leysa. She was pleasing to the eye and her demeanor exuded a clear sense of self-assurance adding to her sexuality and allure.

Stephen swirled the dark red liquid in his glass. He lifted it and looking at it admired its ruby red color. He put his nose inside the opening and gently inhaled to savor the wine's bouquet. "Ah, you always serve superb wine at the aged pinnacle of its life." He sipped and swished the wine around in his mouth, lifted his head, closed his eyes and inhaled through his mouth and exhaled through his nose. "Perfect."

Stephen watched as Arthur swirled his glass just as Stephen had done to admire the wine. After they each sat enjoying the savory liquid for a moment he noticed his patron relax a little.

Stephen nodded toward the crowns and continued.

"You may not know this, but the Scythians became very wealthy because they controlled the trade routes from China and the East to the ancient kingdoms of Egypt, Babylon, Persia, Assyria, Greece and Rome that became known as the Silk Road. It was a perilous route. The land trade routes to the South through multiple kingdoms and empires were treacherous but a smooth flow of goods from east to west and back through the northern grasslands and deserts was assured by the Scythians."

"They particularly coveted gold because of its rarity and properties yearning for Persian and Greek motifs."

"They employed Greek artisans to make the gold objects they used to display their wealth in this life and the next. They loved the horse, lion, stag, deer, eagle and especially the gryphon. But the gold crown was given the highest honor. Only kings who showed the utmost bravery in conquest and leadership could wear them. These would only be worn on special occasions at times when a show of power and prestige was important. Sometimes just riding up to the gate of a town wearing the gold crown would cause the town to capitulate and ask for mercy. If they did not take the crown to their grave they would pass them down to their sons."

Arthur interrupted Stephen to add. "I'm sure you're aware that warrior graves containing women dressed in full battle gear were found in the lower Volga and Don Rivers in Southern Russia and Eastern Kazakhstan. The kings might also pass them down to their daughters."

Stephen answered with some surprise. "I wasn't aware of that, but it makes sense. The discovery of these female warriors gave credence to the Greek tales of Amazons."

Arthur went on, pride in his voice. "Scythian women rode along with their husbands during campaigns. About one-third of the warriors were women. They wore the same battle dress as the men and were as fierce. Women who stayed behind during lengthy campaigns had to protect their villages."

"Scythian children both boys and girls were given the same training. They learned to ride, shoot the bow, throw the spear and were trained to be proficient in hand to hand combat. In fact, they competed with others regardless of sex."

Stephen wondered where Arthur had come up with those tidbits of information. After a brief pause, he went back to detailing his general knowledge. "Herodotus described them as having no right breast because it had been cauterized at birth, so the Amazon warrior could shoot a bow without hindrance. No Scythian woman was allowed to marry until she killed a man in battle."

Having had enough exchange of history, Arthur asked in a controlled, low voice hoping Stephen wouldn't hear any quiver. "How much do you want for them?"

As discussion turned from history to negotiation a palpable tension filled the space between them.

Stephen's tone became more serious as he looked directly into Arthur's eyes. "Five million."

Arthur thought and then met Stephen's eyes causing Stephen to look away first.

Feeling more confident, Arthur began bargaining. He didn't want to seem too anxious, even though new beads of sweat began forming on his forehead. "Five million is a very high price for the pair."

Stephen, knowing he could get a much higher price interrupted Arthur and said evenly, "Arthur we both know five million is a bargain. They are the only two Scythian gold crowns with garnets in existence. We also both know that garnets, while not very valuable today, were very valuable to the ancients. Any red stone was called a ruby."

Arthur knew the crowns were valuable as Stephen pointed out, but while Stephen knew the history one would learn from books, he wasn't aware of their entire history or what they really represented. The price really was a bargain, but he kept this thought to himself.

"I have other wealthy clients from Russia, China and the Middle East who would pay a great deal more for them. However, I know you're a student of Scythian and Eurasian history and will appreciate them more than the others. I'm showing them to you first, before they go on the auction block to be bought by the highest bidder." Stephen added.

He used this threat as a bargaining chip even though he didn't like to auction his antiquities. He preferred the personal connection and knew his clients would reward him with future business.

"You always know my weak spots." Arthur admitted. "And bring unique objects for my collection." He was about ready to burst out of his seat. He could try to bargain down an extra ½-1 million dollars, but this was of no consequence and they both knew five million was a fair price. "Because of their uniqueness and know you could get more for them, I will buy them for the asking price." His voice was slow and controlled hoping it hid any emotion. He didn't want to give Stephen too much satisfaction by agreeing to the quoted price and set a precedent for future transactions. Arthur was done with the bargaining and wanted to get on with taking possession of the crowns.

Pulling out a smaller silk pouch Stephen smiled knowingly. "I'll also throw in this famous gold Scythian box lid seal." Stephen pointed to the design, a lion pouncing on a running stag and continued, "This symbol depicts the power of the Scythians conquering anyone who would get in their way. It is another impeccable object of renowned Scythian design from the same time period."

Arthur could have been more forceful and controlled the situation better as his usual style, but the reemergence of the crowns and the validity of the legend had taken him off guard. He liked the seal. It was a nice addition to the deal. He knew just the place for it.

"You are too kind, thank you." Even though he'd agreed to Stephen's price he was filled with a sense of triumph. The crowns were his and his cheeks flushed with excitement.

After Stephen left, Arthur remained in his drawing room with the crowns and he thought about the rest of the stories his father and grandfather told him as a child.

CHAPTER 2

The horseman approached the gates of the city at a fast gallop. "Open the gates! I have news for the King!"

The gates swung open with the creak of time. Not slowing down, he rode up to castle center and jumped off his horse screaming, "Where's the King?"

He entered the ground floor to the King's throne room, ran up the three flights of stairs entering it out of breath. Alfronex, the King of the walled city of Prax was already on his throne surrounded by his advisers all having been alerted by the horseman's calls.

Alfronex recognized him as one of his emissaries to the east, "Why are you so terrified? What news do you bring?"

Trying to catch his breath he answered, "The Warning Legend is true. *Beware the Thunder from the East.* I have seen it and it is coming our way."

Stunned, Alfronex tried to calm the situation. "Slow down, compose yourself and explain what you mean."

After a few moments that seemed to stretch on for hours, he finally spoke in a trembling voice. "The Scythians are on a rampage. They started farther north and east and are heading west toward us. They are destroying all the towns and villages in their path. The few who have escaped describe it as a blood bath."

"The Scythians are seasoned horseman. They ride as one. The thunder of their horse's hooves proceeds them by a day before their arrival."

The small but expanding dust cloud on the eastern horizon would turn the new day into night, changing the morning sun into the moon. An ominous crescendo of hooves grew ever louder as the approaching tempest threatened.

Alfronex the King of the city of Prax slowly climbed the eastern wall to view the ever-expanding cloud of dust from the approaching horses. His aging body strained in the sweltering heat with each step. By the time he reached the guard tower, sweat poured from his furrowed brow. Shading his tired eyes to gain focus, he looked as if he was saluting the coming attack. By squinting tightly to get a better look, he could almost see the mass of heavily armed horsemen coming his way. As he felt the earth rumble his body began to tremble.

Alfronex, normally a brave man, became terrified. The approaching Scythian's were known to rip whole towns apart, killing all of the inhabitants in their wake. He shuddered to think what would happen to the city and his people. He stood frozen by the horrific sight unable to move.

He thought about his daughter Adantha. His first two wives had not been able to conceive, and his third wife died giving birth to her. He adored his calm, sweet daughter and shook his head rapidly trying to clear his mind of what might happen to her. There was no time to allow himself to worry about her now. The Scythians were approaching rapidly, and it was the first time he was glad he had no male heirs to witness the end of their family line.

He pulled his gaze from the sight to gain some composure. Once calmed he ordered his page to prepare his most trusted advisors for his arrival in the throne room. He was desperate to form a plan of defense and do it quickly. Time was running out. Sullen and still deep in thought he rapidly descended the stairs making his way through the labyrinthine halls that had always provided protection.

As he hurried to his throne room his royal blue silk cape fluttered exposing his white ruffled silk shirt and loose-fitting cream-colored pants. Atop his head sat a cone shaped hat made of embroidered royal blue silk. Around the hat was a gold crown that stood out regally. The tips of his boots pointed backwards, and a deep purple pear-shaped amethyst dangled from the points. The gems flashed brilliant red highlights.

Two lions on their hind legs facing each other were embroidered on his royal crest. They held another deep purple amethyst with the same red highlights. A heavy gold link chain held the crest firmly in place around his neck despite his rush.

The rare and desirable amethyst between the lion's paws had come all the way from Siberia and the blue silk of the crest had been dyed using an ancient formula as blue did not naturally exist outside of lapis lazuli from Afghanistan. The imposing royal crest was designed to honor a long and powerful history, but the Scythian's would have no respect for any of these things and they would not be intimidated.

CHAPTER 3

THE WAR ROOM

Alfronex's father and grandfather expanded the borders of their kingdom in all directions gaining great wealth which they shrewdly shared with their subjects. In return they were considered firm but fair leaders and engendered loyalty. Alfronex followed the example of his forefathers and this resulted in a reign of relative peace and prosperity. Great battles were still fought to ward off neighboring kingdoms, but further conquest was unnecessary. As he approached the throne room he thought of the reputation Prax had as a strong kingdom far and wide, but he realized this might not be enough to save it this time.

The throne room was adorned with the quiet opulence of Alfronex's dynasty. He looked around, as though he was seeing it for the first time. His advisors were already assembled, and they milled around mumbling to each other waiting for their King to begin.

An ominous glow from four large marble and bronze cauldrons heightened the already apprehensive mood in the octagonal room.

War trophies from better times adorned the walls. Shields, lances, swords, bows and arrows from prior conquests were ceremoniously placed each in their own niches. A variety of stone and wooden sculptures inlaid with gold, silver and the green patina of aged copper were scattered throughout the room. A large male lion skin lay on the floor facing east in front of his throne.

Of all directions the East held the highest position of power. The sun was their most powerful deity. It rose in the east bringing light, warmth and the power to grow the crops they depended on.

In a vain attempt to diffuse the overwhelming tension incense had been lighted and now the fragrant smell of sandalwood perfumed the air. A hot breeze slithered through the room like a viper ready to strike when the time was right.

Alfronex walked slowly and deliberately stopping on the lion's back to face the darkening sky in the east. His four chief advisors immediately stopped their milling and assembled around him.

All knew the warning passed down through the generations to maintain an army and cavalry. Skirmishes would be fought with little consequence. *But beware the Thunder from the East.*

CHAPTER 4

THE PLAN

Alfronex tried to muster confidence from his deepest recesses, but his voice did not sound as bold as his words. "The walls of our city are substantial. They are solid and sturdy. Our army is strong. We have a cavalry of 1,500 and 1,000 armed archers and swordsman. We have prevailed in past skirmishes. In spite of our formidable defenses and history, I fear the worst. Could this be the Thunder from the East we have been warned about?"

General of the army, Craladon, bowed his head slightly acknowledging his King's authority. He answered first with confidence in his deep voice. Craladon came from a long line of military elite. His father and grandfather had been generals for Prax. Their leadership, tactics and skill with weapons was legendary. Craladon followed his family tradition and was just as skilled, proving himself in battle. His tall muscular frame exuded strength while impressively clad in his finest battle armor. A deep purple silk cape hanging from his shoulders, sword by his side, made him look intimidating.

The sword he wore was passed down to him from his father who received it from his father. It was made of Damascus steel, the hardest known metal of its time and that made him feel unconquerable. He wore his 37 years well despite the experience of many campaigns.

"Our men are well-trained and disciplined. They hunger for a day such as today. We will maintain our position and bring you victory my King." Pursing his lips and lifting his chin slightly while looking down his nose as he finished, gave him an aura of invincibility.

Always the more cautious and fearful of his future, Senephrax whined in rapid speech, "We can't lose."

Senephrax, the youngest of the King's advisors looked somewhat silly in his long red coat, gold buttons flashing, gold sash around his waist. His high-pitched voice grated on the ears. No one liked him, but as the son of the most influential family in the city they had to tolerate his appointment. He went on trying to be strong. "Our walls, our army are second to none. We are protecting a defensive position, so we have the advantage. Their offensive state puts them at grave disadvantage and weakens them. Perhaps they aren't aware of our strength?"

He was out of breath as he finished his desperate plea.

Gradepon had seen better years. His health was failing from years of battle wounds that never healed right. He fought not only for Alfronex but also for his father. Having served two kings of the dynasty, he was the most experienced of the Council members. He slowly straightened his bent frame with some difficulty. The humility in his voice resonated from the memories, images and emotions of age.

"I have spoken to survivors of the Scythian blight. They tremble and become tearful when speaking of that horrible time. Fear shows on their faces. It appears no matter how big or well-trained the garrisons, the Scythians use sheer force and trickery to overwhelm their foe. The cities and towns are burnt to the ground. Most of the people are killed or taken for slaves."

His clothes never seemed to fit properly on his frail body. He nevertheless tried to look stately as he went on.

"The Scythians will only leave a few elders alive to make sure they tell others what it means to be conquered by Scythians. Exhausted he concluded and bent over again.

Lost in thought Bladacote stared down at the granite floor as the others spoke. He looked regal in his simple black robe. His silver hair shimmering in the light made it luminous. The leather and silver headband held a large gray moonstone which looked like a third eye matching the color of his other two. He was a mystic from a family of mystics. Respected for his predictions which usually came true and his healing powers, he was revered by all.

The most trusted and wisest of the King's advisors, he was always last to speak when in council. Slowly scanning the other advisors, locking eyes to cement their attention, he acknowledged the King with a slight nod.

Clearing his throat with a gravely attention-getting grumble and in a slow deep penetrating voice he offered, "This truly is a difficult day. There are no good options open to us. We fight and win but lose significant property and men. We fight and lose and everything and everyone is destroyed."

He paused for effect and turned his head as he looked out of the corner of his eyes. "Perhaps we can come to some sort of compromise and salvage as much as we can."

As if scripted, all turned toward Alfronex, awaiting a decision. He remained silent while stroking his long white beard, deep in thought. As he began pacing the floor, he argued with himself silently. *Capitulation is not an option! We may be the victors in battle and save part of our culture. Destruction will be great. However, buildings can be repaired. We can give incentives to our people to rapidly procreate replenishing our population.*

We don't know if the Scythians will negotiate a settlement sparing both sides the pain, anguish and destruction.

Alfronex stopped pacing and stood again on the lion's back squarely facing his advisors. He straightened his frame and with a solemn look, he announced his decision. "We don't have all the facts yet. We will attempt to negotiate a compromise, but we will be prepared for their onslaught and fight should they attack."

"General Craladon," he ordered, "place your archers around the walls in strategic positions. Pair the boys of the town too young to fight with an archer. They are to bring them any supplies needed and notify our healers of the wounded."

The General nodded in acknowledgement as the King continued barking orders in rapid fire.

"The women will coordinate the flow of food, water and weapons."

"Split the main body of swordsmen between our main gate and rear gate. Station the remainder toward the middle of the city as reserves to go either way as needed. They are to be ready should a breach in the walls occur. They are to replace the archers as they fall."

"Prepare our horsemen for battle. They are to remain with their horses in the stables awaiting my call. We will not fire the first shot, but we will be prepared for whatever comes."

CHAPTER 5

THE ARRIVAL OF FEAR

The thunder became deafening. Dust choked the air. The smell of sweat from man and beast was sickening. As the Scythians approached, the walls began to tremble. You could taste the dust seeping from the walls. The smell of fear permeated the city. All talking was confined to whispers. Women and children cowered in the shadows. The King and his Court stood on the highest parapet to watch the approach.

Two men riding in front of the broad column of Scythians approached. The older was a large man with a broad, black mustache. His muscular left arm held the reigns tightly, clearly showing control of his horse. His right arm of similar dimension held a gleaming silver sword which was partially hidden by a round shield of leather reinforced by bronze buttons and bands. The younger had a dark warlock braided with leather. This tuft of hair emanating from the top of his head fell to the left side of his otherwise shaved head.

They both wore loose cloth pants. Mid-calf suede leather boots, toe pointing up and back were worn on their feet. Their short-sleeved tunics fell to the upper thigh, one side pulled over the front of the chest.

Alfronex was surprised to see them both wearing gold crowns.

What arrogance, wearing gold crowns into battle is the height of foolishness. Every one of my soldiers would be attracted to them like bees to honey and make them easy targets. Although this may be the arrogance of confidence. He shuddered at the thought.

The crowns of gold sparkled in the sun like beacons as the dust cloud settled. The larger one had tiny four-petal flowers among leaves intertwined with buds, coiled vines and berries of garnet. The leaves on this crown were of Eastern species as seen in China. The smaller crown also with garnets was adorned with leaves of mixed Western and Eastern species. Wreathes of laurel, myrtle, oak and olive as used by the Greeks. These crowns looked similar in construction, but the leaves were different.

Gold was coveted by all from the ancient world, especially the Scythians. They had gold objects made for them as belt buckles, necklaces, earrings, pendants, hair pins, clasps, vessels, horse adornments, plaques and anything they could think of. The most important objects made were Crowns of Gold. These were only worn by Scythian Royalty. Since Scythians were made up of loosely connected bands of nomads, the leaders of each group wore gold crowns. They were used to intimidate those who they battled, for ceremonial purposes, for any occasion where a show of power and strength was required or taken to the grave with them. The only two allowed to be made with rubies (ancient garnets) were worn by the Royal Scythian leaders who connected all of the tribes together. They were unique. The larger of the two had flora from their Eastern origins. The smaller had flora from the Western extent of their territory. The two together cemented the power of the entire Scythian Empire, from east to west. If worn into any of the tribes or beyond, their power garnered the respect of all who saw them. The men who wore them were revered as gods.

Alfronex found himself deep in thought. *Could the Scythian influence run from the Zhou Dynasty to Greece? Could they be a new breed of warrior that has already conquered part or all of the lands east to the sea?*

He had already underestimated his new foe. He became even more concerned at that realization.

The two were accompanied by what appeared to be 750 cavalry. Their King and presumably his son attacking with only 750 men was foolhardy. He saw a beacon of hope and slowly released his breath in a sigh of relief.

As he looked closer he saw scalps hanging from their bridles. Their quivers looked like they were made of the skin from hands. As the bile rose in his throat it had a bitter taste.

He had never witnessed such a show of confidence, power and brutality.

We are not that vulnerable. His thoughts were conflicted as he assessed the situation. Confusion set in while trying to understand the discrepancy. He stood tall trying not to show his doubt and terror to his adversaries or his advisors.

Among the bowed horsemen were large ferocious looking dogs with spiked collars.

His voice was shaky as he spoke to his advisors. "We know they use tricks. 750 men on horseback cannot make so much dust and noise but that is all I see."

He again considered the rumors of their reputation of defeating and destroying all who were in their way. This spectacle confronting him remained both frightening and confusing. There weren't enough men to defeat him, but confrontation was at hand. He didn't want to put his men, resources and city to the test but clearly had no choice. Hopefully he could negotiate a solution.

Just then the two men wearing the crowns approached the walls. The elder's voice was deep, guttural and booming. "I am Theocraxis, King of the Royal Scythians. This is my son Thondurax. You have been raiding and demanding payment from our caravans as they pass through your territory. We will not tolerate this insult. We demand unconditional surrender, or we will destroy all who live within your walls and burn your city to the ground. We will give you until the sun rises tomorrow to make your decision."

They immediately turned and rode back in the direction from which they came. Their column parted in the middle allowing the two gold crowned leaders to pass through. The column closed ranks behind them and followed toward the East.

After this one-sided interaction Alfronex was shaken even more. He had no opportunity to negotiate as he'd counted on. Yet he was hopeful these horsemen could not defeat him. Visibly concerned, beads of sweat formed on his brow and he felt lightheaded. He would again go into council with his advisors to discuss the alternatives, hoping one would come up with a viable solution.

CHAPTER 6

B ack in the throne room the thick air smelled stale. The council, unnerved by the recent events, again discussed the options as Alfronex stood in his place on the lion's back.

General Craladon was first to speak with more bravado than reason. "We are stronger and more in number than their cavalry. We live in a walled city. They will be no match for my soldiers. We have the advantage."

Senephrax was again whining. His high-pitched voice even more grating than usual. "No matter their reputation we have no choice. Capitulation puts us at their mercy. Fighting is too dangerous. We must try to negotiate a better arrangement, so we have some control." He saw that as his only salvation.

With a softer, more trembling voice without much conviction, Gradepon offered his advice. "We must fight. The odds are in our favor."

After hesitating, Bladacote offered his final recommendation, while only looking at the ground. "We can again try to negotiate a settlement before they attack. If they refuse, we have no choice but to defend ourselves. We have the advantage to both negotiate and fight."

Alfronex considered what his advisors recommended. He again paced the room evaluating the options. He returned to the lion's back, faced his advisors and concluded with the finality of a strong leader. "The Scythians only have 750 cavalry with bows to our 1,500. We also have another 1,000 swordsmen and archers. The city walls are high and strong. We have plenty of supplies for a lengthy siege. They do not appear to have reserves. Even if they do, they cannot be more in number than they have shown us."

"No matter the warnings from our past, if we capitulate they will take what they want and murder whomever they choose. There is no guarantee of mercy. They may have a fierce reputation. The sight of their army is intimidating. But we have faced other foes in the past and prevailed. I will attempt to negotiate but fight if we must."

CHAPTER 7

DOOM

The next morning as the sun rose on a bright, cloudless day, the Scythians again approached the walls. This time the King and his son were not wearing their crowns. They were ready for battle.

Theocraxis and Thondurax rode forward toward the main gate. Their cavalry fanned out around the entire wall.

Theocraxis, his right hand held high as his cavalry lit their arrows. His loud threatening voice broke the silence. "Alfronex, what is your decision?"

Alfronex looked defiant. "We will not surrender but we will negotiate terms allowing your caravans to pass through our territory without taxation. We did not know they were under your protection."

Theocraxis was not deterred. "Our only terms are complete surrender or total destruction. If you surrender, we will not kill all who live within your walls and we will not burn your city. You will become part of our Empire and pay taxes in gold, wheat and cattle as we command. You will become vassals to our Kingdom and become one of our many cities and towns. If you fight all will die and your city will be destroyed."

Alfronex looked to his advisors and his bowmen on the ramparts, then faced Theocraxis. "We cannot accept your terms. We are a free people and will remain that way. We are powerful and will destroy you if you do not negotiate a resolution to this conflict."

Theocraxis brought his right arm down sharply as his cavalry raised their bows with flaming arrows and fired their first volley as they turned to fall back.

The archers on the walls were too stunned to react quickly. By the time they launched their first volley the enemy was beyond reach.

Fires broke out in the city. All who were not killed or wounded in that first round tried to put them out.

Alfronex gave orders to General Craladon. "Send 1,000 of your horsemen out of the city gate and pursue them. This will be a battle in our favor."

He was excited at the prospect. "We may have a chance after all."

Little did he know that the Scythian tactics were to split their column in two as the cities' horsemen rode after them. When they were far enough from the city to prevent return to the safety of the walls, the Scythian columns circled around to flank them. The horsemen had no idea they were riding into the face of another 1,500 Scythian cavalry. The flanks closed in back and to the sides, preventing the horsemen from escaping. The battle dogs were unleashed. This caused confusion and panic. They were not able to mount a coordinated counter attack. Those who were not killed in the volley of arrows or by the dogs, turned to retreat back to the city, not having dispatched a single arrow. Of the 1,000 horsemen who left the city only 180 returned, General Craladon among them. The Scythians did not lose a single man.

Craladon reported the rout to Alfronex. "The first 750 were a tease to lure out our horsemen whom they could easily defeat with their cunning trick. Another 1,500 were waiting for us."

"We only have 680 horsemen, 700 archers and swordsmen left."

The city was in flames as the full Scythian force surrounded the walls. They fired volley after volley of flaming arrows into the city always retreating quickly, leaving the city to burn.

The Scythians made camp well out of range of the city archers. Any horsemen that emerged from the city were quickly dispatched. All the Scythians had to do was to send different groups of cavalry from different sides to shoot flaming arrows into the city. The Prax archers did not know where or when they would attack. They became easily exhausted, trying to shoot the fleeing enemy and fight the fires.

Alfronex didn't know the Scythians rotated their cavalry so any who attacked were well-rested. He also didn't know that their support troops included women, some of whom also rode with the men. The rest made camp, tended to the wounded and cooked the meals. The camps had tents for lodging surrounding a central fire pit. Each camp was at a reasonable distance from the other. There were enough to surround the city.

Theocraxis ordered his Lieutenants to lay siege to the city and wait for the city's supplies to dwindle.

Although the city had food and water the constant rain of fire took its toll on both commodities.

All within the walls could hear the drumming and music. The archers could see the camp fires and people dancing around them. It was as though the Scythians were having a party while the city's inhabitants were wasting away.

By the 93rd day, a single horseman with the banner of the two lions was sent out by the King to ask for terms of surrender.

Theocraxis and Thondurax received him. In a clear and confident guttural voice Theocraxis gave his reply. "Tell your King to have his men place all of their weapons: bows, arrows, swords, lances and knives 100 yards in front of the main gate on this highest hill. The King and all his advisors are to give themselves up in front of the weapon's pile. Have what's left of your soldiers line up against the outside of the city walls. Since you are wise to surrender before you are spent, I will show mercy."

CHAPTER 8

RUIN

The lone horseman brought this news back to Alfronex, who, with an ashen face looked to his advisors for their council. There was no incense now. The air was filled with the lingering smoke from the smoldering ruins. The viper had struck a savage blow and was poised to bring home his final thunderbolt.

Badly wounded Craladon had pain in his voice. "My men, the women and children are exhausted fighting the Scythians and the fires. We can only muster 100 horsemen who would be easily slaughtered should they try and face our foe on their battle turf. What's left of my archers and swordsmen can continue to fight from the walls. They have had little success trying to kill the Scythians who show up silently at night. They attack from different directions then retreat out of range. The flaming arrows hit our supplies which are now down to almost nothing. We can't leave the city and use swords against a cavalry. The Scythians don't seem to fear death. They know they are in control of the battle."

Senephrax had a cautious whine in his voice. "We can try to sneak out the back gate and hope to avoid detection."

Gradepon spoke next, frustration oozed from every pore. "We can fight to the last man but that would gain nothing."

Bladacote as always was last to speak. His usual thoughtful manner came through although fear enveloped him. "Should we fight we have no chance to prevail and will lose everything. Escape can perhaps save a few. Surrender might save more."

Alfronex could only produce an exhausted whisper. "We will try to get as many out of the city as possible with a cavalry and soldier escort to fan out in different directions. Some might have a chance to avoid capture. The rest of us will have no choice but to agree to their terms. Let us hope the Scythians do show mercy." He didn't expect much but tried to fool himself into thinking positively.

During the night the gates were quickly opened at varying intervals to let out small groups. It didn't take long to hear the screams of the unfortunate.

The next day Alfronex ordered the main gate opened. As the pile of weapons grew, Alfronex and his advisors moved to the front of the pile on the mound that overlooked the battle area. The last of his ragged wounded soldiers lined up against the city walls as ordered.

Theocraxis and Thondurax again wearing the Crowns of Gold with the rubies slowly rode their horses up to Alfronex and his advisors, their cavalry close behind.

With a quick action, a small group of cavalry surrounded the King and his advisors. The rest rode toward the city gate. As they approached they split into two columns facing the soldiers. As if as one they drew their swords killing them all.

"Alfronex, you and your advisors will witness the complete destruction of your city before we kill you. Your scalp will look good on my horse's bridle. My warriors will place the scalps of the warriors they killed in battle on their bridles. The skin of their hands will be made into quivers. The skull cap of their first kill will adorn their table as a wine cup. Your skull cap will be adorned with gold and I will drink wine from it to remind me of this great victory. Because you capitulated before your complete destruction, I will grant some of your farmers and artisans the chance to join the Scythian Empire. They will remember the power of the Scythians and this mercy shown by our leaders."

Alfronex and his advisers were made to watch as the Scythian cavalry routed the remaining people from the city. They added the captured escapees and separated out the chosen ones. The others were fed alive to the dogs.

They herded the young girls into a corral. Alfronex glanced over to them thinking about his young daughter among the women. Theocraxis offered them to his soldiers. "Choose the ones you want to keep as slaves.

Divide the rest among you to rape and torture to death at your pleasure." He heard a cry of approval rapidly build from his men.

Alfronex looked over to the frightened girls in the corral seeing his daughter in the middle. He shook his head and lowered it trying not to think of her fate.

Dirty and bedraggled, the King's advisors were made to kneel before him. In a loud triumphant voice, he instructed Thondurax what to do next as second in command. "I give you the honor of dispatching these four advisors in front of all. Let the remaining inhabitants see what we do to those leaders who oppose us."

Thondurax giddy and almost drooling responded for all to hear in the same deep guttural voice trying to emulate his father. "I will first cut off your hands after I have them skinned to be made into my new battle coat. I will then take the skin off your backs to be made into a blanket for my bed. Your scalped heads will be placed on spikes in front of this weapons cache to show our power. I will take your skull caps, keeping the best one for myself and award the other three to our bravest lieutenants of this battle. Your scalps will hang from my horse's bridle."

They found the King's daughter hiding amongst the young girls and brought her to Theocraxis.

He gave orders without hesitation. "Cut the clothes from her body and show her nakedness to our troops. Hold her arms and spread her legs while I take my pleasure with her. Thondurax will do the same."

Alfronex was now made to watch as his daughter was first raped by Theocraxis followed by Thondurax. She was then disemboweled and skinned alive as her father watched in horror.

The Scythian army was then let loose on the city taking whatever they wanted. When finished, they burned the city to the ground.

When the holocaust ended, Theocraxis cut the head off Alfronex with one slash of his sword.

CHAPTER 9

Arthur continued thinking of his father's telling of the family legend. "The Scythians rose to power between 800 BCE to 168 CE. They were supplanted by the Sarmatians, who were indeed western Scythians by heritage and just as fierce. The Sarmatians' military armor consisted of overlapping leather scales resembling lizard skin. Feared as dragons, their battle banner became a dragon. This later became the basis of the mythology of dragon slaying knights in the Middle Ages."

"The Scythians were defeated in the West by Roman Emperor Marcus Aurealus in 168 CE. The harsh terms of surrender included a contribution of 8,000 cavalry to the Roman army of which 5,500 were moved to Britain. A portion included the Alan tribe and their Royal Scythian leader. This fierce tribe was located in the western mid-central limits of the Scythian/Sarmatian Empire. Today this encompasses Eastern Ukraine, Southern Poland and Romania."

"These transplants were to protect the uppermost limits of Roman control, Hadrian's Wall. Their families were left behind to prevent them from revolting. The last 2,500 were used as mercenaries by the Romans and remained in Europe."

"Hadrian's Wall ran from coast to coast in northern England for 73 miles from Wallsend on the River Tyre in the East to Bowness on the Solvay Firth in the West. Originally planned to be 12 Roman feet high and

20 Roman feet wide, it was built 8 Roman feet high and 10 Roman feet wide. A tower was built every third mile, a small fort every mile and larger fort every 7 miles. Battles from the Wall were not encouraged. Instead fighting on open ground was preferred."

"The cavalry who were moved to Britain married local Celt women and raised their sons to follow in their footsteps. This way their sons could become Roman citizens while covertly adhering to their Scythian heritage."

"During the late 5th Century CE a war leader arose. Arthur, who was of Scythian/Sarmatian decent from the Alan Tribal leadership, was successful in many battles against the Saxons at Hadrian's Wall. Victory over the Saxons at the Battle of Badon was his pinnacle. He became the legendary King Arthur."

Before he finished going over his family history Arthur took a break. He poured himself a glass of Graham's 1975 vintage port and trimmed a Feral Flying Pig cigar and lit it. He then relaxed back in his soft throne-like chair.

He reminisced about the words his father and grandfather said. "Arthur, you are a direct descendent of King Arthur and Scythian Royalty. We trace our family genealogy back to him. For 1,000 years we ruled northern Britain battling the Vikings, Normans and French."

"Our first ancestor and Royal heir to arrive in the New World came over during the 'great wave of emancipation' from 1607-1624. We count ourselves as one of the FFVs, First Families of Virginia. Our family history continued into colonial times in the Americas."

"In 1603 King James I ascended to the throne after the death of Queen Elizabeth I."

"England, although the victor by destroying the Spanish Armada, was depleted of natural resources after their many years of war with Spain. The King granted a proprietary charter to two competing branches of the Virginia Company which were supported by investors."

"The London Company was allowed to establish colonies between the 34th to the 41st parallel (Cape Fear, North Carolina to Long Island Sound)."

"They left England on December 20, 1606, on the *Susan Constant*,

Godspeed and *Discovery* and landed 144 days later on the shores of current day Virginia Beach. They named it Cape Henry after the King's eldest son Henry Fredrick, Prince of Wales."

Having grown up in Richmond Arthur knew the rest of the Colonial history not only from his father and grandfather but also from school.

Arthur liked to think back to his youth when his family history was told. "They sailed into the Chesapeake Bay and into Hampton Roads, one of the world's largest natural harbors. This area is now surrounded by the cities of Virginia Beach, Norfolk, Portsmouth, Chesapeake, Suffolk, Hampton and Newport News."

"The colonists looked for a defensible deep-water location. They settled on an island in the river they named the James after the King and established the first permanent English settlement in the New World in 1607, Jamestown."

"There was difficulty in maintaining viability of this colony until in 1610 the fleet led by Thomas West, the third Baron De Le Warr, later known as Lord Delaware arrived with new colonists and fresh supplies."

"John Rolfe was among them. He had a new strain of sweeter tobacco seeds. These thrived in the colony and became the cash crop for export allowing the colony to survive and become permanent. New plantations blossomed up and down the James River and other tributaries, furthering Virginia to become a wealthy colony."

"John Rolfe married Chief Powhatan's daughter Pocahontas, cementing a lasting peace between the Powhatan Confederacy and the colony."

Arthur was told that, "King's Granted land was given to the colonists and investors as an incentive to migrate."

He was also told, "In 1624 the King revoked the Virginia Charter and made it a Crown Colony abolishing private ownership. It remained such until the American Revolution in 1776."

His father always became angry at this point. "He fumed that the King could take away what he had already given." Arthur shared his father's anger. He always said to himself, "I'll never let that happen again."

Arthur had a long family history of entitlement through power and cunning, which made him feel invincible. His family's wealth and power came from tobacco, sugar and slaves. The great trading triangle started in Europe and brought textiles, rum and manufactured goods to West

Africa. Local African coastal tribes captured enemies and inland people and held them in slave factories for transport to the New World colonies. The American colonies shipped tobacco, cotton and corn back to Europe. The Caribbean colonies shipped rum and sugar to both the American colonies and to Europe. This started in the 17th century and lasted until the middle of the 19th century. More than 12 million people faced that awful fate. Once enslaved they became property. Any offspring produced also became slaves.

"When slavery was abolished 1861 and with the defeat of the South in the Civil War our family's power and wealth were devastated. Fortunately, the family had the foresight to invest in both sides. Their northern munitions factories and businesses specializing in the production of food and uniforms kept the family coffers afloat when the southern ones were lost."

"Scythian carpetbaggers helped keep our family near the head of the line during reconstruction. The northern holdings were gradually sold off in order to help solidify the tobacco empire. Wars would come and go but an addicting drug like tobacco, especially with all the modern addictive enhancing additives, would remain forever. Or so the family thought."

Arthur continued to mull the fact that the tobacco industry began falling on hard times during the latter half of the 20th century. This was on his watch. The suit against big tobacco stripped it of power and economic clout. The fine alone was a blow. Advertising was outlawed. Gradually feeling the loss of that power and prestige, Arthur vowed to take back what was rightfully his.

He now fumed. *The inability to advertise, the Surgeon General's warning on every pack of cigarettes and the increasing tax on tobacco is catastrophic.*

His mind boiled. *I am having trouble maintaining our position and status under current conditions. Our family has always evolved with the times. I will continue that evolution.*

With this in mind he decided to build his Castle Fortress on the land his family obtained during reconstruction and expand its size. If he was going into the illegal drug trade, he would need a place of safety. He wasn't sure yet how he was going to make that addition work, but he wanted to be prepared. If he couldn't do it, at least his sons would have a head start.

CHAPTER 10

Arthur had two sons. As with every third generation in his family he and his sons or daughters were named after the leaders in the Scythian origin stories. They were all brought up with Scythian training, Scythian history and the legend of the Scythian future. His children would carry out his orders to rebuild a new Scythian empire as the legend predicted.

Although each had a Scythian name, they were also given names appropriate to the country they lived in. This would help them to assimilate but retain their heritage.

His oldest son was named Arpoxais, after the eldest son in Scythian mythology, who was to take up feeding and supplying the troops. His English name was Richard, after the Knight of the Round Table, Richard the Lionhearted. Arthur's eldest son died at birth.

His youngest son was named Lipoxais, after the next in line in Scythian mythology, who was to be the warrior. His English name was Lance after Sir Lancelot, another Knight of the Round Table.

Arthur was given his English name by his parents. To keep the legend alive. They also gave him his Scythian name, Colaxais, after the Scythian mythological leader of royal decent. In every third generation in England and America the firstborn son was named Arthur after King Arthur. There was always a Colaxais/Arthur ready to bring the Scythians back to power when the time was right.

Although Scythians could marry outside their heritage, they were encouraged to stay within the family. There were some who left the fold as expected over time, but a large number remained true. A spouse who wasn't Scythian by birth had to adhere to the Scythian way awaiting the Scythian resurrection.

Arthur's wife died in an auto accident when Lance was young, hit by a drunk driver. She was a true Scythian who could out ride, out shoot and out fight most men. He never remarried and still mourns her passing.

CHAPTER 11

A rthur ran his hand over the medallion which adorned the black lacquer box containing another Scythian treasure. Admiring the medallion's design, a lion sinking his teeth in the neck of a stag, he gently placed the box between the two larger red silk boxes containing the crowns. They were all positioned at one end of the exquisite wooden Ming table in the middle of his drawing room. The table was inlaid with lacquer, ivory, silver and gold. The deep red carpet and long flowing drapes of Royal Blue gave the room an aristocratic warmth. Portraits of his forefathers interspersed with English and Colonial landscape paintings lined the walls. He wanted the room to envelop and caress his family when they gathered there, but he also wanted the atmosphere to give off a regal power to the outsiders he might invite in. He placed the wine bottle and corkscrew to one side.

After setting up his drawing room just the way he wanted it, he called for his son Lance to join him. As Lance entered the room Arthur pointed to the chair adjacent his and with an outstretched right hand he motioned for Lance to sit.

Lance had no idea what his father was up to. He had never seen him act like this before. His father seemed somehow taller and he had a haughty air about him.

Arthur looked at Lance and with an arrogant voice said, "The tobacco industry, while still lucrative, no longer provides the power and prestige it once did. We need to rebuild our place in the world like our ancestors did." He spoke with venom in his voice and his youngest son was intrigued by what his father was saying.

"I have decided we are adding heroin to our Gold Crowns Tobacco Company." Arthur paused to let Lance absorb what he'd just announced before continuing. "The 'War on Drugs' is focused on marijuana, methamphetamines, cocaine, crack and prescription pain pills. They are beginning to focus on heroin in the same way, but it still provides an opportunity to make lots of money." Arthur explained, his eyebrows furrowed in concentration. This was something he'd been considering for a while.

Lance's eyes opened wide. His eyebrows raised as his jaw dropped. Arthur continued, "Heroin remained in the background until the 90s. Before then it was used mainly by Asians, musicians and poor blacks. You had to go to specific locations in small, inner-city communities to get it. It is now becoming a more widely used drug fanning out into the more affluent suburbs. It is more compact to transport and can easily be cut by up to 60%, increasing its final street value."

"We'll buy it through my Chinese friend Wu Jan who lives in Hong Kong. He'll get it from the Golden Triangle where Myanmar, Laos and Thailand meet. He'll export it to the US and once it's here we'll distribute it."

His tone became more serious as he looked Lance in the eye. "There is a fortune to be made. Let the Colombian and Mexican cartels take the heat while we slip under the radar and win the grand prize. Heroin is once again the up-and-coming drug of choice. What's the difference if we change our business focus from one addictive drug to another? And once we build the import and distribution system we'll begin to take over the drug cartels."

He noticed his son silently nodding his head in agreement, a look of awe in his eyes. Just as his father had told him the legend of the Scythians, he'd told his sons, so Lance was well aware of their family history. Arthur had been careful to prepare his sons.

A small smile formed on the corners of Arthur's mouth. "I'm putting you in charge of transportation and distribution. You'll need your cunning warrior skills to fulfill this role. I'll deal with procurement. We'll use our Scythian brothers in politics, banking, real estate, military, transportation, accounting and other unforeseen areas of business to round out our Empire. This will secure our families' finances and power, so we can bring a return of the Scythians for generations to come."

Arthur paused to let his words sink in while he scanned Lance's face for any sign of doubt or hesitation.

Lance questioned his father, "We know we're Scythians but how are we going to connect with the rest of the Scythians around the world to pull this off?"

Arthur's eyes burned into Lance's, knowing he would ask that question, then smiled as he reached for the two red silk boxes and opened them.

Lance nearly fell off his chair at the sight of the gold crowns before him.

Arthur slowly and reverently picked up the larger of the two crowns and placed it on his own head. With Lance still in shock he picked up the other gold crown and with almost as much reverence placed it on Lance's head.

Lance got a lump in his throat, but managed to choke out the words, "These couldn't be the crowns of Scythian legend?"

Arthur smiled at his son as he nodded his head affirmatively.

"How did you get them? Where did they come from?" Lance was still thunderstruck, looking at his father in disbelief.

As the realization of what he was seeing sank in, a smile began to creek up the corners of his mouth. "The legend is true."

"I got them from Stephen Holder. He got them from a wealthy Chinese client. Neither knew what these really were or they wouldn't have let them go for such a small price." Arthur smiled. "Stephen authenticated the crowns as ancient Scythian from around 2000 years ago. With them we will finally be able to organize our Scythian brothers and soon we will be the most formidable fighting force in the world once again."

Then Arthur caressed the black lacquer box with reverence. "This has been handed down in our family for over 1800 years. Inside is the artifact that was used by each patriarch who led the Royal Scythians in their conquests. It came with us to England and later here."

"You remember how I told you that even after Rome relocated our warrior men to Britain we were still a great power. No Roman army in Britain could defeat us, but we kept our treaty with Rome because we had to leave our families behind."

Looking at the box Arthur anxiously moved it around a little with the exciting anticipation of sharing its contents with Lance. He continued, "During the downfall of the Roman Empire, our family emerged in Britain as King Arthur and the Knights of the Round Table. The dragon was our battle symbol." He looked at Lance. "Many consider this myth, but we know differently. The legend followed us to the Virginia Colony and when we saw an opportunity to conquer new territories in the New World, we didn't hesitate. After arriving we became powerful enough to have a major influence in the administration of the Virginia Colony."

Arthur's tone changed to one of annoyance. "Later our family became complacent and started losing influence, first with the abolishment of slavery during the Civil War and culminating in the financial catastrophe of the tobacco suit."

Arthur taking on the persona of Colaxais squared his shoulders and looked firmly at his son Lipoxais, "We only use our Scythian names when we're together. Otherwise we use our English names Arthur and Lance."

"With these crowns we have the opportunity to gain back our power." His eyes moved slowly back and forth to his son's eyes to drive home the point.

Lance understood, the corners of his mouth rose slightly in an approving smile, conquest in his eyes.

Arthur slowly picked up the black lacquer box with the gold Scythian Seal of a lion killing a stag on top and placed it in front of himself. "This Scythian symbol proclaims our power over all who become our subordinates." As Arthur ceremoniously opened the box his eyes sparkled with excitement knowing what was to come. Lance looked on with anticipation. The inside of the box was lined with a beautiful royal blue silk. As he picked up the gilded skull cup lying on a carved wooden stand inside, he placed it on the table. The soft thud seemed to expand, filling the room with power.

"Just as my father did for me, I brought you up on our family's legend. Even though we inherited Castle Arthur in Northumberland, England; Alain Castle in Lucerne, Switzerland; Altai Stables and its 1000 acres in Loudoun County and our Gold Crowns Tobacco Company from Colonial times, I'm sure you had doubts about the whole story. After all many generations of Arthurs have come and gone and nothing happened."

"We now have irrefutable proof the legend is real. We are the beginning of the new Scythian Empire. It's a tragedy that your mother and brother aren't here to take part in this historic moment. I'm sure she would be proud of you."

Arthur picked up the bottle of 1986 Chateau Mouton Rothschild sitting next to him. It made the usual pop as he opened it. Slowly pouring the silky, dark red liquid into the skull cup, he beamed with pride. The room seemed to expand with anticipation of what was to come.

He again looked at his son with pride then picked up the skull cup and toasted.

"With this ancient symbol of our ancestors, we will again rule the world." He took a large swallow and handed it to Lance. Lance tipped the cup toward his father in acknowledgment and took a large gulp as well.

BOOK III

THE SETUP

CHAPTER 1

Arthur continued to share what he knew about heroin production with Lance as they rode the elevator to the penthouse. There was a sense of excitement and concern in the air as the eight-foot cube made its way up to the top of the building.

"The Golden Triangle, the mountains where Laos, Myanmar and Thailand overlap, is the second largest opium producing area in the world after Afghanistan." Arthur's voice was unyielding as he looked directly into Lance's eyes.

"Opium is brought by donkey and horse caravan to the Myanmar-Thai Border where it is refined into heroin. Thai and Burmese Chinese control these operations and use couriers to transport it to the United States via Hawaii and California. Chinese Muslim Panthay and Chinese Chin Haw, both descendants of Chinese Hur Muslims from Yunnan province in China, work closely with non-Muslim Jun Haw and Panthay making up the Triad secret societies."

"The production of opium from Afghanistan was reduced dramatically with the decrease of Taliban influence after the Russians left. The Taliban actually just lowered the amount they grew to bolster their image. In reality heroin funded them. They opened the flood gates once the US came in. Their heroin usually shows up through the southern 'Balkan Route' through Turkey. Here it splits going to Russia and Europe from where it then goes to England and the US."

"Golden Triangle heroin comes to the US via Hawaii and western US ports. It is brought in by mules or containers on both airplanes and ships or through various package shippers.

"Our heroin from the Golden Triangle will be transported to Hong Kong to be repackaged into 25 kilo blocks with an added homing beacon."

"We are going to mix fentanyl from China at the repackaging site to our heroin making it more potent. It has quick onset but short duration. Fentanyl gives less euphoria but causes sedation and at much higher levels causes respiratory depression which can make it very dangerous. It's 50-100 times more potent than heroin. There are at least 12 types of fentanyl. One is 10,000 times more potent. Evan a tiny amount of that can be lethal. Most reported heroin overdoses are actually fentanyl overdoses. We are going to use the least potent variety. We don't want to kill our customers."

Lance was intrigued. "Where did fentanyl come from?"

Arthur answered having researched the chemical before deciding to use it. "It is a synthetic opioid found by Paul Janssen in 1959. He created Janssen Pharmaceutical because of it which was later bought by Johnson and Johnson. It is a better pain reliever that heroin. It can be taken orally, smoked, snorted or injected and can be absorbed through the skin. Once in the body it is hard to stop its action. Some of it comes from Mexico but most comes from China. Some of the street names it goes by include China White, China Girl, TNT, Murder 8, Apache and Dance Fever."

"The Russian Spetsnaz used it as a gas to quickly subdue people during the 2002 Moscow theater hostage crises. 150 people died."

When the elevator reached the top floor, they got out facing an ornately carved door. As they rang the bell the door opened framing a beautiful, petite, Asian woman with shoulder-length straight black hair and golden eyes. The contrast between her hair and eyes was striking. She wore a loose low-cut blouse the same color as her eyes that revealed the outline of her bare breasts. Tight black pants and black shoes with six inch stiletto heels finished off her stunning look. Leading them to the plush living room, she motioned for them to sit on the couch facing the floor-to-ceiling windows. Her perfume lingered, leaving her essence in the air as she glided effortlessly around the room.

A glass tabletop seemed to float between two marble upright sides and on top sat a bottle of 30-year-old Middleton Barry Crockett Irish whiskey with two glasses. As though mesmerized by a siren's song, they couldn't take their eyes off the Asian woman's silky movements as she poured each of them a glass. It was the best show in the room. Lance followed his father's lead as he picked up his glass and took a sip.

It was a beautiful night overlooking Hong Kong Harbor and the city from atop the building. The new modern waterfront buildings in Kowloon were ablaze with the lights of night. On the wall behind them was a priceless collection of antique Chinese porcelain, jade and bronze. The atmosphere in the room was meant to lull them into a dangerous lack of focus.

Arthur had discussed negotiating tactics with Lance before their meeting with Wu. Pretending to catch himself, Arthur blinked and shook his head as if to come out of the supposed trance. He wanted Wu to think he was taken off-guard by the room. He turned to Lance. "Remember Wu Jan is our connection to the heroin supply. I have long known him through our mutual love of Chinese antiques. His collection has no rival."

Lance sat attentively still also pretending to be affected by the mood in the room.

"Wu Jan is charming and shrewd but can be quite dangerous when provoked." Arthur knew full well that his friend was listening to their conversation and watching. He warned Lance this would be the case before they arrived. "We are going to flatter the old buzzard to butter him up to get the best deal out of him." Arthur said.

Lance shook his shoulders in a fake shudder to make it seem like he'd been dreaming. He fired back with a feigned look of concern. "I'm not sure I'm up to the task, father. Wu Jan is surely steps ahead of me. I don't want to disappoint you."

"You'll be fine my son. I trust your judgment." Arthur was reassuring, as a brief smile flickered across his face. *And, I trust your training and pedigree,* he thought.

"We'll make the best agreement we can. After all, it's a no-lose partnership. He'll get the heroin to the ship and arrange transport. We'll provide the pickup and distribution. We all win."

Theirs was a well-choreographed first step.

"G-e-n-t-l-e-m-e-n." The stretched-out word rolled out of the door to their left.

Wu entered the room jovial, smiling and clearly in an upbeat mood. "Welcome to my meager home. I hope you've enjoyed looking at my modest collection of porcelain shards and rocks while sipping on the only bottle of Irish whiskey I had left in my cellar."

His insincere humility brought on a wave of disgust in both Arthur and Lance, but they tamped this down so as not to tip their hands.

Wu was of medium height and a bit rotund from all the excesses he indulged himself in. Always with a smile on his face, he cajoled his opponents into lowering their guard. Behind that smile was a jackal as ruthless as they come. He had no qualms about stealing, blackmailing, kidnaping, torturing or killing to further his interests.

Wearing a magnificent Emperor's silk robe from the Ming Dynasty that oozed stately extravagance and power, Wu stood just inside the room. He was accompanied by two startling Chinese beauties dressed in silk evening gowns. One gown was red and the other blue with side slits that ran from the hem to hip.

The woman in red was wearing a beautiful ruby and diamond necklace and matching bracelet, the other woman wore a sapphire and diamond necklace and matching bracelet. The contrast of the dresses and jewels against their silky pastel yellow skin and dark flowing hair would stop any man in his tracks, taking his breath away.

The smile on Wu Jan's face widened as his guests devoured his "gifts" with lustful eyes.

"I have taken the liberty of bringing companions along for you. Arthur, since you are the oldest you get to choose first."

Arthur looked at the women thoughtfully. "Wu, you make doing business such a pleasure." He always had his pick of the ladies. Those who were reluctant were delivered one way or another. He took his time making his choice wanting to stretch out the decision.

Nodding to the woman in red, she moved effortlessly to his side. While the woman in blue floated to Lance's side.

"So we all feel alike, I thought I would round off our party." Wu

him, but he was intrigued, "How will you take care of the problems I may encounter?" He tilted and lowered his head. His eyes narrowed slightly.

Arthur rose as he took over the conversation. He pulled his shoulders back and puffed out his chest. He looked like a king addressing his underling.

"My son and I are Scythians. Direct descendants of Colaxais and King Arthur, we come from a long line of Scythians who ruled the Asian Steppe from the Western Chinese frontiers to the Balkans and Europe to Britain. I have in my possession proof of my heritage, two gold Scythian crowns with garnets. Anyone of Scythian heritage who sees these crowns will know who I am and the power I hold. You either join me or are destroyed."

Wu knew who the Scythians were. His ancestors spoke of them as barbarian nomads who were ruthless in warfare, but also honest and fair in their treaties. It was because of the Scythians and their Mongolian ancestors that the first Emperor of China, Qin Shi Huang, built the Great Wall. He was also the one who built the terra-cotta warrior army to protect his tomb.

"How do I know that what you say is true? Show me proof." Wu was adamant.

Arthur pulled out a picture of himself and Lance wearing the two gold crowns. "The crowns you see in the picture are only worn by Scythian Royalty. They're the only two with garnets known to exist. They've come to me through destiny. These crowns will bring back Scythian pride and the Scythian nation shall rise up and rule the world!" Arthur's persona as Colaxais was triumphant. His voice lingered in the room.

Wu Jan slumped in his chair defeated. He knew what he heard was true. Scythian descendants lived in countries all over the world now. If they could be brought together through the leadership of Arthur, they could indeed rule the world.

He had no choice but to agree to their terms. Even if this mad man's dream did not come to fruition, he could still make a nice profit going along with the plan.

"Agreed. May our partnership be long and fruitful." Wu lifted his wine glass filled with the vintage port in a toast.

CHAPTER 2

Arthur did not like traveling but the trip to Hong Kong had been necessary. He always felt comfortable and safe returning to his fortress. Being rural and made up of rolling hills and small mountains, it was also the perfect location for riding and Arthur kept a large stable. With the jet lag from his trip gone Arthur decided it was a perfect day to take out the horses.

"Father," Lance began while sitting atop a beautiful gray-blue stallion. He wanted to show his father how much he respected him and express how grateful he was that he believed in him, "I'm honored that you've entrusted me with the pick-up and distribution of the merchandise. I won't let you down."

"I know, my son." Arthur replied. He was proud of the way Lance bested Wu and it showed in his eyes. "I've groomed you to handle the job. I know you'll do whatever necessary to remove competition and make sure this is a smooth operation." Arthur turned his attention back to his horse. "Now let's see what these thoroughbreds can do," he added kicking his heels into the sides of his jet-black stallion. The horse reared up and took off without hesitation.

The crisp autumn air, filled with the woody fragrance of a forest getting ready to sleep, complimented the cloudless blue sky. A gentle wind blew, and Lance followed closely behind his father.

Arthur called back to Lance. His voice powerful enough to carry over the pounding hooves, "The stallions are certainly a refinement of the steppe horses our ancestors rode."

Lance shouted back, "They're faster for the short haul and more elegant."

Arthur loved his steppe horses but also appreciated the sophistication of his thoroughbreds, "They'd never make good cavalry horses, too high-strung. Try to shoot a bow off one and you'd miss your mark every time. For sword play they'd run the other way instead of charge into battle with a taste for it. For the sheer pleasure of running with the wind and floating on air, there is nothing like them."

Loudoun County had a thriving equestrian industry and Arthur raised thoroughbreds to race the Maryland-Virginia racing circuit. He used to break them in at Colonial Down racetrack twenty-five miles south of Richmond. This track closed down in 2016. He also raced at Laural Park in Laural, Maryland and Pimlico Race Course in Baltimore before deciding which horse had what it took to move up to the big league. The horses that didn't make the grade were butchered for his table or specialty markets. He would also keep a few prime cuts for the Scythian hunting dogs he bred. While he loved the beautiful creatures, he had no tolerance for weakness.

After returning from the ride Arthur and Lance settled on the raised back patio. The cobblestones on the floor matched the stones of the Castle, only much smaller.

Arthur wiped his brow as Leysa, a petite brunette attendant dressed in an above-the-knee black uniform with a white lace apron poured fresh-squeezed lemonade. "OK Lance, give me your rundown on how things work starting from the pick-up."

Like his father Lance was fascinated by history and as he researched the best route for the heroin he discovered a number of interesting things about the region. In fact, he learned they wouldn't be the first to run illegal goods into the area. He knew his father would be interested in this parallel as well, so he decided to begin with the history. "Before I looked into it, I had no idea Hampton Roads and the Outer Banks had a long history of pirates and smuggling."

Arthur settled into his lounge chair eager to listen to his son as Lance pulled his chair closer.

"It starts with a man named Peter Painter, an early pirate from Portsmouth Town, North Carolina, who plied his trade along the Atlantic Coast to the Caribbean. He would often go to Port Royal, Jamaica, a neutral meeting place for pirates of the time."

"Captain Henry Morgan, another famous privateer, was named governor of Jamaica by King Charles II in 1675. He was not a pirate and sailed under the English flag. Fighting against the Spanish gave him legitimacy. He raided and sacked the Spanish at Panama City and made away with millions in gold and silver."

Arthur smiled as he closed his eyes imagining in his mind's eye the story his son was telling him.

"Port Royal, Jamaica became a pirates' haven under his governorship. Morgan's leadership was fair and consistent."

"Oh, as an aside since you love your wine, Father, I know you'll love this bit of trivia. Morgan's flag ship *Satisfaction* was found in 2012 and contained the oldest known bottle of Heidsieck Champagne."

"That would be great for my collection," Arthur mused nodding his head. "I wonder who owns it?"

Shrugging his shoulders, Lance went on. "After Morgan's death, 'Red Legs' Graves took his place and was as ruthless at governing as he was at pirating."

"Painter came to Port Royal not knowing a change in leadership had taken place. He was slapped into chains and imprisoned for not paying his 'port tax,' which he did."

"His crew sold their booty to get him out of prison. As he sailed out of Port Royal, he swore a pirate's oath to the devil and all the spirits of the sea to avenge his treatment."

"At that moment a great earthquake and a tidal wave destroyed and swallowed Port Royal beneath the waves forever."

"To this day the coastal people refer to this as the 'pirate's revenge.'"

Arthur listened intently, surprised by Lance's depth of knowledge. He very much enjoyed the history his son was telling him.

"It's OK to be ruthless but to maintain control you must also be fair," Arthur instructed his son. "That's why our Scythian ancestors were so successful."

Lance thought about that for a minute before returning to his story about the Outer Banks.

"You've heard about Blackbeard, the most famous of the Outer Banks' pirates. He came on the scene after Painter. He was born in Bristol, England, and sailed the biggest and best of the forty-gunned captured French slave trader, La Concorde. He renamed it the 'Queen Anne's Revenge' in honor of the English Monarch whom he sailed for from 1702 to 1717. After that he sailed for himself developing his fearsome reputation. He lived on Ocracoke Island, just south of Cape Hatteras."

Lance took a sip of his lemonade, "North Carolina was a lawless colony at that time. The merchants there petitioned the colony of Virginia for help. Governor Spottswood of Virginia sent Lt. Robert Maynard to capture Blackbeard 'dead or alive.'" Lance paused to create a little suspense before continuing. "Well, Maynard killed him in battle in 1718 on Ocracoke Island, sailing back to Virginia with Blackbeard's head dangling from the bow sprint. They never found Blackbeard's treasure though and even today people from the Outer Banks to Hampton Roads look for his lost gold."

Arthur cut in, "Yes, an acquaintance of mine who lives in Virginia Beach tells me there are folks who still think his treasure is buried on a small island in Lake Joyce, off Shore Drive which once open to the Chesapeake Bay."

Lance smiled knowing he had grabbed his father's attention. "In 1996 Mike Daniel who found some gold-laden Spanish galleons also located what appears to be the Queen Ann's Revenge in 25 feet of water off Beaufort, North Carolina. They are still excavating the site. Though no treasure yet."

He added, "There are many stories of smuggling in the Outer Banks and Hampton Roads during the Revolutionary and Civil Wars. Prohibition was a boom time for smuggling. Scottish and Irish whiskey from Great Britain, rum from Jamaica, Tequila from Mexico, Vodka from Russia and wine from Europe were all on the menu."

"There are still houses in Virginia Beach in Bay Colony and Thalia with basements and tunnels to docks where contraband would be brought ashore and stored for distribution."

"The Outer Banks with its hidden coves and rambling shoreline remains a great smuggler's hideaway even to this day."

Lance paused for effect, while he took another sip of his lemonade, as he brought his adventure tale up to date.

"It's no wonder the Cavalier Hotel, in Virginia Beach became a hot spot during the Roaring 20's. The railroad lines to Norfolk brought the wealthy to the oceanfront and the alcohol to distribution points north, south and west. They smuggled liquor just like we are planning to smuggle heroin with cars and trucks."

Lance noticed his father lit up at his mention of the famous hotel.

"I always liked the Cavalier. I'm thrilled they brought her back to her old glory." Arthur added.

Lance segued to his well-thought-out plan. "Since most of the East Coast heroin is coming in through Miami, New Jersey, New York and Boston, we're going to bring the merchandise in through Virginia Beach and the Outer Banks. No one is looking for it to come in at the Mid-Atlantic locations."

"I've tapped Lepordaxis, a Ukrainian of Scythian descent, to coordinate the pick-ups. He's well connected with fishermen in Virginia Beach and the Outer Banks of North Carolina. Using him will provide a layer of distance between us and the smugglers."

"How have you vetted him?" Arthur's voice contained concern.

Lance was a bit miffed by the question. It suggested he didn't do his job thoroughly and it was important to him that his father consider him competent. "Through the channels you set up and I refined." His voice had a tone of sarcasm in it. Lance took a deep breath and let it out slowly then continued. "After your agents throw the packages overboard off shore near Virginia Beach and the Outer Banks, two long-time smugglers who Lepordaxis hired will coordinate a pick-up in the waters off of Virginia Beach and the Outer Banks with smugglers in the fishing trade. This will provide another layer between the goods and us."

Hoping his father understood, he went on after a brief pause. "Using the homing beacons inside the packages to zero in on the shipment, they'll be easy to pick up with little chance of raising any suspicion."

"The pirates we are using have large Hatteras, Bertram and other major deep-sea fishing boats and they've established themselves in the charter business. We'll also use the commercial fishing fleet in Wanchese, who can hide the merchandise on their boats and offload it at various places in the Inner Banks without suspicion. Lepordaxis will make sure there will be many boats of different types in rotation."

Arthur was puzzled by Lance's mention of the Inner Banks and interrupted him to ask, "What are the Inner Banks?"

Lance smiled with satisfaction that he knew something his father did not, "They are the western shoreline of the mainland as opposed to the Outer Banks which are barrier islands."

Lance picked up the plan again, "Some fishermen in the Wanchese fleet have been small-time pot smugglers for years so they know the drill. They can bring in the merchandise anywhere from Wanchese to the Inner Banks and keep the ports of entry changing. It will be a shell game that will confuse the authorities and keep them guessing. This tactic was passed down to them by their pirate ancestors."

Lance went on to explain the next step, "Lepordaxis will set up distribution starting in Baltimore to give us some distance from the import site then move to Richmond and DC. Once those places are established he'll move up the Northeast to Philadelphia, New York and Boston. He'll select each regional leader by Scythian heritage and vet them through our psychological, drug and lie-detecting techniques. Their genetics and genealogical pedigrees will also be screened through our people." Lance paused for effect, "They will be vetted the same way we vetted Lepordaxis."

Arthur stopped Lance and asked, "Where is Lepordaxis going to get his Scythian muscle?"

"He'll get them from Eastern Ukraine where they are currently battling the Western European Ukrainians. You know the battle from Scythian times for that territory is still going on, but there are people who can be spared. The Warrior class will run our distribution and supply muscle while the Agricultural class will run our accounting and office needs."

"Being Royal Scythians, we will lead management. I've already located Scythian lawyers, bankers, business men and government officials using the lists you've given me, and they are excited to work with us. All I had to do was show them our picture, wearing the crowns. It's happening just like you said, the crowns have started to unite our people."

Arthur was finally satisfied and praised his son for his great knowledge of history and smuggling. He was also impressed by Lance's work to track down the current day warrior Scythians. He took a sip of his cool lemonade, looked over his domain, and smiled as he thought, "*Life is good.*"

Arthur concluded, "Now all I have to do is to tell Wu Jan to set the date for the first shipment and set a shipping schedule."

CHAPTER 3

FBI Director Bergin's face was flushed and beads of sweat began forming on his forehead and across his upper lip. He slowly looked over the Terrorist Task Force seated in front of him in the small auditorium knowing he wouldn't be giving his men much to go on. Clearing his throat, he began the briefing with a firm voice.

"Representative Groves from Maryland was shot as he was leaving home yesterday in Bethesda. Senator Mullins from California was gunned down yesterday evening as he was leaving his favorite restaurant, Marcel's, at Pennsylvania Avenue near K Street. A silencer must have been used since no one heard the shots. We've recovered two CCI mini mags from the heart of each body. Clearly these were hits. Strange as it seems they were scalped, the top of their skulls removed, and their hands skinned. We have reports of similar hits on CEO's from banking, industry, lobbying, and major law firms."

"Clearly, we have a problem and we have no leads, so we'll have to look at everything to connect the dots. Now get to work and find out who is behind this. The White House wants answers now."

CHAPTER 4

Fluorescent lights reflected off everything in the room, creating a stark brightness that made it feel like there was nowhere to hide.

Stan Ferguson, ASAC (Assistant Special Agent in Charge) of Baltimore DEA District Office, called his newly formed group of veteran agents together. "Gentlemen," he began. "You already know one another so I'll skip the formalities. We have a big problem and little time to solve it, so I'll start from the beginning with a history of the problem. I apologize that this is going to sound like a lecture so stop me at any time with questions or comments."

Although balding, his prematurely silver hair gave him a look of distinction and authority. He had a mustache and goatee and all who knew him well called it his schnauzer look behind his back, but they meant it affectionately. His agents liked him because he always had their backs.

The men were used to high-priority missions, but from Ferguson's tone they could tell this was something on a whole different level. Ferguson continued, "You know Baltimore has been a Mob Town since the 1850s and we also know that like most other American cities the local drug trade is run by black and Hispanic gangs. None of that has changed, but I have a report from Washington that says there's been an increase in violent activity possibly linked to our area. I need an update on the gang war between the East Side Brothers and the Walnut Hill Gang and I want to know what's up with the new fentanyl-laced heroin showing up on our streets. Where's it coming from, who's moving it and where's it going." Stan went on, "I want to go over some history here that some of you may know better than others. I think it is important for background purposes, so we are all up to speed and starting on the same page."

Stan's voice showed the frustration of dealing with a media that was more interested in hyping a story and creating controversy to sell advertising, rather than reporting the news.

"Low-level dealers move through the systems' revolving door, getting little jail time. With the closing of the General Motors plant and Bethlehem Steel mill in Baltimore, good paying blue collar work dried up. There is now little work available. Making minimum wage if you could find a job versus making hundreds of dollars a day selling heroin on a street corner is no contest. Although dangerous it is the best way to thrive for an uneducated, unskilled person growing up in the inner-city ghetto. People in this position have to become violent to protect their turf from competition. Beatings and killings are commonplace."

"Our guys in law enforcement always seem to come up with the short end of the stick. As you are well aware our jobs are dangerous and split decisions often have to be made. Sometimes the outcome is not pretty."

"It doesn't help that there are some bad apples and departments in our ranks that cast a dark shadow over the rest of us. The media seems to jump on the bad ones without reporting that the greater majority are professionals doing a good job. Even so there is a very credible evidence that black Americans are targeted more by the police and their treatment is more violent. So, the Black Lives Matter movement has validity and is important. The media often lacks the balance necessary to remain credible by not telling the entire story."

Stan paused to let the information sink in and give everyone a breather. He looked round the room ready to field questions. Since there were none he went on.

"The street corner boys don't make the big money. That is reserved for the top levels just like in any corporation. These bosses buy mansions in the suburbs."

"The gangs are run like corporations. They have to protect their brand and territory and have to market their product and maintain supply. They are divided into geographical regimes or bubbles. There are commanders, lieutenant commanders and ministers of justice, education, finance and defense."

"Nationally, heroin is a $60 billion a year industry. In Baltimore there are an estimated 20,000 occasional users and 60,000 chronic users."

"This epidemic started with our troops in Vietnam. Drafted to fight an unpopular war, anger and frustration combined with cheap heroin fueled the beginning of the epidemic. The CIA's involvement in heroin with Air America made it readily available. After coming home, the addiction continued for many. Their kids also became users. However, the crack cocaine epidemic which began in the 80s, overshadowed heroin."

"The current heroin epidemic started with Oxycontin. In 2007 Perdue Pharma pled guilty to knowingly misleading doctors and the public about its addicting qualities with false information. It is similar to heroin. Perdue made $2.8 billion from 1995 to 2006. It was fined $600 million, and its top three executives were fined $34.5 million. OxyContin is oxycodone in a time-released form. Percocet is Tylenol mixed with oxycodone. Oxycodone alone is available in generic form and is inexpensive."

"In 2010 'pill mills' were restricted from distribution because of overdoses, making it more expensive on the street. As pills became scarcer, 4 out of 5 pill users switched to street heroin which was much cheaper."

"A single dose pack or bubble of heroin consists of 0.1 gram. A bag is 10 packs or 1 gram, a bundle 10 bags, a sleeve 10 bundles and a kilogram is 10 bundles. It is going from $15-20 per pack depending on quality. Users will start out with occasional use. This will increase with time as they build tolerance to it. Once addicted they can use 3 to 10 doses per day always fearful of overdose. That can cost $50 to $180 per day. They will do anything to get their next hit which is why it is so dangerous."

"Mexican and Columbian farmers switched from growing marijuana, which is now coming mostly from the US, to growing poppies. The price of heroin has been halved by these larger supplies.

Mexican heroin is usually brown or black tar. This occurs because the morphine from the poppy is not completely acetylated. This makes it a base which doesn't dissolve in water. Making this doesn't require special skill and can be done in someone's kitchen. It is usually smoked and goes by the street names: Mexican Brown, tar, Mexican Mud, Chiva, boy or dope. The purity can run between 25-80%."

"Increasing numbers of Latin American groceries and Mexican restaurants have been cropping up in our cities. Most are legitimate businesses but for some the Cartels have taken a page out of the Arabic Middle Eastern playbook mimicking a "hawala." This is a way to launder money outside the banking industry. People will bring in illicitly gained money to the store. The store will put it in their daily deposit. The Cartel will give a small portion of it to that person's family back home. The laundered money is then free to be used in any way the Cartel wishes, locally or transferred back home via legitimate means."

"Pure white heroin, China White, requires a chemist's skill to turn it into a salt which is easily dissolved in water. This is usually injected." China White can also refer to fentanyl or a combination of fentanyl and heroin since they are both white and are opiats.

After a brief pause, Stan turned his attention to Agent Charlie Cass, liaison with the Maryland State Police. "What do you know about our gang war, Charlie?"

Charlie started his career in Desert Storm in the military police. After his tour, he came home to join local law enforcement for a few years. He then transferred to State Police, moving up through the ranks to become liaison with the DEA. He was 6 foot 2 inches tall and muscular but had an almost sweet baby-face that hid his strength and determination. He replied shaking his head, "The State Troopers, their agents and CIs (Confidential Informants) are drawing a blank. It is happening under our radar."

Stan turned toward Fred Sierles next dipping his head slightly to acknowledge his turn to report. "Fred, what have you found from your liaison with local law enforcement?"

Fred Sierles was an old timer with the DEA after starting out as a local cop. Almost 6 foot tall and skinny with wiry, black hair, he spoke in a controlled fashion. He had been at his assignment for the past 14 years. He was well-liked by his liaison and friend, Tommy Green at the Baltimore City Police Department. "I've spoken with Tommy. He's canvassed his department from the detectives down to the beat cops and their CIs. There's a gang war going on but it's a strange one." He had a perplexed look on his face, eyebrows raised as if to physically express the bizarre nature of the information to follow. "The gang leaders of both groups are being taken out and it looks as if they're taking each other out. However, some have been shot with Tavors. This is not their weapon of choice. The other strange part is that some of them have arrows in their bodies and the principal leaders have been scalped, the top of their skulls removed, and their hands skinned."

"Our informants don't know anything about a turf war. Up until now they've had a workable truce since neither group appeared interested in extending their territory. Plus, the same bullets and arrows used on the leaders of both gangs doesn't make sense. They use different weapons and ultimately the minor players in the area don't have the muscle or guts to pull something like this off."

"There appears to be a new player in town we know nothing about. One of the beat cops followed a trail of heroin overdoses in his neighborhood and brought in a couple of packs."

He was referring to how the heroin is packaged. It comes in kilos, kilograms, which is broken down to grams which is then broken down to a pack which is 0.1 gram, the user level. One pack costs $15 to 20. This is usually injected, rarely snorted. "The new packs are costing $12 each and are high quality."

Stan interrupted. "That's a big price difference. Someone seems to be undercutting the gangs and taking them out at the same time. How about the purity?"

Fred was compulsive and known to go down rabbit holes while investigating. Fred cleared his voice and everyone in the room knew they were in for an aside. He liked to "school" the young agents.

"In the late 80s to 90s street heroin was cut with baking soda, baby laxative, lidocaine or detergent to 17% pure. Now it's 30 to 40% pure. If the purity climbs any higher a lot of people will OD. Recently fentanyl has been added to the heroin. This is called a hot shot. This gives heroin a faster and stronger kick. It also makes it more dangerous. These recent ODs may be another batch of fentanyl-laced heroin like we had a few years back, so I'm going to send the packs to our DEA Mid-Atlantic Regional Chemical Lab at Largo, Maryland to check purity, what it is cut with and where it comes from. As you know purity is important to the street buyer who prefer to go to whoever has the best stuff."

Stan nodded in agreement with Fred's thoughts and next he turned to Evan Stahl. "Evan, what can the FBI add?"

Evan had been FBI liaison to the DEA for only four years but easily fit into this niche. His red hair caused him to stand out in a crowd and his mild manner made him likable. He shook his head as he offered apologetically, "I've checked with my field agents, who pushed their CIs. I've checked with our lab at Quantico. We have nothing."

Quantico is located 40 miles south of DC. This is where the Marine Core Base Quantico, the "Crossroads of the Marines," was established in 1917. On its campus 547 acres is dedicated to the FBI Training Academy. Within the FBI academy there are the Chemical Labs, Biometric Analysis Unit, Forensic Response Unit, Terrorist Explosive Device Analysis Center, Behavioral Analysis Unit and Scientific Analysis Unit.

Stan turned again, this time to Lou Reynolds, Customs liaison. Lou was as straightlaced as they come. He always wore black pants, black shoes and a white shirt. Stan lifted his head slightly in a nose point, eyebrows raised. "Customs have anything?"

Lou answered in his usual monotone, "I've checked with our people. It appears that new high-grade heroin is coming in from somewhere in the mid-Atlantic. It is not showing up in the usual New York, New Jersey or Miami locations. It's not the Mexican Brown and it's purer than the Columbian or China White we usually see. We've collected some packs through undercover officers. I've also forwarded them to the CBP (Customs and Border Patrol) Lab in Chicago for identification."

Lou added, "We also have word that small amounts of this new heroin are beginning to show up in DC, Richmond and Hampton Roads."

Lastly, Stan turned to Ryan Thompson, ATF liaison, and waited for his report. Ryan was of medium build. The pockmarks on his face from adolescent acne made him look mean and menacing. A mixture of confidence and question filled his face.

"We've received the arrows and shell casings from local police and sent them on to our NIBIN — National Integrated Ballistic Information Network. The shell casings are 5.56. Fred is right the gun we recovered is an Israeli Tavor. It was lodged underneath a pallet, hidden from view. That is probably why the shooters missed it. From the looks of the scene, the perps had plenty of time to clean up. The arrows have us baffled too. We've checked with our field agents who have pressed their informants. We don't know where the guns are coming from, let alone the arrows." Stan looked over the group slowly, his eyebrows deeply furrowed now.

"We have a big problem. It's not just gang leaders but also politicians working on bills to reign in laundered money from drug cartels and other leaders outside of politics opposed to the drug trade. All are showing up with the same wounds. I have a bad feeling about this. My guess is that this is the beginning of a much bigger problem. The new player appears to have a quality product and equipment, intel, muscle and money and that's a powerful mix."

"The Head of the NSA decided to make us Task Force Alpha of Homeland Security. Our role is to coordinate information as it comes in, but since this seems to be the beginning of a much larger operation, they have decided to create an even higher level ultra-secret task force called Talon Of Security Homeland located at the Joint Expeditionary Base Little Creek in Virginia Beach. We will report to TOSH and I know you understand this information stays in this room."

He again slowly looked over the group sitting before him, stopping briefly at each one, locking eyes to bring home the point.

CHAPTER 5

Joint Expeditionary Base Little Creek-Fort Story is the major operating base for the Amphibious Forces in the United States Navy's Atlantic Fleet. It has four locations. Three of these are in Virginia Beach.

The Norfolk-Virginia Beach Base totals 2,120 acres of land. It is a large Base running from the end of Little Creek Road in Norfolk along Shore Drive to Independence Boulevard in Virginia Beach. It is home to the Naval Amphibious Warfare Forces, Naval Special Warfare Group Two — SEAL Teams 2, 4, 8 and 10 and Explosive Ordnance Disposal Group Two.

Another of its locations comprises 350 acres located just north of Fleet Training Center Dam Neck in Virginia Beach just south of the resort strip, home to SEAL Team 6.

The Fort Story location is at the tip of Virginia Beach, the site of the First Landing of the Virginia Colonists from England in 1607. This is where the Atlantic Ocean meets the Chesapeake Bay. It's also the site of the Cape Henry Lighthouse built in 1792. This was the first Federal construction project authorized by George Washington and overseen by Alexander Hamilton.

Training, operations and support facilities located at Little Creek are geared predominantly to amphibious operations. This makes the base unique among bases of the United States and Allied Navys. It is the largest base of its kind in the world.

The entrance off Shore Drive to Helicopter Road ran past the always stinking sewage facility. The turn onto Gator Road to Signal Point gave TOSH a fairly secluded location.

The building was concrete, World War II era. Its white paint and green roof were typical of the area's buildings. It had seen better days. The paint was pealing, the roof needed repair. The reception area wasn't much better. The old cream-colored paint on the walls made them look dirty. It smelled musty. The gray linoleum tile floor was chipped and scuffed from long use. The small, wooden reception desk and several metal chairs looked beat up. The whole place looked uninviting. The pass code push button security lock on the door behind the desk looked out of place. The security camera on the wall facing the front door was well hidden, as were the outside security cameras.

Brad Johnson, a retired SEAL, and his longtime best friend and former SEAL buddy, TJ Daniels, worked undercover in Hampton Roads. They often worked with local, state and federal agency including local vice, DEA and ATF.

Brad was put in charge of TOSH by the NSA and wanted the building to look uninviting. Once through the old painted, beaten-up wooden door, the main office took up most of the rest of the building's space. Here Brad had it painted in earth tones. New florescent lighting with warm white bulbs softened the ambience along with wall-wash incandescent lighting. A rectangular oak conference table faced a cork board and 90-inch HD TV screen. The chair at the head of the table was designated the commander's.

Other modern oak work desks for team members were placed strategically along two other walls allowing ample personal space but were still close enough to allow easy contact with each other. Each had a computer and a secure land line phone. The final wall had a men's and women's restroom, a shower, a large storage area and a small kitchen.

Brad had a marine staff sergeant maintain the facility. He kept it clean; the refrigerator always stocked with bottled water, soft drinks and snacks; the coffee pot always brewing fresh coffee.

While Brad wanted the outside to look uninviting, he wanted the working area inside his facility to be warm and pleasant. He knew it was going to be a home away from home for some time. Taking good care of his team would pay dividends, given the long hours they would spend there.

Brad called for the group's attention in a firm voice as he slid comfortably into his chair and swiveled effortlessly to face them.

"All right people, let's get started. We'll go around the room and introduce ourselves and give a little background so we all get to know each other. Connie, you go first."

Connie had soft, wavy blond hair pulled back in a ponytail and was fairly attractive, although she always wore loose street clothes and no makeup, hiding her beauty.

"My name is Connie Huffnagel. I'll be in charge of computers and communications. I've been working at NSA for the past 11 years after they caught me hacking into the CIA, Defense Department and NSA computers."

Brad shifted his gaze to Godfrey and pointed gently with his chin. "Godfrey, you're next."

Godfrey took in deep breath and exhaled slowly.

"I'm Godfrey Washington. My specialty is lab and chemicals. I grew up in the Oakland ghettos, but I was lucky. They saw that I had a talent for chemistry and that was my ticket out. I've been working at the Quantico FBI Labs ever since. Occasionally they lend me to Customs or DEA."

Brad then looked at David Friedman and motioned him to speak with a nod.

"My name is David Friedman and I'm a specialist in archeology, ancient civilizations, and ancient weapons. I have dual citizenship—American and Israeli. I was born in Miami Beach, but my parents moved to Israel when I was 6. I graduated from Technion University in Haifa, receiving my PhD in archeology and ancient civilizations. The Israel Museum in Jerusalem gave me special training in ancient weapons. My time spent in the Israeli Defense Forces was in weapons design and tracking the origin of weapons. I did get frontline experience in the Palestinian Territories. The US Military and NSA hired me 10 years ago for my special skills after I got my second PhD in engineering at MIT."

Brad looked at TJ, a small smile of recognition and a shine in his eyes. "TJ, give 'em your rundown."

"TJ Daniels here. I grew up in Portsmouth. My daddy was a Norfolk cop killed in the line of duty when I was 18. He made me promise to go to Virginia Tech in Blacksburg on a football scholarship and that's where I met Brad. He was quarterback for the four years I played tight-end. We became a team and good friends. I followed him into the Navy and then SEAL Team 6. Since discharge we work together undercover for a number of agencies: narcotics, terror or whatever comes up."

Brad finally looked at Sergeant Walters.

"Hi, I'm Jim Walters. I joined the Marines during Desert Storm and saw action in Iraq. I went back to Iraq to serve two tours in Enduring Freedom. I also served two tours in Afghanistan where I was wounded several times. Before I was released medically they gave me the opportunity to serve here with you, making sure the mechanics of this place run smoothly. I jumped at the chance. I just can't see staying home watching TV or playing golf." An appreciative tone in his voice was recognized by all.

All eyes went back to Brad.

"I'm Brad Johnson. I grew up in Virginia Beach and played football for First Colonial High School. TJ covered much of my story with his, so I'll keep it short. I'll just add we've worked undercover mostly in the local drug trade for a while now."

"Moving on to why you're here, I'm sure you all saw the news about the Congressmen who were shot. After those shootings, a number of Baltimore gang lords who trafficked in heroin were killed using the same M.O. and a new fentanyl-laced heroin is turning up on the street. The President wants this stopped ASAP so he appointed an Ultra Black Special Congressional Committee to oversee TOSH. Two-star Admiral Mack Davis will be our liaison to DC. He's been a SEAL for 32 years. In addition to being our liaison, he's the SEAL's liaison to both the NSA and Department of Defense."

"There's a new player moving in whose brutality and scope of operation far exceeds what the agencies are used to. They're not only taking out the competition at the local level but also those in import, distribution, money laundering and politics."

"Homeland Security Task Force Alpha in Baltimore will lead the regional hunt and wherever it takes them and report back to us."

"TOSH will coordinate and refine the information and plan our ops. We're the spear. T J and I will remain undercover when we are in the field and be the tip of the spear making the deals as we climb the ladder. We use our real names and have developed a tough reputation as pissed off forms SEALs."

"Word is the fentanyl-laced heroin is coming out of this area. Our mission is to find out who's behind the new heroin on the street. This is a top priority, so we've been cleared to request aid from any agency, but if you run into problems contact Mack. He'll smooth it out whether with CIA, FBI, NSA, Joint Chiefs, DEA, Customs, Homeland Security or any branch of service and other state and local agencies. He'll also take care of any interagency problems at home and abroad."

CHAPTER 6

Lou Reynolds asked Stan to call a meeting. He had some news to share. "Guys, Lou has some follow-up. See if any of it rings a bell."

Lou looked around the room before starting. "As you know I'm our liaison with Customs. We've received word from one of our local agents in Hampton Roads that there seems to be a lot of activity with the sport fishing fleet out of Hatteras. Some are going out without charters and the fish haul seems to be limited when fishing's good. Also, the crews are beginning to spread money around. It's come to our attentions because as you know this is very unusual for early spring since the big blue fin tuna are running."

"I'm having my agents press their informants and we're identifying ex-wives and jilted girlfriends to see what we can uncover about the crew. I'm requesting that the rest of you do the same."

Fred Sierles took the lead. "I've been getting vague reports from the local police in the Outer Banks of more money showing up in their economy too. I'll press harder with our connections to see what more they can dig up."

Evan Stahl chimed in. "We've been hearing a low buzz but nothing specific to report."

Almost apologetic in his response Ryan Thompson followed up. "We've heard nothing yet about the arrows and shell casings we found at the hit in Baltimore. I've sent an arrow, the Tavor and some of the bullet casings to David at TOSH. He's the weapons expert so if anyone can put it together he can. We'll see what he comes up with"."

Stan left his report for last. "I also have some news. The lab at Quantico has analyzed the heroin we found. It is coming from the Golden Triangle and seems to be a special shipment, not the usual stuff. It's 40% pure with fentanyl added and cut with mannitol. We assume the enhancements are added here."

Stan summarized. "Contact your liaisons at TOSH and bring them up to date. Maybe they'll have something to add."

CHAPTER 7

Calling his team away from their desks for an update, Brad settled into his chair. "All right folks, what have we learned from Task Force Alpha and what more have you found out through your own digging around?"

All eyes shifted to Godfrey as he started out. "We have confirmed that this is indeed new heroin. We've checked it against heroin from Afghanistan, Mexico and Columbia. It's coming from the Golden Triangle, but it's DNA is different from the other heroin from there."

Connie was a little upset that Godfrey beat her to the start. It surprised her to realize how much she wanted to be the center of attention. "I've checked with my contacts at NSA, CIA and DEA with the information Task Force Alpha gave me. I've also done a bit of searching myself. The DEA Agent in Ho Chi Minh City got hold of some of this new stuff but isn't sure why it was there or where the heroin goes after it leaves the Golden Triangle. We're picking up a lot of chatter online, but I can't yet determine what happens to it."

David followed up with surprise and wonder in his voice, his eyebrows raised, a sparkle in his eyes. "The arrows are really interesting. They're an ancient Scythian design, but they're new! Through chemical analysis on the wood, Godfrey determined that they're being made in the Altai Mountains where Siberia, China and Mongolia meet. The arrow heads are barbed which tears the skin when pulled out. They also contain snake venom, dried human blood and dung. This is typical of what the Scythians added to make them more lethal. Really incredible. I've never seen anything like it. Someone went to a lot of trouble and expense to make these."

He added, "The scalping, removal of the skull caps and skinned hands like we found on the victims is also part of Scythian history, but their empire hasn't existed since 168 CE. Why all of this is showing up now is anyone's guess."

Trying to make up for lost position Connie blurted out. "I've been following up on the leads from Task Force Alpha regarding the Outer Banks. Agents from all departments tracked down the spending habits of ex-wives and jilted girlfriends. I've hacked into various computers, emails and social media. There's a connection with increased money and activity to the charter boats in the Outer Banks, but more so to the commercial fishing boats in Wanchese."

Brad was always the last to speak to sum things up and set a plan to proceed. "I'll connect with Stan at Task Force Alpha to see if he's found any leads for TJ and myself to follow in the Outer Banks. Connie, you do the same."

Connie was pleased that Brad singled her out and by the way he looked at her.

CHAPTER 8

Brad was FaceTiming with Stan from the computer on his desk. "I need a name and location of one of your agents on the Outer Banks, so TJ and I can make a connection."

Looking a little tired from all the action, Stan was slow to respond. "We know both Pirates Cove Marina in Kitty Hawk and the commercial marina in Wanchese just over the bridge on Roanoke Island are a hotbed for small-time smugglers. Most of the folks there are hardworking and clean but there are always some ready to jump into fast money. They use their charter boats and commercial fishing boats to make the score. Moose Delaney is our undercover DEA man down there. Connect with him for the introductions. I'll let him know you'll be calling." Brad signed off. "Copy that, we'll make the move.

CHAPTER 9

Brad and TJ entered Mimi's Tiki Bar at Pirates Cove. The grass tiki hut in the center was where charter boat captains and crew went to unwind after a long day at sea, hooking the big ones for the tourists. Because tourists often joined the captains and crew it got a reputation as the place to be. TJ and Brad found Moose outside sipping a tall one under an umbrella at a picnic table overlooking the harbor. The afternoon was exceptionally warm for early spring. Wispy white clouds floated effortlessly in the sky. The gentle breeze brought the pleasant, salty smell of the Sound to the waiting nostrils.

"Hey Moose." Brad approached the table in an upbeat manner. "I'm Brad and this is TJ. We've been looking forward to meeting you." He knew Moose was a master of deception from the jacket he read.

Moose acknowledged them and pointed to the opposite bench motioning for them to sit. "I've been looking forward to doing business with you. Welcome to my neck of the woods." His open casual manner was a ruse to suck in anyone who might be around observing them. He could smell them out like rats on the waterfront.

His infectious smile and jovial tone set the stage for this first act of the play.

Missie came over to take their order. "What'll you have gentlemen?" Hoping it was her, she batted her eyelashes flirtatiously at Brad.

Brad answered, "Two of the same as he's having."

Brad, TJ and Moose's eyes all followed the tall, thin, black-curly-haired, high cheekboned beauty and her skimpy tight shorts as Missie walked back to the bar.

TJ shook his head, a grin on his face. He was always astonished that Brad never seemed to come up short. "Man, how do you do that? You don't even have to give them any encouragement and they offer themselves up. Amazing."

Moose smiled thinking back to the days when he had that magic. Even with age he didn't do so bad, but the tarnish took its toll.

She returned quickly with their beers and gave Brad a wink as she set down the bottles. She put an extra sway in her hips this time as she slowly walked away looking back to see if Brad was watching.

Brad questioned Moose nodding Missie's way, "She one of the locals?"

Moose answered knowingly, "Yeah, grew up here. She loves fishing and men, and in that order"

"Maybe I'll have to get to know her better." Brad then theatrically lowered his voice, hoping that anyone listening would hear him. "We're interested in scoring some big-time white. We're told you're the man to see."

Moose answered in a similar low voice. "Right. My sources tell me you're clean. If you weren't, I wouldn't be sitting here."

The men bantered on for the next 20 minutes giving each other background information on themselves to set the stage further.

Having spent enough time for anyone interested to observe, Moose was ready to move. "This isn't the place to talk business so let's go to a more secure setting. Follow me to the 1587 Restaurant in Manteo across the bridge on Roanoke Island. We can talk and catch some dinner there."

Missie watched them leave, a little disappointment on her face until Brad looked her way. She beamed a seductive grin at him while slowly running her tongue across her lips.

The exchange between the men had been well choreographed in advance so the local bad guys and lookouts could easily see the connection being made. They were not too happy about the attention Missie showed to Brad. Even though she was easy, she was selective, and they weren't on her menu.

Roanoke Island is just west of Pirates Cove in Kitty Hawk and lies east of the mainland. The North end, named for Chief Manteo, is more refined than the South end, named for Chief Wanchese. Wanchese, the South end is known for its working commercial fishing boats.

The two tribal leaders had been friends prior to the first English expeditions to the new World, but when Sir Walter Raleigh arrived the Indian Chiefs were persuaded to accompany him back to England in 1584. There Manteo learned English, Wanchese refused. Chief Manteo's warming up to the English angered Chief Wanchese. They never repaired the rift. In 1587 the first English colonists arrived on Roanoke Island.

John White, the Governor of the First Colony, returned to England that year to bring in more supplies. He was detained by Queen Elizabeth I who needed all ships to fight the Spanish Armada.

When he was finally able to return three years later, there was no trace of the Colony except for the word "Croatan" written on a log. This became "The Lost Colony."

Dare County was named after Virginia Dare, the daughter of John White. She was the first English colonist to be born in America. The town of Manteo puts on a yearly drama commemorating the event. She disappeared along with the other Colonists.

This learning experience led to the first successful permanent English settlement in Jamestown in 1607.

CHAPTER 10

1587 Restaurant faces the waterfront in Manteo. Its location inside the Tranquil House Inn, a charming boutique hotel on Queen Elizabeth Avenue, is central. The friendly interior walls are blond pine with tables to match. An upscale local's hangout for the captains of the commercial trawlers and charter boats, business could always be conducted discretely.

Moose said in a not so low voice, "I love coming to this place. The food, the atmosphere is great. Look at that view." Moose walked his friends through the restaurant to the windows knowing anyone interested would see them.

Moose wanted Brad and TJ to be noticed so the smugglers would see them with him and start to think they were OK. He found a booth in a corner that was out of the main line of fire but where they would still be seen.

Brad ordered hot Shrimp Dip with Pita as an appetizer and fresh grilled Tuna Steak. TJ wanted the Crispy Shrimp Wraps for his appetizer and Flounder Stuffed with Crab as an entree. Moose got his usual Scallop Chowder followed by Crab Cakes. A round of Corolla Gold from the local Weeping Radish brewery, was ordered for the table.

The food and beer were great. They talked about fishing and football. TJ was getting a little antsy and said, "Well?"

Moose smiled knowingly and said, "Be patient my friend. This is like fishing. Sometimes you just have to wait for the fish to bite. The school is in and the sharks are circling."

As they sat there enjoying the last of their dinner, Nick Hollaran came over. He had been watching them with intensity after their arrival. Moose was delighted by this move. In fact, he was expecting it. He knew that Nick was a major player in the area and often organized the locals when necessary. Nick was also the person who everyone looked to for resolving conflicts among them. Nick thought of the local smugglers as his boys.

One of Moose's informants told him Nick's ex-girlfriend said he'd come into a lot of money recently and that he'd be at the restaurant tonight. The informant also told Moose the ex was jealous because Nick had ditched her for a younger model, so he wasn't sure how accurate the information was. Moose crosschecked the intel with Connie over at TOSH and it held up.

Nick seemed to ask with genuine curiosity, but he already knew the general answer, "Who are your new friends Moose?" His cautious attitude didn't go unnoticed.

Moose tried to break the ice gently. "This is Brad Johnson and TJ Diggs from just north of the state line. They played for Virginia Tech—quarterback and tight end. You may have heard of them?"

Nick's face flushed red with anger, his words slow, "Oh yeah, I remember you guys, quite a pair. I wasn't too happy with you when you trounced my Tar Heels. That last quarter hail Mary in the '89 game was unbelievable."

Moose broke in to ease the tension. "Well, you can be happy with what they do now. Take a seat and join us for a whiskey." He noticed their waitress hovering a little too close. Giving her one of his get lost looks with a menacing glint in his eyes she backed off to give them ample distance for privacy.

Nick knew Moose and was well aware of his connections to the drug trade. He also knew that Moose would only deal with legitimate players. He could forgive the transgression of winning the football game if it meant filling his pockets with cash.

Nick's shoulders relaxed as did the expression on his face. He wasn't sure why, but Moose had a way of doing that to him. He slid into the remaining available seat at the table. Moose ordered a bottle of Crown

Royal Black and a bucket of ice. He wanted to soothe Nick's football pride and loosen him up before getting down to business.

Moose was his usual jovial self. The low soft music playing in the background kept the atmosphere calm. The ambient noise from the casual conversations in the room gave them enough cover to get to know each other better.

"I've worked with Brad and TJ's contacts for years and they've been telling me I should get to know them." Moose explained, "These guys aren't just going to make great business partners, they're fun to hang around and the ladies come to them like moths to a flame." Moose raised and tipped his whisky glass in respect toward Brad and TJ.

Nick was skeptical. "How do I know they're not cops?" His question turned the atmosphere around the table tense. Nick trusted Moose, but how much could you trust anyone in their trade? They were either cops, players trying to rip you off, or kill you and take over your territory. Even if you have worked with someone for a long time, situations change. This business was fluid and you could never let your guard down.

Moose shook his head with a tight-lipped smile, eyebrows together, his growl low and angry. "I know the people they came from who speak highly of them. My sources tell me they're clean and I trust them. Do you think I would do business with them if I thought they were cops or even fly-by-nighters?"

Moose didn't beat around the bush now as he became serious turning the conversation to more fruitful turf. "Brad and TJ are looking to score large amounts of China White. Know where they can fill their order?"

Nick paused a minute looking around the room not wanting to appear too anxious. He wanted to mull the information over. He picked up the bottle of Crown Royal and poured himself two fingers. Still deep in thought he slowly picked up 3 ice cubes. They made a clink as they dropped in his glass. Satisfied with Moose's answer, he carefully started to open up. He could check with his own sources later. "I know a couple of guys who are bringing it in for a new big-time player. We have to account for everything we bring in, but for the right money we could lose some of the shipment. Or if that's too rich for you, we can get you larger amounts of Columbian White or Mexican Brown and all the pot and meth you want."

Brad didn't hesitate, keeping on target. "We're only interested in the primo China White we've heard about. We can get all the other stuff we need."

Nick sipped his whiskey slowly switching to small talk in order to better size up Brad and TJ. "You guys live in Virginia Beach?"

Brad knew what Nick was up to and indulged him, so he'd get comfortable with them.

"Yeah, we decided the easy life at the Beach was a nice way to go. Lots of action and chicks, especially since they updated the Cavalier and north end along with the rest of the strip. Businessmen, celebrities, politicians and military brass are flooding in to partake of the action. It's good for business, if you understand my meaning."

TJ's eyes sparkled. He wanted to be a part of the action. "Rubbing elbows with the upper crust is lots of fun. They have the money to party right and only want the best."

Brad and TJ carried it off perfectly and Nick felt reassured after getting a better feel for his new acquaintances. "I'll talk with some of the guys and see what we can do."

CHAPTER 11

The aroma of fresh coffee permeated the warmly lit war room. Jim poured a cup for anyone who wanted one. He had Brad's usual waiting, 2 creams, no sugar. He grabbed a Diet Pepsi out of the fridge for Connie. He always enjoyed treating her special because he knew she'd smile at him and he wanted to become friends.

Brad included Moose in the meeting this time and introduced him to the group. Then gave him a brief rundown on each of the team members before asking, "Moose, give us your background."

All sat in their chairs separated by the conference table in the middle. Moose was next to Brad in a chair Jim brought in from the store room.

He began, "I was with DEA for 20 years and looking forward to early retirement when the higher-ups offered me a sweet deal to move to the Outer Banks. I just had to go undercover." Moose looked over the room then continued, "fishing is my first love, so it was a no-brainer and now I've been here for the past 6 years. Through my undercover work I've been able to gain the trust of all the players in the area, so I can get access to anyone."

"Let me fill you in on the area a little. The Outer Banks are filled with tourists and occasionally a charter boat will do a bit of smuggling, but it's the big commercial trawlers out there fishing for scallops, oysters, shrimp or fish that do the majority of the smuggling. Those boats mainly port in

Wanchese but they can go anywhere along the Inner Banks."

"Wanchese is the commercial south end of Roanoke Island. The fishermen there started the backyard boat building industry. Three or four Captains having nothing to do in the winter would come together to build a fishing boat in a backyard shop. It might take a year or so to finish their custom boats. But what boats they were."

"They'd put their experience on the water together and designed a boat with the 'Carolina flair' at the bow. The knife edge in front would slice through the waves of the Atlantic while the wide flair would deflect the water away from the boat keeping the fishermen dry. This sacrificed bow space which they didn't need in favor of some degree of comfort, especially when the weather and water turned cold and the witch's breath blew."

Moose paused for effect. "It differed from the production 'clorox bottle' boats which had a broad front allowing for a large cabin. This gave comfort to the sport fisher which they required. Those lazy bastards try to be gentlemen fishermen, hiring a captain and mate to do the dirty work while entertaining each other with tales of conquest in business, politics and women. The less wealthy would try to emulate the big fish but did most of the scut work on their own. B and B Boats (Buddy and Billy) are one of the few backyard boat builders left. They make a nice boat."

"Some of the boat builders got out of the fishing business as word spread of their fast sturdy boats. In the 1960s this morphed into the finest performing sport fishing boats in the world."

Everyone listened intently, knowing nothing about the subject, drawn in by the tales of the sea with the drama of exploration and conquest. The atmosphere was hushed. Even Brad and TJ who were very familiar with boats and the water from their experience with the SEALs knew nothing about this area of expertise. All eyes focused on Moose. Surprise and longing showed on their faces. Moose could see they were paying close attention to his every word. He loved being the star since his job afforded little time to be in that position.

Moose continued his history lesson after a long pause, looking each person in the eye, including Jim Walters who stayed in the background, to draw in his audience further. He often wore a broad grin which he knew made people relax in his presence. That grin gained him entry to places that were hard to get into for most.

"They then went into the yacht building business. Now they have an international reputation. Bayliss Yachts and Spencer Yachts, two of the best custom boat builders in the world used to be built out of cypress and cedar in the 1970s."

"Their boats are now built out of what they refer to as 'space age plywood.' This consists of a space age polymer core with an overlay of fiberglass. They use a computer-controlled router to cut the necessary precision pieces that fit together perfectly. The bottom and top are built over a 'jig' or wooden frame that is then cold molded with fiberglass surrounding a lightweight polymer core. The jig is then removed."

"I've visited their shops. They're amazing. It is hard to believe that computers and space age technology are now used to build such beautiful creations. Each is a work of art."

"Some boats can be up to 90 feet long with a 20-foot beam and can do in excess of 43 knots. They're lightweight and strong. Some can cost up to $11M and often have a hidden compartment with a retractable wall allowing access to the armory."

Brad knowingly nodded as he listened.

"We ran across one of one of those boats in the Philippine Sea when TJ and I were in the SEALs. We were trying to route Al Quaeda terrorists from Mindanao who were running guns."

"It was the rainy season. We went in at night in a heavy rain. Our target was a senior Al Quaeda operative visiting the base camp. Our mission was to bring him back alive if possible or kill him if necessary."

"We came in over the horizon in our Z-bird towed behind an indigenous Filipino fishing vessel as our support craft."

"The Z-bird is a CRRC, **C**ombat **R**ubber **R**aiding **C**raft. It's an inflatable 'Zodiac' boat 15.5 feet long with a 6.3-foot width. The ones the SEALs use is the F470 which can be paddled or motored with a 55 horsepower 2 stroke engine. It is lightweight, stealthy and easily stored when deflated. It has multiple chambers preventing deflation and can be launched from aircraft, surface vessels or submarines."

"Our inlet was acquired as we came in at low speed and hid the

Z-bird in a mangrove swamp. Patrolling in about ½ mile from the base camp we started making unexpected contact with overwhelming fire. We decided to abort and broke contact. Returning to the Z-bird we made a seaward exfil."

"Several hundred yards out we encountered an enemy vessel. They took us under fire with a 12.7mm machine gun. We returned fire and ran in the opposite direction fire walling the throttle. To our surprise the boat gained on us."

"The only reason we evaded it was because we turned shoreward to shallow water and hid the boat in the surf zone between waves and swells."

"We barely got away from the son-of-a-bitch. That was one fast boat especially for the seas." Brad seemed apprehensive, still in the moment.

"Pictures later identified it as a Spencer-made yacht. Impressive!" Brad appeared a little spent after reliving that harrowing experience.

Moose smiled in acknowledgement. "Paul Spencer is honest and is a good friend. He's a real gentleman to work with. His boats are some of the best made. He doesn't always know what the boats are going to be used for or how they're going to be refitted. How that boat was used is no reflection on him."

"Paul also owns O'Neal's Sea Food Harvest located at Wanchese Seafood Industrial Park next to his factory which provides some of the freshest seafood in the area. It has a small seating area for those who want to eat in and a few tables outside for those who don't want the confinement. I often go there for lunch." He paused as he reflected on meals he had eaten there… "that's good food."

Moose came back to the present. He wanted to move on with the background of the area to take the spotlight off Paul who was clean and was a friend.

Moose continued, "Wanchese has two different groups living there, 'holy rollers' and 'hell raisers.' As you can imagine they mix like oil and water. Informants come from both groups because of the usual greed, jealousy, getting better deals from the authorities or just plain 'doing God's work.'"

"The main group of smugglers work out of the 'Inner Banks,' the western side of the Pamlico Sound. Engelhard is the only small town in the area. It lies along the Pamlico Sound with its numerous coves, inlets and docks. This is in the middle of nowhere. It is located south of the Alligator River National Wildlife Refuge. Just to its west is Lake Mattamuskeet."

"The big trawlers, gill netters, shrimpers, scallop boats and oyster boats are ported there on Far Creek at the Big Trout Marina. The smaller boats can get out of Oregon Inlet which often silts in. The bigger ones have to go south to the inlets at Ocracoke or Hatteras. When they come back, it isn't unusual to see them offload at out of the way docks for various reasons. These are some of the last entrepreneurs left in America. Government rules have crushed the others. Of course, the big players get the rules bent in their direction through payoffs to the politicians in the way of lobbyists and PACs."

"There are lots of derelict boats lying around to cover their movements. They have a saying, 'Where she quits is where she sits.' When the life of the boat is spent they leave her where she dies. It costs too much to haul her away."

"The surrounding area is mainly swamp and kind of looks like the Everglades. NC 264 is the only road from Roanoke Island and the Outer Banks to Engelhard. This also connects to NC 94. These are both small but good roads with little traffic."

"NC 94 connects to NC 64 at Columbia 54 miles away, where it turns into a four-lane divided highway similar to an Interstate. From there you can easily connect to I-95 at Rocky Mount or go on up NC 17 to connect to I-64 in Hampton Roads and on to I-95."

Moose chuckled, his infectious jovial personality showing through the serious mood in the room lightening it. Moose loved to tell the stories. Everyone continued to listen, fascinated by the facts and history of the area.

"Back in the 70's, before I first came here, the Poparena located just north of Engelhard was the place to go. It used to be a rough hangout with fights and blood every night. All that's left of it now is a cinder block shell. This happy time lasted until the big drug bust in the late 70's along the next door 5th Avenue E canal. Lots of folks from the Outer Banks and Roanoke Island were involved. The feds had a tip and were ready to pounce when the drug boat came in, surprising them."

Moose went on with his background of the area, enjoying himself as he looked over his audience whose rapt attention hung onto his every word.

"All along the North Carolina coast during colonial times smuggling was rampant. There are even tales that Blackbeard was in cahoots with North Carolina's Colonial Governor Eden at Edenton. They had houses with tunnels to the sound to bring in the booty."

"During the Civil War sugar was at a premium. This was smuggled past the Yankee Blockade into Middleton, a dot on the map just south of Engelhard. The *Star*, a sugar runner, was scuttled there with ballast after they cut her mast to prevent it from getting into Yankee hands. It's still there."

"Then there were the heady days during prohibition after the 'booze yacht' ran ashore on Hatteras Island. A good time was had by all."

"In the middle of town is Duck's. It used to be named Duck's Pool Room after the owner's nickname. This is a wooden shack about 20x20 feet with a plywood floor. The pool table is now gone. It has a small bar with four large help yourself apothecary jars on it filled with boiled peanuts, nabs, pickled pig's feet and pickles. There are several comfortable chairs, including a coveted rocking chair. The main action occurs on the benches out front on the wooden planked porch, just like out of the wild west."

"During the summer it's filled with the locals telling tall tales and adventures. The owner, the local Maritime Officer, is straight arrow. However, he can't help what might go on there."

Moose went on, having difficulty containing himself, to tell the tale of the 'Summer of Sea Weed.' His words came a little faster. His mood brightened even more.

"1979 was a 'high' time for the residents all over the Outer Banks." His emphasis on the word 'high' didn't go unnoticed. "The Coast Guard was chasing a small Panamanian freighter, *Freedom IV*, in the fog off shore. When they caught up to it and searched it, all they found was a small amount of marijuana and cocaine residue. The freighter was empty."

"Only one charter boat dared to go out that day. While trolling they saw bales of marijuana floating by. The locals call these square groupers." Moose chuckled at the words for effect as well as his own entertainment.

"They didn't pick any up but told one of their dock neighbors about it. He went out and landed a large amount. The next few days, bales of marijuana kept washing up on the beaches. The locals were out in numbers to reap the harvest. It's rumored that a number of charter boats, restaurants and small business got their financing and start from that haul."

Moose settled in continuing on with his tale. "Now, these guys don't see themselves as pirates or smugglers, just opportunists like in days past."

He was on a roll, gratified that everyone in the room continued listening intently, all eyes focused on him. He prided himself on being a good storyteller.

"The US Government felt compelled to put up Life Saving Stations along this coast in the mid 1800's. These 'opportunists' would often kill the survivors of shipwrecks in order to claim the cargo for themselves. The Outer Banks was very isolated in those days and the residents lived a subsistence lifestyle. Anything that washed ashore was heaven sent and they took advantage of it."

He couldn't contain himself and just had to expand the history of this era.

"The people manning the Life Saving Stations were daring and heroic. The Grand Cross of Honor Medallion has only been given 11 times. Six of them were given to the men from the Chicamacomino Life Saving Station at Rodanthe. This is where the seas become treacherous at the confluence of the Labrador Current and the Gulf Stream. The ocean off Cape Hatteras is known as the graveyard of the Atlantic."

"Patrick Edwards, the Captain of the Station, was known to have said to his men at a particularly dangerous rescue, 'The book say you have to go out. It don't say nothing about coming back.'"

"One of the most famous rescues occurred during World War I when a German U Boat sank the British oil tanker *Mirlo*. They saved 42 of the 51 on board."

Brad cut in wanting to get things moving along and up to the present.

"Moose has introduced us to Nick Hollaran, one the local smugglers. He's based out of the commercial fleet in Wanchese. This gives him vast connections including the Charter Fleet at Pirate's Cove Marina and the trawler fleet in Wanchese and Engelhard. These guys stick together like stink on shit."

Moose nodded and added, "Although I know most of the players in the Outer Banks area, they will send out Carolina Skiffs or duck hunting boats to meet the pick-up boats. These small boats can be run by anyone the captain of the larger boat chooses. These guys are a dime a dozen. They can off-load anywhere."

"I don't know schedules for pick-up at sea or distribution from the drop spots. I'm hoping you guys can fill in the gaps."

Connie saw a chance to use her expertise and have the spotlight shine on her. She was becoming more assertive. She was beginning to feel more comfortable around her new family. The energy and testosterone were palpable. Being this close to the action began awakening her sexuality. She was surprised that she began checking out the sailors as she drove in and out of work.

"Give me the names of who you know, and I'll run traces on them and see if we can expand our knowledge."

Brad asked if anyone had any questions for Moose or the team. Since all remained silent lost in thought, he brought the meeting to a close.

"Moose is going to run point for TJ and me as we flesh out and infiltrate their system. These guys are a tight group, so it'll be challenging. We'll use all the info you can dig up."

CHAPTER 12

Moose, Brad and TJ met with Nick outside on the deck of Poor Richards Sandwich Shop over the water. The view across to Festival Park, the site of the First Colony and the *Elizabeth II*, a replica of a 16th century merchant ship was delightful, and the food was always fresh and tasty. Their Carolina pulled pork BBQ sandwich with slaw and hot sauce was famous.

They each ordered a beer and BBQ. The sky was again blue and cloudless. The Mid-Atlantic has perfect weather. There are three and one-half months of spring, three months of summer, three and one-half months of fall and 2 months of winter. You get a taste of all of the seasons, but the best seasons are the longest. The cool air was filled with the aroma of hickory from the BBQ pit. After the first round, Moose directed the conversation toward Nick.

"How's it coming? Any news about how much we can get and when?"

Although he knew Moose well, Nick was a bit unnerved by his directness. He sipped his beer and waited a bit to answer so he could consider Moose's sudden shift. After sizing him up he decided Moose was just excited about the deal. It would be a lot of money and heroin, but he wanted to maintain as much distance as possible.

"The shipments are sporadic. Each of the boats get a turn. The big trawlers will be called on when the seas are high, and the small commercial trawlers will pick up when the seas are friendly.

Occasionally a charter boat will do the pick-up, so we can keep it varied. We never know when we'll be called on until the night before the drop. They're starting out small but tell us the amount will increase as they get established."

"How much we can deliver will depend on the size of their order. We'll try to divert as much as we can, but I think we can safely get you 3 kilos, give or take, per week. Cost is $50,000 per kilo starting out. The price can vary depending on the amount you want and the resistance we get from our source. We'll deliver it to Moose at a time and place of our choosing."

Focusing directly on Brad and TJ he said, "You'll have to get it from him."

Brad had a look of disgust as he flared up. "We want to start with 10 kilos per week at $36,000 per kilo and want more as our business spreads."

Nick expected bargaining and tension. "Look, this is the beginning of the whole operation. We have to let the system unfold to know what's possible. I'll settle for $42,000 per kilo and get as much as I can."

Brad tried to tease out more information by agreeing to his revised terms. "We can live with that. Where does the rest of it go?"

Nick snapped back. "You already have as much information as you are gonna get."

Brad spoke calmly so he didn't get Nick more agitated. "OK, don't get so uptight. I'm just curious."

Moose broke in trying to change the subject and calm everyone down. "Great! We have a deal! Now let's just enjoy the beer, food and setting."

CHAPTER 13

Brad called a team meeting with Moose again present. Jim was now getting everyone coffee and adding snacks each time he served them. Everybody liked pastries and croissants from Gateaux Bakery and Cafe on Independence Boulevard in the morning. Sometimes instead, he brought bagels and lox cream cheese from Bruegger's Bagels at Virginia Beach Boulevard just west off of Independence Boulevard. Occasionally he would bring in a pound of smoked nova lox and cream cheese from the Restaurant Depot at Witchduck and Virginia Beach Boulevard.

Lunch included sandwiches from The Leaping Lizard Cafe on Shore Drive. For a special treat, he would bring in mile-high corned beef and pastrami sandwiches with coleslaw and kosher dills and slices of New York Strawberry Cheesecake from the 58 Deli at Loehmann's Plaza. Sometimes lunch came from farther away. De Rican Chef on Holland Road and Buckner Boulevard had the finest Cuban sandwiches north of Miami along with other fantastic food.

For dinner he brought in Chinese food from Judy's Sichuan off Constitution Avenue or the best Peking Duck and Dim Sum in town from Jade Villa near Virginia Beach Town Center. Occasionally he would get fried oysters from Surf Rider Restaurant on Diamond Springs Road.

Other times he would bring in a platter of sushi from Kyushu on

Newtown Road or salads from multiple sources. He knew the work they were doing was very important. Having led teams, he knew when his people were focused on a mission they often forgot to keep themselves properly nourished. The food breaks would also give them some down time to get away from their tasks and refresh themselves.

With everyone in their chairs, beverages and snacks served, Brad called the meeting to order.

Moose brought them up to date on the meeting they had with Nick.

"Nick is going to supply us through me with what they can slip out of the shipments the different boats pick up. Problem is, we won't know when the pick-ups occur or who gets them. It may be days later. He is tight-lipped about the others he'll be getting stuff for. I'm checking who they might be through my contacts."

Connie was always eager to add her information. She was beginning to feel more comfortable around these testosterone-filled men. She had been used to working around nerds. She found this job more to her liking and that surprised her.

"I've done some checking through bank accounts, cash purchases and credit cards to see who has new-found wealth. I'm checking the fishermen and also their wives, kids and girlfriends. I'm getting a picture of who to zero in on. I'll give Moose the information as it comes in."

Godfrey couldn't hold back any longer. His demeanor spoke of his concern.

"We'll need samples of the heroin to make sure it matches the heroin we're after. I don't want us to waste time chasing the wrong stuff."

Moose finished up. "Even though I've vouched for Brad and TJ, Nick will only do business with me. However, by meeting Brad and TJ, Nick believes that I'm connected to some big-time players with good financing. He's ready to deal."

After the formal meeting Moose stayed around to chit-chat with the group. He wanted to get to know them better and wanted them to feel comfortable with him. He liked the interaction with people on the same page, where he could relax and let his guard down. He also loved the food that was great and always in fresh supply.

CHAPTER 14

Connie and Jim were becoming friends. He recognized the beginning of her transformation and wanted to help it along. Being sensitive he knew she was somehow damaged in her childhood and initially tried to keep herself in the background. He could see her beginning to develop so he took her to dinner at Le Yacca at Hilltop, a wonderful French restaurant that made you feel as though you were in Paris.

Connie was wide-eyed as they were led to their table. "I've never experienced this quiet elegance before. Is this the way rich people eat out?"

Jim just smiled, "I want to broaden your experience. If you think this is nice you ought to see the top restaurants in Paris, Lyon, Bordeaux and the Rhone Valley. This is a good example outside of France and gives a similar feel."

"I decided to take you here first, but the best restaurant in Hampton Roads is Coastal Grill on Great Neck Road in Virginia Beach. Every meal is perfect from seasoning to temperature to presentation. The wait staff is knowledgeable and attentive but not intrusive. They have the best sautéed soft-shell crabs I've ever tasted. The atmosphere is quiet and comfortable. Let's enjoy tonight. I'll take you there on our next foray."

Jim was a foodie since childhood. "I'll order for you since you are probably not familiar with the food."

Connie was beginning to relax and absorb the ambience. "Go right ahead. I like it so far."

"I'm not going to get too exotic for you since this is your first experience at French dining," Jim said reassuringly. "We'll start with onion soup, a French staple, then go with the Veal Normandie for you. This is thin-sliced veal scaloppini with apple brandy under a mushroom cream sauce. I'll order the duck breast with caramelized white peach and foie gras which is pan-seared goose liver in a port wine sauce for me."

"OMG," Connie said with excitement. "Sounds delicious."

"It is. I've had both here before. They do a nice job. I'll order a red wine from the northern Rhone Valley which will pair nicely with the food." Jim said relishing her excitement.

As the bread and wine were served Jim started. "I believe we could become good friends. You might not know but I am gay, so we could have a special bond that even girlfriends can't get. We have no sexual attraction or competition between us. I just want you to know I am here for you."

Connie smiled, relaxing even more. "Oh, that's great. I felt the friendship and thought my reluctance to engage was keeping a distance. I'm glad you persisted and brought me here. Now I know where I stand. It was confusing."

"Well, I've met folks like you. What happened in your childhood that scared you away from getting close to people?" Jim questioned, hoping he didn't push the envelope too far.

Connie looked down at her wine glass, picked it up and took a deep swallow. "Working with this team has actually been a very good arrangement for me. I continue to hack into the world's most sophisticated systems and get paid for it. Having given up my family of online hackers for a new one when offered a job at the NSA made a big difference. The job at the NSA was with people who worked together in person. I fit in OK since they were a bunch of nerds and the only competition was who could hack the best. We never interacted outside the office, which was fine with me. This new family has shown me there is a new way to interact. I'm glad you warmed up to me from the start. It made me feel comfortable enough to open up a little."

Connie paused, looking Jim straight in the eyes, and sensing no malice, decided to let him in on her childhood. "I grew up in the foster care system abandoned by my mother when I was four. She was a heroin addict and couldn't take care of me. My new family kept me fed and clothed but there wasn't much love. They took in 5 other foster kids and seemed only interested in the money they received from the State. The other kids also came from desperate situations. We only interacted when necessary for survival. I started to learn computers in school and found I had a real knack for them."

Connie again paused looking for Jim's reaction. Seeing only compassion she went on. "I was sexually abused by my foster father starting at age 12. This went on until I was 15. I finally ran away from home and lived on the street. I visited the library a lot and improved my computer skills enough to be able to use them to get adequate income to live on. I had my own place with enough computers and hardware to keep me happy. The nerds online were a family and I fit in well. I was finally busted when I was 18. They saw my potential and put me to work at the FBI, later transferring me to the NSA."

When the onion soup came in time to take the heat off her, she changed the focus to Jim. "This soup is great. What about you? How did you get here?"

Jim smiled after a nice spoonful of soup. "I grew up in a loving, nurturing family with a brother and sister. I was the youngest. My mother was a great homemaker and a fabulous cook. I used to help her in the kitchen. As I got older I would read cookbooks from all cultures and pull out recipes to try."

"I realized I was different when I was 8 and gravitating toward things my sister was more interested in. This didn't prevent me from liking male things too. I joined the field hockey and football teams and was quite a jock. This might have been overkill after I realized my difference was being gay. It was tough during my teens, trying to hide my feelings and sexual orientation. I joined the Marines at 18 and moved up the ranks to Master Sergeant allowing me to command a team. I had to hide being gay. Thank God for 'don't ask don't tell.' I doted over my men, so it wasn't difficult to have a line waiting to come under my command."

"The Marines gave me the opportunity to travel and eat at some of the world's great restaurants to compare how my mom and I did. We're still very close."

With that ending, the main course arrived. Connie's eyes were sparkling with anticipation as she sank her fork into the first bite. "Boy, this is wonderful." Looking over at Jim's duck he gave her a bite, first of the duck and then the foie gras. "This is exceptional. I didn't know food could taste so good."

"I now have another surprise for you. I have ordered a Grand Marnier Soufflé for desert. There is nothing like it."

As the meal went on Connie became more comfortable and recognized what an awesome friend Jim was becoming.

CHAPTER 15

Brad brought the team together for a conference. They took their respective seats.

Jim made his usual rounds of refreshments, drinks and snacks. He was beginning to learn what each team member liked and made sure he had their favorites on hand. Jim's sensitivity made him pretty astute at reading his team. He learned this in his leadership positions in the Marines.

Godfrey was the first to speak. "Boss, I check that sample you brought in and it matches, we've been getting reports from Task Force Alpha of the same high-grade fentanyl-laced heroin showing up not only in Baltimore, Richmond and DC but also beginning to show up here. Task Force Alpha also reports even more dealers are showing up in the morgue. There definitely seems to be a major turf war going on."

David added, "Nobody has ever seen this heroin/fentanyl combination before. The quality beats anything on the street. This stuff has one hell of a kick and is also cheap."

TJ shot back. "There are no big-time dealers or importers we know of here in Hampton Roads. Task Force Alpha has put a flashlight on every rat and roach in the area. They seem as bewildered as we do."

Connie leaned back and when she did her shirt tightened,

showing off her perfectly proportioned breasts. The pink cotton crew neck clung lovingly to them, so you could see her nipples were hard. Connie chimed in, "On the intel I'm getting it seems there is a widening circle of heroin like ours coming from the Ebony Bar, Catch 31, the refurbished Cavalier, and the Meet Market. Maybe you guys should sniff around there." She unconsciously thought they should sniff around her.

CHAPTER 16

B rad snorted as he and TJ ordered their first round at the bar. "At least the drinks are half price on Wednesdays and Fridays until 9."

TJ was looking forward to mixing with the crowd. They were here as dealers and they dressed accordingly. Brad had on beige linen pants with a light blue long sleeve cotton shirt. He'd left the top three buttons opened and his lightweight darker beige linen and silk jacket finished off the look. TJ was outfitted in his designer jeans, a thin off-white long-sleeve silk shirt and a pseudo suede light-brown jacket.

"Not a bad place to hang out for the eye candy and dinner. At least it won't be boring."

The Meet Market near the end of Great Neck Road where it ends at Shore Drive, is not only one of the hangouts for SEALs, but also for locals. The location is easy to find.

The food is good and the drinks always flowing. At the entrance, the restaurant and bar are divided. Food and drink are served in both areas.

The restaurant has booths and tables. Attractive modern chandeliers hang down above them. People who aren't looking for a connection feel comfortable eating in this part of the restaurant.

The real action happens in the bar.

The large horseshoe-shaped dimly lit bar is large enough to hold a lot of people but cozy enough for intimate talk. The bar top is made of oyster shells covered with a thick plastic coating. The empty beer bottles encased in a fishnet above it, framed by wooden compartments, give it a nice touch. On one side of the room are booths that can fit four and the other side has tables for two for more intimate conversation.

Brad spotted an old wannabe slinking around the bar. "Hey Parnell, you pretending to be a SEAL again?" Brad hissed, his eyes slightly closed for further effect. Parnell really irritated Brad. SEAL's put a lot on the line to keep the country safe for people like Parnell and he'd mingle pretending to be one just to pick up girls.

"No, I promise, Brad. I'm not doing that anymore since you broke my arm for doing it last time. It still hasn't healed right. See?"

Parnell moved his arm up and down rapidly with a pained look. It didn't have full range of motion and he looked like a chicken flapping its wing.

Parnell disgusted Brad so he was pleased the lame arm was a reminder that kept his behavior in check, but Brad knew he could lean on Parnell for information. A small smile crossed his lips and he paused for effect before leaning in close to Parnell.

"I want to know who's peddling the new China White that's been showing up around town."

Brad's actions made Parnell nervous and he began jibbering, "Yeah, that's really been good stuff and cheap too. I got some from Roosevelt."

Brad looked at TJ and raised an eyebrow.

TJ caught the pass then growled slowly. "Roosevelt who?"

"Roosevelt Watkins. He hangs out at Ebony's on Atlantic around 21st Street. He's the man." Parnell hoped this was enough to satisfy the threatening ex SEALs standing before him.

Brad finished up. "We'll see about that. Keep out of trouble and you'll stay in one piece. Remember, you're not a SEAL."

Brad turned and headed for the door. TJ followed.

"Yes, Sir!" Parnell snapped back with a sense of relief.

They got into Brad's car. He turned toward TJ and said, "Looks like it's your turn buddy."

TJ smiled. "Roosevelt Watkins." He nodded his head remembering the name. "We went to school together. I knew him well, a real sociopath. He'd sell his mother if he had a chance. It'll be 'nice' to renew our acquaintance."

TJ was smacking his lips and had a twinkle in his eyes. He continued in a sarcastic tone. "Well, boss, it looks like I'm going to have to play with the slime and grime. I'm not thrilled to go to the Ebony. It is a sleaze joint, but duty calls."

Brad followed up quickly. "TJ, don't get too eager to play in the dirt. It might get messy."

TJ just kept smiling as Brad drove him home. He wanted to wait for Saturday night when he was sure Roosevelt would be there.

TJ lived on the west side of Atlantic Avenue at 72nd Street. His house backed up to First Landing State Park. His front and side yards had Russian Olive bushes blocking it from any prying neighbors. They also smelled great starting in August when they bloomed. Their perfume permeated the whole back end of his street. They were also a bramble patch no one could push through, giving him some security.

He also installed front and backyard security lights that popped on with any movement. John's Brothers installed and monitored his alarm system. His backyard opened to the Park through tall arbor vita trees which concealed his 8-foot-high chain-link fence with concertina wire on the top and throughout the fence. In the middle was a Japanese-style tori gate with eight-foot-high 8x8 inch cedar posts on each side. The top was made up of two 2x10 crossbars both turned up at the ends, the bottom shorter than the top. The door of the gate, also of cedar, was made of vertical 2x4s long and short alternating with three 2x4 crossbars. All had the 2-inch side facing front and back.

TJ liked his privacy and wanted as much security as he could get while living in a small residential neighborhood. He liked the Japanese motif which made up the outside and inside of his house creating a deeply spiritual atmosphere.

He turned toward Shintoism during his stint in the SEALs. He had done things, following orders, that bothered him. He came to realize that politicians controlled who he killed. Most were clear enemies of America. He had no problems with those. But some didn't fit his definition of enemies. Those were the ones he had difficulty with. It brought him to an existential crisis.

The Shinto religion with its tie of the individual to nature and a belief in a sacred power *kami* in both animate and inanimate natural things just felt comfortable to him. It soothed his restless soul and made him feel right with the world. He could go out and do necessary things and come back to his sanctuary. Since retiring from the SEALs he didn't have to take any assignment he didn't want. He could pick and choose.

The house had eight-inch horizontal overlapping cedar planking and the roof was low pitch with the corners turned up making it look like a Shinto Shrine. The interior of each window had natural cedar trim and ³/₄-inch cedar strips in eight-inch squares inside of them continuing the Japanese feel.

The interior of the house was decorated in a minimalist tradition. The entrance housed a tokonoma with a Japanese mountain landscape painting hung on the back wall. Below and to the right was a simple rosewood stand with a Meiji Satsuma vase on it. The walls were a plain cream color throughout. There was a large framed calligraphy art piece centered on the largest wall in the living room which overlooked the backyard Japanese garden. The calligraphy spoke of the balance of yin and yang. He saw the word balance as a guiding force. A low natural maple square table surrounded by four almost flat pillows were placed around it. A bronze incense burner and tea set were tastefully displayed on top. His bedroom had a thin queen-size tatami mat on top of a natural maple platform. There were natural maple cubbies and cabinets for clothes and storage. There was no TV anywhere in the house.

CHAPTER 17

EBONY BAR
ATLANTIC AVENUE
VIRGINIA BEACH VIRGINIA
MEMORIAL DAY WEEKEND—SATURDAY NIGHT

TJ's father was in the first group to integrate the public school system in Norfolk in 1959 as a senior. He was bussed from Portsmouth to Norfolk to attend Granby High. It was tumultuous at first, but he was a great football player, tight end. This helped quiet the dissent once the white majority found they now had a winning team. His father later became an Army Ranger for 10 years and fought in Vietnam, winning the Bronze Star. He went on to become a Norfolk policeman and was killed in the line of duty in 1987 when TJ was a senior in high school.

TJ and his father loved muscle cars. He still drove his father's 1966 red GTO convertible. It had a Ram Air setup with a new 744 scammed Tri-Power engine, a close ratio 4-speed manual transmission and, of course, black Stato Bucket seats. This car could move and sounded like it.

TJ worshiped his father and all he stood for. He hoped he could live up to his expectations.

Playing football was reward enough. Becoming a SEAL and member of the elite SEAL Team 6 was frosting on the cake even though his father didn't live to see it. Now joining his buddy Brad in these new adventures was beyond his wildest expectations.

TJ slowly cruised down Atlantic Avenue from Laskin Road, the top down. His car, as always, drew looks from the hoards on the sidewalk. He loved the attention. Turning onto 22nd Street and pulling into a parking lot, he gave the attendant a fifty.

"Keep an eye on it."

He walked around to Atlantic Avenue through the throngs of tourists and found the entrance to Ebony which was mostly a black haunt. The city tried their best to keep order, but there were always unsavory characters hanging around outside. He pushed his way through the crowd and went inside where he approached 2 Dice, the bouncer.

"Anything interesting?"

2 Dice answered without hesitation as he continued scanning the crowd for trouble. "Not yet, just the usual Saturday night ruckus for the start of the season, but the night's young."

The large rectangular room with a smaller matching rectangular bar off to one side was plastered with small booths along the wall. There was plenty of room to float through the crowd, gain some privacy or secure a prized vantage point.

TJ mingled. The black foxes were out in force. There was some prime white meat along with some white wanabees. The white squids, who tried to be black, were always amusing and dangerous. They always had a chip on their shoulder to be knocked off. The Hispanic mulattoes would willingly oblige, as would the black locals who were cocks of the walk. It was the kind of place you always came packing and ready to use. Even though he knew it was stupid, he enjoyed testosterone-filled situations like this.

He was cruising slowly around the periphery watching the pick-up game unfold before him when he spotted Roosevelt sitting in a strategically placed booth. He was surrounded by three amazingly beautiful black ladies and one blond knockout. Roosevelt was loud and obnoxious, smiling his pearly whites. His gold front tooth with a diamond in the middle matched a diamond in his left ear. His green striped jacket blended with his light green patterned shirt, four buttons opened showed off the thick gold chain with a scorpion medallion hanging from it. His green pants and shoes matched the broad green stripes in his jacket. There was a magnum of Crystal champagne on the table.

As TJ approached the table, he quickly lifted his chin, looking Roosevelt straight in the eye. "Hey, Roosevelt, I see you crawled out from under your rock. Where've you been hiding?"

Roosevelt shot back. "In yo mama's ass." The woman flattered Roosevelt with their laughing and the side-eye they threw at TJ.

TJ slammed down his drink on the table. "Let's not get so nasty. Ditch the women. I want to talk."

Roosevelt flicked his head slightly and the women quickly slid out of the booth and disappeared. They sensed the troubled atmosphere that blew in.

TJ sneered, "I was generous that time, Roosevelt. Next time I won't be so kind."

Losing the ebonics Roosevelt apologized. "Sorry man, I just didn't want to lose face in front of my women. What can I do for you?"

TJ faced Roosevelt squarely. His voice was matter-of-fact and direct. His eyes were like spears drilling into Roosevelt's brain. "I understand you have a source for the new China White coming to town. I want to know who it is, or I can't promise you'll leave with a face your ladies will recognize."

Roosevelt hoped the information he was about to give TJ was enough to satisfy his old nemesis. "I got some from a couple of guys, Bubba and Danny. They're a couple of hillbillies. I think they are out of here, maybe the Outer Banks. They sometimes hang out at some of the low-life bars in Portsmouth, Granby Street and Ocean View. That's all I know. Don't blow my position or I'll be back to whacking by hand."

"What do they look like?" TJ wanted a description.

"If you see them you can't miss them. They are both about six feet tall. Bubba is stocky and has orange hair. Danny is thin and always wears a work shirt and jeans."

TJ continued to look straight through Roosevelt. He wanted his message to sink in. "As long as you're giving me all you know, I'll let it go. But if I find out there's more to the picture than you're telling me, those fag photos you posed for will find their way around and you and your hand will become good buddies."

Roosevelt started pleading. "I swear that's all I know."

"Give me a pack." TJ demanded.

"I didn't know you started using?" Roosevelt looked at TJ truly surprised.

"I don't. It's for a lady friend." TJ lied.

"I got a better idea, I was just getting ready to go out back to score a key of Columbian White. Why don't you come along, I'll introduce you, maybe you can score some prime stuff too?" Roosevelt was hoping this additional offering would endear him to TJ.

As they left the bar together, they rounded the corner, walked to the back of the building and rounded another corner. It found them on the edge of the parking lot in the alley. TJ followed Roosevelt to an area secluded by bushes. As they approached the figure waiting in the darkness, TJ recognized him as one of the new DEA pukes. It wasn't hard for him to realize that he walked into the middle of a bust.

Before the agent could blow his cover, TJ coldcocked him. The man went down, and TJ grabbed Roosevelt to make a run for it before the other agents could react. They bolted into the crowd of tourists to take cover, but one of the agents recognized TJ and pulled the other agents back.

Roosevelt couldn't stop thanking TJ. "Oh shit! Anything you need man, just let me know 'cause I owe you." He kept shaking his head, "Shit I can't believe I almost walked into a bust. Man!"

As TJ drove back to headquarters, he wondered who the hillbillies were.

CHAPTER 18

TJ called Connie and wanted a meet to discuss the news. He thought going to First Landing State Park would be a good change. He wanted to get to know Connie better and thought a walk in the woods would do them both some good. The cathedrals of nature were always both soothing and energizing.

Connie pulled up next to TJ's red convertible, top down. "Wow, I've never seen one of these." TJ usually drove his Ford Bronco to work leaving his baby for special occasions.

"Yea, my dad bought this used when I was in high school. We rebuilt it together making lasting memories. Every time I take it out I feel him with me." TJ had a distant look, lost in his past.

"I didn't think you've found this magical place yet, so I figured we could go over some new information while enjoying the setting before the weekend is over. I've seen how good you are at digging up information. Maybe you can give us direction to the next rung when we meet with the team."

"Sure. This place looks interesting. I'm ready for new experiences, Connie said as she headed for the Bald Cypress Trail.

CHAPTER 19

B rad entered the war room with TJ. He loved the ambience he created, wanting his team to be comfortable and to feel special, knowing he would get the most out of them. The team members were hard at work at their desks and didn't notice him. Brad cleared his throat loudly and in a cordial tone asked his team to take their positions at the conference table. His mood was upbeat which set the tone of the meeting.

"Hey guys, let's get a current rundown from everybody. TJ, you go first with your news."

TJ attempted to mask his enthusiasm. It came through anyway. "I've wallowed in the mud a little and think I have a lead."

The Team chuckled. They began feeling comfortable with each other.

TJ filled them in on his encounter with Roosevelt. "We have to find the hillbillies, Bubba and Danny, and follow where this lead takes us. I've already discussed this with Connie."

Connie didn't realize how excited she was getting to be the center of attention. "I've already looked into them following your preliminary report to *me*." She emphasized the word "me." This personal communication from TJ before reporting to the rest of the group made her feel special.

"They came from the western Virginia coal mining area around Bluefield and moved here as teens. They're in the charter boat business and have a 60-foot Hatteras named *Shaft 6* which is usually docked at Rudee Inlet. Sometimes they dock in Hampton and sometimes at Pirate's Cove in Kitty Hawk."

"The prime place I could find for you to meet them is Greenies in Ocean View. From the GPS readings on their truck, they seem to like it best especially on Wednesday nights when it's half-price beers." Her voice became soft and dreamy. "And by the way, it's rumored to have the best Old Bay boiled shrimp on the East Coast. Too bad the City of Norfolk bought up all the land on the Bay side and is going to knock down all the buildings including Greenies. It is an institution that will be sorely missed."

She fantasized that one day Brad would take her there before it was leveled. She was too scared to go by herself.

David was always business. He rarely smiled or joked. It wasn't clear how many pairs of jeans he had since that's all he wore. Connie, Godfrey and TJ had a pool going on the number. Most often he wore a T-shirt with some nondescript design. When it got cold, he wore a long sleeve T and a black leather jacket. No matter the weather he always rode his custom hand-built black-and-chrome 1949 Indian motorcycle. It had a track master style frame, all aluminum tank and seat, brass light covers and fender, modified GSXR windscreen, Pisa LED headlights, and gold leaf and pinstriping. He loved this unique antique bike for its rarity and beauty as he did all antiques of similar quality. The fact that it always turned heads was of little consequence.

"The chemical analysis via Godfrey on the wood from the arrows has been matched to wood coming from the Altai Mountains in Western China and Southern Siberia. This makes no sense. They could get wood from anywhere."

"Still no word on where the Tavors are coming from."

David went on showing a rare bit of pride in his voice.

"The Tavor is an interesting choice of weapon. It was designed by an Israeli, Zalman Shebs in 1995 for house-to-house street fighting. It is a compact bullpup design with a long barrel for high muzzle velocity. It has a long-stroke piston system similar to the AK-47 which is more reliable than the short-stroke piston. It can be semi or fully automatic."

"It is also designed for ambidexterity. It can easily convert for right-or left-handed shooters. Versatile, small and compact it packs a wallop. It can use both 5.56x45mm or 2.23x45mm bullets. Other street guns can only use the 5.56 bullets. It has won a number of awards and has been added to the Israeli arsenal as a weapon of choice."

Brad was the last to speak, hoping to keep up morale by showering the team with praise. "You guys are doing a great job."

"Word from Task Force Alpha is that this new heroin; same quality, same cutting material and same price, is beginning to show up in DC, Richmond and Hampton Roads. They are seeing the same carnage in these cities as in Baltimore. The major gangs are being taken out. 5.56 bullets from Tavors, arrows, scalped heads, missing top portions of skulls and skin from hands seems to be the modus operandi at all locations."

"Great work Connie on the tip about Greenies. TJ and I will head over tomorrow night and try to run into the hillbillies."

CHAPTER 20

The growl of the engine and crackle of flying gravel ceased as the slick gun-metal gray Mercedes AMG 550 came to a stop. Brad Johnson didn't look forward to sipping beer at Greenies, the sordid West Ocean View bar.

He had a lot on his mind and going to Greenies wasn't going to help. In fact, it made things worse. Being with TJ would be fun, but he knew even that prospect wouldn't make up for what lay in store for him.

"TJ, I don't want to do this tonight. I'm not in the mood."

They closed the car doors with a solid clunk that only a well-built car can make.

TJ was puzzled by Brad's hesitation. "What's up? This is what we trained for boss. The team has done great so far."

Brad shuffled his feet on the gravel. "Putting this team together at the last minute without seeing if all parts fit is like putting a new carrier in the fleet without first taking it out on a shakedown cruise."

TJ was always there to help Brad find clarity and put him back on the right path when he was getting lost or bogged down, but he didn't understand what was eating at Brad.

"It might not be so bad boss. After all we played together for Virginia Tech. I caught plenty of your passes for touchdowns. For the life of me I can't understand why I followed your ass through SEAL training and on to SEAL Team 6. My momma told me you were going to get me killed."

Brad slowly shook his head back and forth while looking at the oil-covered rocks. "I guess you caught the same case of stupid I have. Always trying to win."

TJ countered in a strong voice, looking Brad in the eye. "Win? You're just an adrenalin junky posing as a Boy Scout, always trying to make the world better, good versus evil."

Brad reluctantly surrendered. "Yeah…yeah…let's just get in there and do our job so we can see if the rest of the team is up to it."

TJ came back. "Look, the President and Select Congressional Committee on Intelligence didn't tap an ultra-select group of top military brass, CIA, DEA, ATF, and Customs to create Task Force Alpha and TOSH to get some real bad actors for fun."

"They couldn't have put a better person in charge overseeing the operation. You have to agree Mac Davis is the finest man we've ever worked for and he picked you to lead the Team in the field."

Brad regained his composure. "Yeah, I know. I'm just a little tired and a bit cranky that's all."

He was closer to TJ than anyone else in the world, but he still didn't want to disclose the real reason for his reluctance to go into Greenies.

TJ sounded confident. "I know we haven't worked with Connie before, but she is the best damn computer and communications wizard there is. Godfrey is a miracle worker in the lab. David is a genius with weapons. Being stationed at Little Creek along with SEAL Teams 2, 4, 8 and 10 is the perfect spot. Plus having SEAL Team 6 at Dam Neck, the Atlantic Fleet headquartered at NOB Norfolk and Task Force Alpha in Baltimore gives us access to all the personnel and materials we need to carry out our mission. We are in good shape."

Brad knew TJ was right about the team and he was trying to help, but that wasn't the real reason Brad was out of sorts, he just didn't want to see a certain someone from his past. "You know as well as I do that the SEALs aren't allowed to operate on home turf. OK, we can talk all night, but talking isn't doing. Let's get in there and see what we can dig up."

They entered the stinking, dimly lit room and selected a large table in the center. The bar was filled with shirtless beach bums with pierced nipples, middle-class locals with their wives, older gray-haired women and a few bikers. They took in the odd mix. A waitress approached with a big smile, surprise in her eyes.

Brad smiled back. "Evening Nell, the natives treating you okay tonight?"

Nell had on the same outfit as all of the other waitresses, hot pink short-shorts with a tight sleeveless T-shirt, but somehow, she looked far better than any of the other girls. On her left shoulder was a tattoo of a large red fox with green eyes that matched her own hair and eye color. Nell's smooth slinky gait even looked like that of a fox.

She purred back slyly, thrilled to see Brad. "I keep them in line. What'll you have?"

Brad winked while trying to be charming to make the best of a difficult situation. "The usual."

TJ ordered the same and when Nell was out of earshot said to Brad, "Umh, umh, she certainly is a fox and hasn't changed much. That's the real reason you were dragging your feet to come in. I forgot she worked here."

Nell and Brad went back a long way. They were an item while Brad was in high school at First Colonial playing quarterback and she was a cheerleader. This continued at Virginia Tech where he was a star quarterback for his four years.

Things between them started slipping while he was at Tech. He became something of a ladies' man in college, but she was all right with that knowing she couldn't control him. She continued to see him whenever he was available, but once he joined the SEALs they rarely saw each other and drifted apart. She was his first love and he would always have a special place in his heart for her. Brad hadn't seen her in years, but he had to agree with TJ. She was still hot.

Nell lingered at the table after delivering the beers hoping to renew their relationship. "I haven't seen you for a while. How's the knee?"

"It still gives me problems, especially in the winter, but I push through it." Brad tried to keep the conversation superficial. He didn't want to encourage Nell. "How have you been?"

"I'm still single." She looked for Brad's reaction hoping it would be positive. "I tried a few office jobs, but I don't fit in well, too confining. Waitressing gives me the flexibility I need to keep me sane."

Nell tried to get the conversation back to Brad. "Are you still angry with the military after they botched your knee and retirement?"

"Yea, there are some things I just can't forgive," he said trying to maintain his cover.

"Are you still into the dark areas of society?" Nell showed genuine concern.

"I get along." Brad tried to end the conversation as he picked up his beer and took a swallow looking away.

Nell got the hint and excused herself. "I've got to get back to work. Nice seeing you."

Brad looked at the table with a blank stare. He pulled himself away from his thoughts and back to TJ. "All right, quit ogling the ladies and look for our prey."

TJ now understood why Brad uncharacteristically made up the lame excuses stalling to come in. He felt his pain. Trying to change the subject he said, "Well, boss, maybe they just haven't gotten here yet."

Just then the door opened with a loud whoosh and two men who could only be the hillbillies came rolling through.

Bubba Spruill was dressed in orange overalls with a multicolored Alexander Julian long-sleeve shirt. His left front incisor was gold, outlined with a dollar sign in the center. His 260 pounds, which filled his clothes, along with his curly orange hair and bull neck, made him look menacingly comical. He was accompanied by his business partner and boyhood friend Danny Winston. Danny was tall, thin and had on the blue jeans and work shirt they were expecting. He wore a ball cap that said, "Trojan Condoms." Their walk was an Appalachian lumber, slow and clumsy. They had about a three-day growth of beard each.

Bubba and Danny grew up together in the coal country of

Bluefield, Virginia. Their friendship was cemented when they were ten after their fathers both died in the same cave-in at Shaft 6. Right then and there, they made a pact never to work the coal mines. They would do whatever it took to get out of Bluefield and become rich.

Going east, they started working on fishing boats out of Hampton. Being young, they were brought under the wings of the fleet, learning everything from oyster dredging to scalloping to drag lining to deep sea fishing. They heard all the old tales about the pirates on the coast of Virginia and North Carolina and of the "rum runners" during prohibition. Learning the current smuggling trade was part of their education.

Using their connections back home in the coal-filled mountains, they could earn enough running MJ and meth from there to Hampton Roads and Richmond to afford a beautiful 60-foot custom built Hatteras they named *Shaft 6* to remind them where they came from. They would occasionally use this to pick up drugs from mother ships coming from Mexico or Columbia but mostly used it to charter going after the big game: tuna which only ran in the late winter and marlin which ran in the summer. If you brought in big blue fins you could ship them directly to Japan's Tsukiji Fish Market via Norfolk International Airport to Washington/Dulles Airport, after they were flash-frozen with nitrogen. They would get $3-5,000 each. Once in Japan some were worth upwards of $100K at the auction block for bragging rites. Most sold for $8-12K.

Bubba bumped Danny with his elbow, "Grab me a beer. I'm gonna hit the outhouse."

Danny nodded with a smile as he turned his attention toward Nell as she approached him. "Hey, honey, two cold ones for the table and bring us 2 baskets of your boiled shrimp, heavy on the spices."

Danny looked around the bar drooling at the eye candy. He had no trouble finding the guys who owned the cool Mercedes in the parking lot. They were the only overdressed customers who stood out.

When Bubba returned to the table Danny nudged him. "Check out those two. They look like the type we need to connect with if we want to increase our business."

As Bubba scrutinized them, he wondered why two rich guys

would come here. He was really skeptical, and his antennae were up. "Yeah, they look the part, but this is way too easy. Call Nell over and see what she knows about them."

Danny called out, "Hey Nell," and motioned her over with a twist of his head. "What do you know about those two?" Almost whispering to bring her closer she bent over the table flashing a little cleavage. That always increased the tips.

"Oh, that's Brad Johnson and TJ Diggs former star quarterback and tight end for Virginia Tech."

The admiration in her voice went unnoticed. Her cleavage didn't.

"They come here occasionally. Rumor has it Brad got dropped from the SEALS after a knee injury in Afghanistan. The VA didn't fix it right and after his hazardous duty and retirement pay took forever to come through, he got pissed off and went into the drug trade. Anything he can do to make up for lost time. He and TJ have been buddies since college football. Where Brad goes, TJ follows."

"Interesting." Bubba didn't realize he was licking his lips as he thought to himself, "*What easy marks.*"

He focused deeply into Nell's eyes. "How do you know so much about them?"

"We were a number while he was quarterback at FC. I followed him to Tech, but you know things change." Anyone would have noticed the forlorn look on her face. Not these guys though. They were more interested in the two well-dressed men three tables down.

Bubba called out to Brad and TJ, "I understand you guys played ball for Tech. Come on over and join us. Let me buy you a beer."

They made small talk about football, the crazy wars in Iraq and Afghanistan and the western Virginia coal miners. The conversation finally got around to fishing.

Bubba told the boys about their boat and how they loved to go after the big ones.

"Maybe we'll take you out sometime and see if we can hook into a trophy." He chuckled to himself knowing that would never happen.

Brad motioned to TJ with a head point. "Well, we'd love to but I've gotta get my girlfriend home. His momma doesn't like me keeping him out past his curfew."

Bubba laughed and shouted as Brad and TJ were leaving the bar, "I'll call you."

TJ followed along, but he was surprised by the fast retreat. "Why did we leave so quickly?"

Brad stretched his shoulders back as he squeezed out a grunt. "I didn't want to seem too anxious to get together with them. We'll let them chew on the bait a little before we set the hook."

They got back into the Mercedes and peeled out of the parking lot with a roar of the finely tuned engine. "Now let's go see what the Meet Market has to offer."

CHAPTER 21

The Meet Market is always packed, especially on Wednesday and Friday nights. Dressed in anything from jeans to cocktail dresses women position themselves at strategic spots near the bar where they can show off their best. Men are drawn to them like fish to bait, hovering in groups around them.

Brad and TJ slowly wandered up to the bar and ordered their usual, Jamison neat in a shot glass and a Grey Goose martini. Brad had to settle for the regular Jamison since they didn't carry his preferred 18. They noticed many of the women checking them out.

As they watched the ebb and flow of the hopeful hookups, TJ noticed a nice-looking brunette with deep blue eyes alone in a corner booth get up and go to the ladies' room. She came back with a glazed look and a slight stager, head nodding. He pointed her out to Brad. Brad recognized the signs of heroin intoxication immediately and went over to introduce himself. "Hi gorgeous, I'm Brad. Mind if I sit down?"

She smiled sheepishly, "I'm Lannie. You come here much?" Her voice was as soft and smooth as a warm breast on a cold night.

Brad answered, "Nah, only when my astrologer at the Cayce Center tells me I'm going to meet the woman of my dreams at the Meet Market."

"Mmm," cooed Lannie, smiling a little more now.

Brad gently moved closer oozing charm. "Looks like you're riding the horse, darlin'. Know where I can score some?"

She turned her head and blushed. "Sure, but you can't get it the way I can. I just flash my eyes and they give it away."

Brad raised his eyebrows and smiled. "Yeah, that's a trick I just can't use. But I got plenty of green."

Lannie was in the zone, her body rocking back and forth, her eyelids drooping. "Well, I just go down to Catch 31 and hook up with two goofy-looking guys that always want to have a good time. They seem to have an endless supply, but they aren't always there."

"What do the guys look like?" Brad questioned.

"'One is heavy-set with curly orange hair and always wears these funny orange overalls. His friend is thin and always wears blue jeans and a blue work shirt. Sometimes in the summer he wears a T-shirt that says, 'I Heart Beaver.' He says it's from Beaver, Utah.'" She offered as she was drifting off.

Brad began distancing himself from Lannie. "*The Hillbillies,*" he thought to himself.

After some more small talk it was clear Lannie wanted Brad to take her home. And when she started to get aggressive, Brad signaled TJ to come over and get him out of there gently. He was hoping she wouldn't get into more trouble considering the condition she was in; always wanting to help a damsel in distress. Brad figured that she was used to it and would probably score with some high-roller. She had to make money for her habit somehow and the Hillbillies would only supply enough for their night of pleasure.

When they got to Brad's car, TJ noticed the smug look on his friend's face. "Well, what do you know, partner, she also fingered Bubba and Danny as the source" Brad said.

TJ pursed his lips, wrinkled his nose and squinted his eyes. He was annoyed and a bit jealous that these two could afford the better things in life that he couldn't. This was part of his motivation to follow Brad hunting the bad guys.

"I knew those two hillbillies had more money than brains. I felt it in my bones that they were into more than just deep-sea fishing with a little grass and meth on the side." TJ agreed.

Brad looked skyward questioning their position and concluded. "Yeah, we'll get Connie to see what more she can dig up on them and see how they fit into this. They can't be the importers or distributors. They must be somewhere in the middle. Let's go back to headquarters in the morning and see what the team has come up with. We'll report our confirmation that the Hillbillies are the source and we've connected. We have to be careful though. I have a bad feeling we'll be going up against some new heavy players."

"Roger boss." TJ snapped back.

CHAPTER 22

B rad marched into Headquarters anticipating forward movement. Most were already at their workstations. TJ was standing next to David discussing their finds.

"All right guys, let's see where we are," Brad ordered as he approached the corkboard. They dropped what they were doing and almost ran to the table filling their appointed chairs. They loved their job and the camaraderie that was developing. Most of all they began to love the thrill of the hunt, each hunting in their own way. There was no one way to get to their goal. They knew that each were the top in their field or they wouldn't be there. This was where the action was coordinated. The room was electric. They knew they were part of a much bigger picture. Anytime they ran into a problem they had a myriad of options to choose from to solve it, including brainstorming with each other.

Drinks and snacks were delivered as the team settled in. Everyone appreciated the attention Jim showered on them. He always gave a little extra to Connie, assuming her metamorphosis was partly due to him. He wasn't too presumptive to think it was all his doing. He was attracted to her as a friend. Since he was gay, he wasn't interested in her as a lover. He was more attracted to Brad for that, but he knew that was a mountain too high to climb.

Connie jumped in first. Although she was used to gaining respect for her sharp mind and work quality, she was beginning to see a new side of herself. As the operation went on, she began wearing clothes that were more stylish and revealing. She secretly began having feelings for Brad and hoped he would notice. The connection to the team began bringing her out of her feminine shell. All the interaction with the fast crowd, beautiful women using their assets and the power of the pussy made her feel more feminine. She had never experienced anything like this. She wanted in on the action.

"Looks like our hillbillies are the pick-up. Their credit card bills have jumped dramatically, and they have been throwing cash around their usual hangouts. Both have new Ford 4x4s bought with cash, decked out with all the bells and whistles."

Godfrey was next to speak. "The pack that TJ got from Roosevelt is the heroin we're chasing."

Brad turned his attention toward David. "David you have anything for us?"

David was always thoughtful and thorough. "The weapons purchase comes from accounts that bounce around the Middle East, Asia and Europe before ending up being drawn out of a private account in Switzerland. Connie and I haven't been able to crack the source of the money yet. We'll keep working on it."

Brad concluded. "David, call Stan at Task Force Alpha. I want you to go to Ho Chi Minh City and connect with his DEA liaison there. We know it's coming from the Golden Triangle. I want to know how it's getting here."

CHAPTER 23

As the plane doors opened, the hot humid air slapped David in the face. Sweat began leaking from every pore. He wasn't thrilled to be in Vietnam. Between South Florida and Israel, he'd lived in hot locations and could take the heat, but this humidity made it several layers worse. Ralph Walker met him at the plane.

"Welcome to Vietnam. I'll take you to the hotel where you can get a shower and maybe a little sleep before we get started. Then I'll take you to buy water-resistant boots. This is, after all, the beginning of monsoon season."

David packed light, just a small carry-on hanging from his shoulder, only the bare essentials inside.

"I slept on the flight, so I'll be ready to go after I shower. I don't want to waste any time and I want to get out of here as quickly as possible. Even though I was in the Israeli military and am used to uncomfortable conditions this place doesn't fit me. Humid jungles are not my cup of tea."

David was already irritable and became sarcastic. "By the way, nice shirt. Is that for the monsoon too? Your lack of professionalism makes everything worse." David was direct and blunt as he temporarily reverted back to his Israeli persona.

Ralph tried to soothe his new friend's discomfort. "Oh, the shirt yes, I wear it to look like a tourist. The camera finishes off my look. I can go anywhere I want, sometimes I even pretend to be lost. When we travel up north, I'll dress appropriately for that too."

David realized he didn't give Ralph enough credit. He was sharper than he originally thought. David reminded himself being on the frontline like Ralph was different than what he did behind the scenes. He hoped would adapt quickly. "OK, bring me to my hotel and pick me up in an hour for our shopping spree."

An hour later David was waiting outside his hotel. As David climbed in the car, Ralph said, "Before we start our adventure, I'd thought you'd want some background. First, I'll take you to HQ."

The DEA office in Ho Chi Minh City is located in a small nondescript building in an out of the way corner of the city. The inside is typical government fashion, depressing and gloomy.

Ralph started a brief history lesson. "You might want to read '*The Politics of Heroin in Southeast Asia*' by Alfred McCoy, first published in 1972. The latest edition was published in 2003. It talks about the CIA's involvement in heroin during the Vietnam War. Air America was covertly owned and operated by the CIA. It's not clear whether they are still involved today."

"Although the military junta was replaced by a nominal civilian government in 2010 in Myanmar, the Army still controls the drug trade along with human trafficking and slavery. Myanmar Oil and Gas Enterprises has no assets and makes no profit but has millions of dollars in Singapore bank accounts. Banks in Rangoon will launder money for a 40% commission."

"Opium and heroin production here was reduced by 80% from 1996 to 2006 but is coming back in a big way. They are now also producing methamphetamine and designer drugs."

Since this was a learning as well as exploratory visit for David, Ralph pulled out a map of Southeast Asia.

"We are going to fly north from here to Luang Probang airport in Laos. From there we will go by car to Chaing Sean, Thailand, the heart of the Golden Triangle. We'll stop at the Hall of Opium Museum in the city, an 'edutainment' opium theme park in Golden Triangle Park. This will give you a broader history of opium production in the Golden

Triangle and the involvement of the British."

"Then I'll show you Nam Akhu in Myanmar several kilometers away. This is a Muslim area you might have heard of. This is where the Buddhists are killing the local Muslim population, trying to purify it. People in the area live below poverty level. Even so this is a major drop-off point for the horse and donkey caravans from the poppy fields and refiners. Adjacent to the Salween River, the product is put onto small boats for the journey to Moulmein on the Bay of Bengal. From here it is taken to Rangoon. It can also be taken to the Irrawaddy River further away and down to Rangoon where most is then taken to Bangkok. Once there, mules board commercial airliners eventually bound for Hawaii or California. We'll try to zero in on who is producing your heroin."

Ralph's next recommendation was a surprise to David. He wanted to make sure David had overcome jet lag and started adapting to the weather. "Pack a bag for a couple of nights. We leave the day after tomorrow."

CHAPTER 24

David was glad the temperature and humidity were both a little lower at the 1000-foot elevation since Ho Chi Minh City is at sea level. However, traipsing around in the monsoon season wasn't much to his liking. He was glad Ralph suggested he buy water-resistant boots, more appropriate clothing and a couple of non'dos, the conical bamboo hats worn by locals to keep the rain out during the monsoon or made wet, so evaporation would cool them when it's hot and sunny.

David was now dressed in his usual T-shirt but wore new khaki cargo shorts and sported a non'do. David even took Ralph's advice about wearing a camera. Despite the annoying strap around his neck, it did complete the tourist look and he decided that returning with photos would help his team see what they were up against.

Ralph wore a different flowered Hawaiian shirt but also had the same pants, boots, hat and camera as David. He was amused by his new friend's wardrobe discomfort and had trouble hiding his smile, turning his head, holding back a laugh.

"David, loosen up. You are supposed to be on vacation having a good time. Let me take a picture of you for your people back home."

Ralph couldn't contain himself any longer and burst into uproarious laughter, wiping tears from his eyes.

David sneered at Ralph just as the camera clicked the photo.

"I'll email this to your friends, so they can see what a great time you're having." This time he roared with obnoxious laughter so loud it caused people to stare.

After he settled down, they went to the rental counter where Ralph rented an old beat-up jeep.

"Four-wheel drive is a necessity in these parts. We are going to be driving on some very muddy roads."

They found a jeep which had clearly seen better days and jumped in. Ralph told David, "This jeep had once been owned by Air America. The CIA set up a dummy corporation during the Vietnam War. It funded itself by transporting and selling heroin and marijuana. It was able to service and maintain all of its equipment like this jeep. Rumor is that it is still in business today. So no matter what it looks like this jeep will hum a beautiful tune."

David was not thrilled with the afternoon rain. "Couldn't you find one with a roof and windows that don't leak?"

Ralph broke out in laughter once more. "This is part of the adventure."

David just stared at Ralph and said, "What a jerk!"

"Hang on we're off to Chiang Sean, Thailand on the banks of the Mekong River," Ralph shouted as he floored the gas pedal.

As they were driving Ralph continued, "I have a special treat for you. Anytime I'm in the area, I make it a rule to stop at Sala Mae Rim Restaurant at the Four Seasons Hotel. It has the best Northern Thai food in the area. We'll sit out on the deck overlooking the lotus pond and rice patties. Sometimes you can even see elephants in the jungle."

David sat back trying to enjoy the ride while he filled Ralph in on what his team knew.

David was startled as the jeep slid to a stop in the hotel parking lot. Ralph let out a deep sigh, "Driving in the rain takes its toll. It tires me out. I'm glad it usually only rains in the afternoon but we can get steady rain for days on end. We really lucked out."

On their arrival, David was again thrown off guard. He looked at Ralph with fire in his eyes, "This is a very plush hotel. I feel a bit under dressed."

Ralph chuckled. He liked keeping people off-balance. He especially liked doing it to David because he was such an easy target. "Aw, don't worry about it. The eating area on the deck is low-key. Everyone dresses casually." He hoped David would relax as they entered the outside thatched roof eating area. The air smelled clean with a hint of rotting twigs and leaves, almost a mushroom jungle smell that didn't offend the senses.

"Let me order for you." Ralph was insistent.

David was not too comfortable with anything Ralph said. He felt trapped and had no choice but to go along. "I hope we're not staying here?"

"Nah, I got rooms at a Country Inn where you'll feel more comfortable. I know the owners well. They'll treat us right."

The waitress came over to take their order. She was very charming and pretty in her silk pha nung, a beautiful piece of rectangular cloth wrapped around her lower body. Her matching silk sabai was draped diagonally over her chest, covering one shoulder, with the end dropping behind her back.

She smiled at them coyly as Ralph ordered dinner in fluent Thai. She smiled and dipped at the knees before turning toward the kitchen.

The Thai beers arrived ice cold, followed by appetizers of Fried Crab Claws with Minced Shrimp and Crispy Shrimp Cakes with plum sauce. "This food is amazing. I've never had anything like it." David was impressed, especially since Ralph ordered in Thai and he had no idea what he was eating. He began to relax, not just because of the beer.

Ralph was pleased with himself knowing David would tell his team back home, hoping his hospitality would get back to his bosses in DC.

"Wait 'til the main courses come out. They're a house specialty."

David heard trumpeting and scanned the jungle for elephants. While David was looking for the animals, the next course arrived, and Ralph described the dishes. "This dish is Northern Thai Dry Spice Curry with Pork and Small Pickled Garlic, the other is Fried Prawns with Hot Basil Leaves."

They shared them the same way as the appetizers.

David was again blown over by the subtleness of flavors, mixing them with jasmine rice. "Man, you've outdone yourself. The food is remarkable. I'm stuffed."

Ralph accomplished his task as he saw David finally relax.

"We'll go to the Hall of Opium Museum before traveling on. This was financed by the Queen Mother, probably as penance for getting the Chinese addicted to opium. We've got a lot to do."

They got back into their jeep and headed down a paved road toward their next stop.

The approach to the Hall of Opium Museum on the outskirts of Chiang Sean was beautiful. The modern white stucco buildings had pyramidal roofs and were surrounded by grass.

Ralph was sure of himself and it showed.

"We're going to take the shuttle bus to the entrance in back and work our way to the front of the building. I think you'll find this interesting."

The beginning cave-like entryway with its dark blue lighting was disorienting. It was made to simulate the disorientation of being high on opium. "I don't know if you know this," Ralph began. "Opium is thought to have originated in the Mediterranean around 1000 BCE and its literal translation is 'fruit juice.' It was brought to China and India by Alexander the Great around 330 BCE. Although Alexander admired Cyrus the Great of Persia, whose Empire stretched from Egypt to the Indus River, he took over his empire through a series of battles, bringing the opium with him."

David cut in. "My training is in ancient cultures and weapons, so I know most of this, but my education didn't include anything about the history of opium. Go on, this is fascinating. Maybe we have something in common after all."

"Great, I'm glad I can teach you something else besides the cuisine of Southeast Asia." Ralph was delighted that David was an interested student.

Ralph continued, "After barely opening China by the West in the early part of the 19th Century, Britain was shipping tons of its silver to China to quench the English thirst for tea, silk and porcelain.

France also found itself in a similar boat. They found a diabolical way to stop it. Britain started shipping opium grown in eastern India to China, addicting many Chinese of all ranks and reversed the flow of silver. The Chinese Quing Emperor tried to put a stop to this in 1839. This resulted in the First Opium War which China lost. In the Treaty of Nanking, they had to cede Hong Kong Island to the British and open five ports to trade."

"This was a terrible deal for the Chinese and they stalled full implementation. In 1850 the British and French again attacked China, resulting in the Second Opium War. The 'Treaty' was renegotiated. This time opening the ports to all British ships and legalizing the opium trade."

"This lasted until the downfall of the Quing Dynasty in 1911. The Republic of China was born in 1912 and lasted until the communist takeover in 1949 establishing the Peoples Republic of China."

David was in awe, "How do you know all of that?"

Ralph pulled his head back and smiled broadly. He was proud of his knowledge of history.

"Well, I'm a history buff. Ancient history is fascinating to me and how it pertains to today's world. That's why I requested this post. It's the closest I could get to China and the Golden Triangle. I take pride in understanding the history and culture of the area to interact better with the locals, whether government or gangs. It helps put me on a more even footing with them, knowing why they act and react in the way they do. We don't learn much about the history of the far east in American schools. If you come here as a novice you will get blindsided and won't be very effective at your job."

David began to respect Ralph the more he got to know him. "What else does the museum have in store for us?"

They returned their attention to the displays. Ralph continued, "The museum also gives a history of the consumption and consequences of the drug. Once addicted, it is very difficult to escape. People would shoot it, smoke it or snort it to get its pleasant dream-like effect. This leads down a rabbit hole of doing anything to get the next fix, whether selling one's self, stealing or killing. Nothing is out of bounds. The destruction in its path is full blown and leads to a life of depravity."

The final display showed pictures of long-term heroin users. The exhibit was incredibly moving and very powerful, going from cerebral to emotional. Exhausted they exited the museum two hours later and David was glad for his new hat since it was raining. He put it on as they walked to the jeep.

"That was really impressive. I would like to see similar museums placed around the US. Maybe kids would learn heroin's dangers and avoid it." David was thinking out loud.

"That's a great idea. We can go through our agencies and try to get it done. You know, I'll bet adding the same type of information on meth, cocaine, hallucinogens and designer drugs would educate our kids to the danger of these drugs too. Hopefully persuading them to steer clear." Ralph was lost in thought at the possibilities as they got back into the jeep.

As he started the jeep Ralph explained, "We're now heading for Nam Akhu about 18 clicks away in Myanmar. After the pavement the road is going to get really muddy so hang on."

They traveled as far as they could on the paved road before Ralph turned off onto a dirt trail just wide enough for the jeep. The puddles, ruts and small fallen trees made the travel slow. It took 35 minutes to travel the next 14 kilometers. David found it hard to enjoy the ride. The rain seeped in from the roof and windows and the jungle seemed to close in, trying to devour them like Seymour in the "Little Shop of Horrors." Ralph stopped briefly to show David a spectacular small waterfall which filled a pool at its base. This was an ideal setting, a hidden paradise. Periodically the jungle would open revealing a mountain rice paddy and quickly closed back up. It didn't seem to want to divulge too much. Ralph stopped at one of the openings.

"Even if farmers have their own water-filled rice paddies in the valleys, they will also grow mountain rice on slopes they clear. This rice has a distinct flavor and is only irrigated by rain. We'll have some tonight at dinner."

Ralph drove a little faster than David would have but he had been this way before. He seemed accustomed to it. "We're approaching

Nam Akhu. We crossed the Myanmar border at the waterfall. This is one of many morphine refining sites. The opium poppy is grown all around this region. It is usually refined to morphine, then sent to villages like this to be further refined into heroin."

As the jeep slowed, the rain mercifully stopped. They began passing thatched roof dwellings with living platforms raised about 3 feet above the ground. The residents peered out wondering who was driving through their domain, making sure it wasn't the army, police or others looking for protection money.

Ralph commented, "The living areas are off the ground to keep the occupants dry and to keep out undesirables like snakes and insects. If critters get in they're much easier to spot. The thatch works well to keep the rain out. This village is typical for the refiners. The villages have between 4 to 10 dwellings each. The refining areas are set up further out in the jungle to conceal them."

David asked, "I have no idea how the poppy is grown, and heroin is produced. Could you fill me in?"

"Thought you'd never ask. I'm going to drive around the area a little and go back a different way. Since the rain stopped and the clouds have cleared, you might be able to see some of last year's growing fields. I'll point them out as we drive by."

"The opium poppy, Palaver somniferum, blooms one time. From seed to harvest is about 120 days. The one main stem contains a terminal pod but can have another 3 to 5 stems each with terminal pods. The flowers are beautiful from white to various shades of red. The pods are about the size of a chicken egg and are tapped or scraped to get the opium. It can grow in any soil but likes sandy loam best."

"They are grown in a family plot of about one acre in size." Ralph stopped the jeep at a small break in the jungle. "Over there to the right is one."

David strained his neck to get a good look. "How many people does it take to cultivate the plot?"

"The highlanders nuclear family consists of 3 to 5 people of ethnic origin, usually Muslims, as opposed to the indigenous tribes. The fields are located at the 3000-foot elevation on westerly facing mountain slopes with a 20 to 40% grade. This is best for sun and water drainage."

"The fields are prepared in March by slashing the forest and burning it in April. The seeds are planted at the end of the rainy season in August to September and no later than the end of October. They mature in the long days of November to December. They are usually planted with corn to keep weeds down and to feed to their pigs and ponies. The corn is harvested in September and October."

David wanted to clarify what he was looking at. "So, this plot has been burned and has been prepared for planting in a couple of months from now?"

"You got it." Ralph began driving again and resumed. "The poppies bloom from the end of December to the beginning of February. The 3 to 5-foot-high plants can have 3 to 5 pods each. The pods are scored or tapped 2 weeks after the flower petals fall off. Each can be tapped more than once. The pod is ready to harvest when the points of the crown on the top of the pod turn upward."

Fascinated, David said, "I didn't realize you had such vast knowledge about the opium poppy. You are a walking Wikipedia. You sound like you've given this lecture before."

Ralph came back, "I've given this lecture many times to people who need to understand the business. I just love the subject."

He took in a deep breath and stopped the jeep at a clearing after wiping his brow. "You see that mountain with the fallow fields along its western side? Those, my boy, are resting poppy fields like the one we just saw close-up." His voice was triumphant as though he'd just discovered a vast treasure, which he had. "Now I'll go into the harvest side."

"While I'm doing that, I'm going to continue driving back to our hotel. These roads can become even more treacherous at night."

David agreed with a loud, "Great!" This surprised Ralph and surprised David even more.

"Sit back and relax. The harvest and refining process are even more interesting." Ralph said in a voice that was smooth and flowing, trying to take the edge off his new friend because he was beginning to drive a little faster on the debris filled muddy road.

"The villagers use a wooden stick with 4 blades to vertically scrape the sides of the poppy from top to bottom. This is done in the late afternoon, so the sticky white opium latex can congeal overnight. This process oxidizes and darkens it. The next morning it's scraped from the pod. The pod continues to drain for several days and is scraped daily. Each pod produces between 10-100mg of opium. Each field produces 8-15kg."

"After it's dried for several more days it turns brown and is then wrapped in banana leaves awaiting sale, barter or for smoking. This opium is like plastic. It seems indestructible. If it's stored correctly, it can last forever."

"Fascinating. I thought it had a shelf life." David was intrigued by the information.

Ralph continued, "To begin the refining process, it's cooked to remove the leaves, twigs and sticks. The resulting thick sticky fluid is then drained through cheesecloth. It's cooked again to remove its water content, turning into a dark brown paste. Dried in the sun to remove even more water it becomes a darker brown putty. 80% of its weight is removed by then. When sold in the States from Mexico it's called Black Tar or Mexican Brown."

David again broke in, "I always wondered how that was made. How do they get heroin from it?"

"I was just coming to that," Ralph replied.

"There are 35 different alkaloids in the putty. Morphine is the main one but only comprises 10%. The other useful alkaloids are codeine and thebaine. Thebaine, by the way, is named after Thebes, the Egyptian City in the upper Nile. It is used to make the semi-synthetic painkillers Percodan, Dilauded and Vicodin."

"German pharmacist, Fredrich Sertuner, isolated morphine in 1805. He named it after Morpheus, the Greek God of dreams. Refining it from opium is relatively easy and only requires a few chemicals and a water supply, so this part is done near the fields. This lightens the load by a total of 90%, making it easier to transport."

"Refining morphine into heroin is more complex. This is done at larger clandestine cook sites like Nam Akhu, across the border in Thailand."

"Since you like history, I'll add, that in the early 1600s, the Dutch introduced opium to China along with tobacco. They were mixed and smoked in their clay tobacco pipes. You have probably seen some. They are usually white and have a long stem and small bowl."

"In the late 1700s, the British East India Trading Company controlled the prime growing area in Northeast India. By the 1800s they controlled the supply and were able to set the price."

Ralph finished as he pulled their jeep into the parking area. "We'll be staying here at the Gin Guesthouse. It's a cozy out-of-the-way place. We'll go to town to grab some dinner, then mingle. I've already made contact with my local informant Blatha Colthan. I call him Viking because he loves riverboats. He'll meet us later."

The brief rest and shower prepared them for the night's activities.

Entering the Khua Imjang restaurant in early evening, they sat down to a smorgasbord that Ralph had preordered with the family who owned the restaurant.

David was confused, and his face showed it.

"This food is wonderful. We didn't even order and they keep bringing out different dishes. How is that happening?"

Ralph chuckled to himself again throwing David off balance.

"I know the family and I told them we were coming."

David shook his head and said in a frustrated voice, "Man, you did it again."

As the dishes were served Ralph explained what they were eating.

The two appetizers were Thai Basil Rolls and Chicken Satay. The first was a rice noodle roll with basil, lettuce, carrots, chicken and shrimp served with plum sauce. The second was thin-sliced chicken breasts marinated in Thai herbs and coconut milk, placed on skewers and grilled. It was served with peanut sauce.

The three entrees included Crispy Duck, Tamarind Grouper and Pork Pad Thai. The duck was roasted till the skin was crispy then sliced and served with bell pepper, onion, and Japanese eggplant. A sweet spicy basil sauce was poured over it. The grouper was broiled and was swimming in a tamarind sweet-and-sour sauce. The Pad Thai consisted of noodles with thin, sliced pork added. The meal was washed down with Thai beer.

David was stuffed from the delicious delicacies. He said, "Ralph, thanks for yet another memorable experience. You have your fun with me, but then you try to make up for it with a peace offering. Quit doing that would you. I don't like the seesaw. I'd rather not have the peace offering if it is going to be at my expense."

David looked Ralph squarely in the eyes, with fire in his own. "Don't do that anymore." His voice was firm and words direct.

Ralph looked at David apologetically and nodded.

After dinner they slowly walked to the riverfront, both in deep thought but for different reasons.

Ralph's demeanor changed to one of heightened awareness as they approached the river. The air was breezy. A light rain fell. A woman passed them trolling the riverfront for business.

"We're going to meet Viking here. I've worked with him for many years and consider him a friend. That doesn't mean he hasn't changed loyalties and set us up."

He pulled out the .45 from the small of his back and tucked it in his front waistband, hand on top.

David was baffled, surprise on his face.

"Where did you get that?"

Ralph didn't want David to know how potentially dangerous the meeting might be.

"I pick it up at the restaurant when I need it and return it when I'm done."

Just then Viking stepped out of a bush one hundred feet away.

"Hello Yankee." His voice was friendly, his stride easy as he walked up to them. "Good to see you, my friend. What can I do for you?"

Ralph relaxed, sensing no danger and introduced David.

"My pal here is looking for the source of new pure heroin coming out of the area. It has been showing up on the East Coast of America and it's different from the usual."

Viking was curious about Ralph's new friend and became cautious.

"Who is this pal? Does he want to buy some?"

"No. Look, I've known David for quite a while. He's clean. Nothing to worry about with him."

"He won't be able to buy any. It's a new operation that's tightly controlled. This new stuff's being refined to higher standards. What do you want to know about it?"

Ralph was genuinely eager to know. His eyebrows and voice both raised.

"We want to know where it goes from here."

"Ah, that's easy. The regular stuff travels south to Yangon or Bangkok. The new stuff goes down the Mekong to Ho Chi Minh City."

Viking was relieved, his shoulders relaxed.

Ralph really looked puzzled now. This was indeed a new trail to follow. It would cause him endless work.

"Can you get me some? I want to make sure it's the stuff were looking for."

Ralph put his hand in his pocket and pulled out a wad of bills, giving them to Viking. He was paying as much for the information as the sample and knew Viking would deliver.

"No problem, I'll drop some off, same spot 9AM. When I see you, I'll drop some trash. It'll be inside."

Viking turned and walked away. He didn't want to linger, bringing suspicion on himself from anyone who might be watching.

David asked, "Where is Yangon?"

Ralph answered, "That's the new name for Rangoon. Each time a new government takes over they change the names of their cities. This time the military government thought it would reflect better on them to lose the old colonial names and revert to old original names."

CHAPTER 25

HEADQUARTERS TOSH
JOINT EXPEDITIONARY FORCE LITTLE CREEK
VIRGINIA BEACH, VIRGINIA
LATE JUNE

Jim was watching the surveillance cameras and said, "Here he comes." The atmosphere was somehow different as David entered the room, kind of hushed. His eyes crept around the corner as he heard a giggle and muffled laughs. He scanned the occupants, who he thought of as friends now, trying to hide their amusement by turning away or covering their mouths with their hands. It was then he noticed them looking hesitatingly at the 18x24-inch picture of him at the Luang Prabang Airport on the corkboard, sneer and all.

David blushed with embarrassment, "OK guys, give me a break. It's not that funny." His voice rose. He wondered what he was doing to continually put himself in a position of ridicule. He had been working on this sort of thing because he was bullied as a youth which lowered his self-esteem. He wanted to do away with old sick behavior patterns and create new more healthy ones, like sticking up for himself.

TJ couldn't help himself. "It sure is. You're never going to live that one down." He blurted out followed by a full roaring laugh unable to contain himself any longer.

David wasn't sure if he should make a beeline for the door or sit and take the humiliation in stride. Since he was trying to boost his self-esteem at the suggestion of his therapist, he decided to sit and reflect on the circumstances. He was beginning to recognize how this situation was just plain fun and lightened the interaction of all. They were helping him to come out of his shell. He took himself too seriously, hiding his feelings and distancing himself from others. He needed to round himself out.

After the fun was over. The team settled down. David relaxed. He put a memory stick in the computer and turned the projector on.

"As long as I was playing tourist, I decided to take pictures, so you could get a feel for the area." He felt more composed than he ever did in his life, smiling at the insight, allowing forward movement in his personal development.

He gave a rundown on his adventure. The first slide was a map of Southeast Asia. The next a blow-up map of the Golden Triangle. He wanted to orient his team. He also posted these as paper maps on the corkboard. He had a picture of the airport and DEA office in Ho Chi Minh City. He liked photography and took pictures of the major tourist sites that Ralph rushed him through even though he didn't want to spend extra time seeing them. But Ralph had planned an extra day in Ho Chi Minh City so he had no choice. He felt this would make the explanation of his trip more palatable. Next came the Luang Prabang Airport in Laos. The team already saw the hats in Ralph's picture. The beat-up rental jeep gave everyone a chuckle.

"You and Ralph rode around in that rattrap?" Godfrey's tone was incredulous. He raised his eyebrows in surprise and had a shocked expression on his face.

"Yeah, it was CIA surplus, but the mechanics were sound."

Feeling ever more comfortable now, David went on with his slide show.

"Ralph loves food. He took me to great restaurants and ordered in fluent Thai." David took pictures of each dish to make the team a little jealous.

"Wow! That food looks amazing. Did it taste as good as it looks?" Jim entered the conversation. He usually stayed in the background, but this was part of his territory.

"Sure did," David said as his mouth began to water.

Jim replied, "Looks like I'm going to have to take it up a notch."

Jim didn't want his hospitality outdone. He was thinking of adding Bangkok Garden to his repertoire of takeouts for the team. He knew them to have the best Thai in the city.

David continued, "The Heroin Museum, ten miles north of Chiang Sean, Thailand, was terrific. You came out of there not wanting to get anywhere near the stuff. Ralph and I think we should petition Congress through the DEA to have it duplicated in major US cities, adding the other dangerous street drugs. We think it will be a much better deterrent than the foolishness that is currently used. The DEA Museum in Pentagon City, Arlington, which is not well known, doesn't hold a candle to it."

David continued his slide show, which included pictures of their meals at the Four Seasons Hotel and the banquet at Khua Imjang restaurant.

Everybody oohed and ahed. Some were even smacking their lips. All were jealous, Jim again the most.

"This is the Gin Guesthouse. My home away from home," David said jokingly.

He then described the meeting with Viking.

"Ralph is pretty resourceful. Not only does he speak fluent Thai but he also knows the best out-of-the-way places to stay and eat. To my astonishment, he picked up a gun at the restaurant. He gave it back when we left the area."

Brad took the lead, recognizing that David was becoming more open, and smiled. "Wow, what a presentation. I wish they were all like that. Maybe you can become a tour guide in your next life."

He stood and approached the corkboard posting what they knew so far.

"Godfrey identified the heroin David and Ralph got in Thailand as the same stuff we're following."

"We now know the heroin is coming from the Jun Haw Chinese from the Golden Triangle. It goes down the Mekong River to Ho Chi Minh City. Ralph has traced it to small ships headed for Hong Kong. We lose it there."

"We pick it up again first on the streets of Baltimore, then on the streets of Baltimore, DC, Richmond and Hampton Roads. We think the hillbillies have something to do with the import and we think it is coming in from offshore Virginia Beach and the Outer Banks. We're filling in the pieces of the puzzle, but we still don't know who is leading this organization."

He looked around the room to see if anyone had any questions. Since the room remained silent he continued, "David, you're back on the road again. I want you to go to Hong Kong. Call Fred at Task Force Alpha and connect with his DEA liaison there. Find out what happens to the heroin once it gets there."

The rest of the team was envious that David got these plum assignments. Brad chose him specifically, not only because of his expertise, but also because he was too introverted. He wanted his team to be comfortable with each other. David had the biggest problem fitting in. Going on these assignments forced him to interact with strangers. Coming back forced him to tell the story of what he found. To everyone's surprise he was a great storyteller.

Brad is a team player and good team leader. He wants his people to improve themselves while under his command. Although not typical of leaders in this position, this was part of his uniqueness. People were always better after serving under him.

CHAPTER 26

David didn't much care for the new assignment but saw it as another opportunity to learn. At least it was better than wandering the humid jungles of Southeast Asia. He quickly caught himself reverting to his introverted self. He wanted to look at this as a new adventure that would further his psychological growth. He walked outside the terminal to the curb and saw a car heading toward him. The driver's eyes caught his as the car pulled up to the curb.

Andy Goodlet stopped in front of David. The passenger window was already rolled down as he moved toward it. "Hello David, put your bag in the trunk and hop in."

David complied. As he entered the passenger side, the car pealed out before he could even close the door. He brought his trusty camera along, so he could keep the team back home informed. Actually, he began enjoying the limelight and wanted to try it out again.

Andy held out his hand to introduce himself, "I'm Andy. I hear you love tours so I'm going to give you my $10 tour instead of my $5 tour before I take you to your hotel." Andy started laughing at his little joke. He caught David looking at him as he slapped the driving wheel still laughing, "Hey I'm just teasing you a little. Ralph told me about your trip."

David looked askance at Andy, wondering what else Ralph told him.

"Hong Kong is a very interesting place. The Chinese took it over in 1997 when the British lease from 1841 with various extensions expired. They tried to incorporate it into the Chinese State but ran into lots of opposition from the locals. They had to compromise and leave it as an independent trade zone. There is still an overlay of British colonialism with an international presence and Chinese tentacles slithering into all aspects of its business and politics."

"We've been monitoring the boats coming from Vietnam. They offload at the docks on Fai Road next to the West Kowloon Highway. I'll take you there this afternoon, so you can see the setup. Then we'll take a little tour of the city before going to your hotel where you can get some sleep. I have a meeting with my CI planned for tonight, so I'll pick you up at 7 o'clock."

Getting off Kowloon Highway, Andy took the adjacent Fai Road to the docks. They were filled with small freighters and barges unloading containers. The grounds were soiled with oil, waste water and garbage. The sharp smell of diesel and acrid smell of rotting organic matter filled the air, burning the nostrils. David took photos as they traveled.

Andy briefed David on the area. "This is the only harbor in the world that does mid-water loading because space is at a premium. It's not a very pleasant place to hang out as you can see. I hope you weren't expecting a resort."

David pursed his lips and turned up his nose almost pinching it closed with his fingers because of the smell.

Andy was a bit put off by the smell himself. "I agree. Coming down here always puts me in a bad mood for the rest of the day. I just wanted to show you where the action is."

"My CI works down here. I've advised him which boats from Vietnam to look for courtesy of your good friend Ralph."

"By the way, he showed me your picture. Nice look." Andy laughed trying to disguise the chuckle with a cough which didn't work out too well.

"All right, not you too. That damn photo is going to haunt me for the rest of my life." David was annoyed once more but again took this as another opportunity to change his reaction. He was becoming aware of his troubling behavior patterns which was the first step toward changing them. He was pissed at Ralph and thought about why. Was he a mark or did they do this to everybody? If they did then his being overly sensitive made him a mark. He would ponder that thought and ask his therapist about it at his next session. If he ever saw that bastard Ralph again, he would somehow even the score. He turned toward Andy and said, "What a schmuck."

Andy just smiled as he drove around Hong Kong giving David his famous guided tour.

"Hong Kong means 'Fragrant Harbor' and is also known as 'The Pearl of the Orient.' It's the most highly populated metropolis in the world with stunning modern architecture, feng shui approved. Public transportation connects to 90% of its population. It has many parks and is connected to Kowloon on the mainland. I'll take you to the Sky Terrace at Victoria Peak on Hong Kong Island for the amazing view of the entire area. It is 1,811 feet high. The area is really beautiful." Andy had more than a hint of pride in his voice.

Andy drove to Garden Road to take David on the Hong Kong Peak Tram. That funicular was opened in 1888 with a modern rebuild in 1989. It is a beautiful ride. On the ascent the high rises seem to tilt toward the mountain in a visual illusion.

Even though Andy had been up here many times, he never got tired of the view.

"Most people here speak English, so getting around is easy. I'm proud of the way this city takes care of its people and guests." Andy seemed to puff out his chest a little at his statement. His posture straightened ever so slightly.

David caught the change, thinking maybe this guy has some humanity in him after all. "This is really beautiful. Is that Kowloon over there?"

Andy replied, "Yeah. That sliver of land with all the boats next to the highway is where we just came from."

Back in the car Andy announced, "We'll go past the quaint Aberdeen fishing village and on to Stanley Harbor. Tourists take small motorized junks around the harbor. I won't subject you to that."

David breathed a sigh of relief. "Thanks."

He appreciated Andy's pride in his city and the insight, but he was here for a special purpose and wanted to get on with it. He set his jaw firmly and looked out the window trying not to enjoy the sites. He didn't yet have the insight to recognize he was doing it again. Never allowing himself to enjoy the pleasure of the moment, he was focused on the job. People could unconsciously read that and easily bait him. He brought the bullying on himself by his actions.

"Mainland China is a different story. China has used 50% of the world's concrete for the past 20 years. They have been knocking down old buildings and farm houses and have been putting up 20 to 30 story apartment complexes 4-5 of the same buildings, next to two other similar complexes of different design. The Chinese banks have been funding the developers to build these 'new cities.' Speculators buy the apartments and try to rent them out. Even if they can't the value continues to rise. Many of them remain empty. The wages in China keep going up causing manufacturing to move to Vietnam, Cambodia, Thailand and Bangladesh. The national bird of China seems to be the construction crane. The displaced farmers are a new wealthy class. When houses are torn down, the occupant is given the same amount of space in the new apartment buildings. Farmers, many of whom have large houses, get large spaces, creating their wealth. The slowing down of China's economy, the empty factories and apartment buildings are going to cause a major bust at some point. The government is trying to balance the crash, so it comes to a soft landing. Everyone around the world is holding their breath."

Andy's eyes scrunched closed; his face followed, lips pursed.

"If you think we have a heroin problem now, wait 'till this house of cards falls in China, pulling the rest of the world with it. Drugs will be the only escape for the out-of-work masses. Heroin will lead the way."

He didn't like the way he was beginning to sound like a recording. He'd have to work on that.

David was impressed with his grasp of the situation and began to relax.

"Now we're going to leave Hong Kong Island which is the business part of Hong Kong and go to Kowloon which is the tourist and working-class area of Hong Kong. I'll let you off at the City View Hotel for R and R. I'll meet you in the lobby at 7."

Andy was silent for the rest of the ride. He needed some R and R himself. Looking at his watch he knew he had four hours to recoup.

Andy walked up to the hotel at 7PM sharp with a determined gait. The sidewalks were crowded as usual. David was outside waiting. He decided to put on a collared shirt for the occasion and wore his trusty blue jeans. Andy had on a flowered Hawaiian shirt and cotton pants.

David looked at Andy with a perplexed expression.

"What's with you guys and the Hawaiian shirts?"

Andy had an impish smile on his face and a snicker in his voice.

"Ralph told me you liked them."

David was angry at the answer. He knew these guys liked to fuck with him. With a screwed-up face, he said, "I just don't get you guys, what gives?" As he tried to regain some composure, he straightened his back and bore his eyes into Andy's.

Andy backed down and confessed, "Dealing with the refuse of society is pretty tough. We've got to have some fun at it or we'd go crazy. You're a great escape for Ralph and me. So, lighten up and let's have some fun tonight."

"I'm not interested in being the brunt of your humor. Cut it out or you're not going to like what I turn into."

Andy lowered his shoulders slightly and hung his head a bit, a pout on his face. He hoped David got the message.

David walked beside Andy, feeling better about himself, to Nathan Road, a major north-south thoroughfare. His step had a bounce in it. The endless line of buses was noisy and smelly. The streets had almost no litter but seemed dirty. People crowded the sidewalks. The gaudy multicolored neon signs advertised the shops and restaurants along the way.

They turned right. After a few blocks they came to Temple Street. Andy broke the silence. "This is named for the Tin Hau Temple. It was built in 1864 on the Kowloon waterfront after supposedly a statue of Tin Hau, the Goddess of the Sea, was found. She protects all boat people. After several land reclamations, it is now almost a mile from the water."

As they walked down Temple Street, they entered the Night Market. This open-air market ran several blocks with souvenir stalls on both sides. Shops in the buildings faced the back of the stalls, neon signs blaring.

Andy went back to his old tricks as they ran the gauntlet. Stall owners brashly approached them to get in their face. Andy knew to look forward and ignore them. He chuckled under his breath, a hidden smile on his face as David was attacked by the onslaught of merchants hawking their wares. "Hello, you come look, hey, good price, cheap, how much, come look."

David was overwhelmed and looked to Andy for help. "Get me out of here." He noticed the smile growing on Andy's face as he burst into boisterous laughter.

He grabbed David's arm as he headed for the next street to exit the Market. As they left the commotion, Andy let out a loud belly laugh that almost doubled him over. "I guess you don't like playing tourist?" Another round of laughter came out of Andy.

David just stood and stared. "You guys are sadistic pricks," David's voice was angry. He didn't like bullies or tricksters ever since he was on the receiving end of many attacks when he first moved to Israel as a young boy. He shook his head trying to figure a way out of this union.

Andy wiped the tears from his eyes. "Aw, I'm just having a little fun. You're too wound up, I'm trying to loosen the knot."

David looked down at the ground, kicking his feet a little. He felt the tightness in his stomach and realized Andy was right. Having been accused of this before, he decided right then and there that he was going to try to have more fun and put business in its proper place. He also got more of an insight into how closed off his emotions were. His fear of giving in to experience them was what they might ultimately reveal. He knew he had to work on this.

"All right let's move on." David's voice showed not only surrender but also conviction.

"We're going to Kam Shan Seafood Restaurant. If I have some business in the area this is where I eat. They have great food, some of the best seafood in the area. They have two restaurants. The one farther down Nathan Road is modern with the main dining room on the 7th floor. That version is mainly for tourists. The original one is on Woo Sung Street around the corner. It is a bit rundown but this is where the locals go. Since I know the place well, let me do the ordering."

David thought, "Here we go again," then realized the last time he was in a similar position it turned out great.

The restaurant was better than he expected. It wasn't fancy, but it was clean and inviting. There were fish tanks along the wall with all kinds of live fish, crabs and lobsters. There were also basins on the floor with live abalone, various kinds of clams, oysters and shrimp. The place buzzed with people having a good time.

As they walked to their table David realized they were the only Caucasians in the place. The air was thick with the aromatic smells of exotic dishes as they were led to their table. As they sat two menus were dropped in front of them. Andy smiled reassuringly as the Tsingtau beer arrived at the table. He ignored the menu and looked up at the waiter and began speaking in Cantonese. Surprised that Andy ordered in Chinese, David was more than curious. He was concerned.

"Tell me what we're eating. I've heard they eat funky things here. I don't want to eat fried rat or BBQ dog. You're not having more fun at my expense, are you?" His voice was firm, eyes focused directly at Andy's, jaw set.

"I'm not messing with you. I didn't order anything exotic. The Lobster Noodles are one of their specialties along with their Steamed Abalone in Black Pepper Sauce. Their Fish Cakes are the best in town. Eggplant in garlic sauce will round out the meal. I know you'll enjoy them all. I had some fun at your expense. I just want you to know I'm not a total asshole." His voice was soft and humble.

David was relieved and began to calm down. He decided to go with his newly experienced emotions to see where it took him.

As they waited for the meal to arrive, Andy asked David what he thought of Hong Kong.

David said, "It's very different from what I thought it was going to be.

The hustle bustle and contrast between junk and high end is fascinating. I understand you can get anything you want here, anything."

Andy said, "If you can think of it, you can get it."

The dishes began to arrive in quick succession. They looked more than delicious as David dived into them.

"Man, this stuff is great. I've never tasted anything like it." His voice was as excited as his palate, not knowing where to start seconds. After eating his fill, he leaned back, belly full, his mind at rest with a delicious meal and a satisfied experience. David thanked Andy. "I appreciate you're not fucking with me. I really enjoyed that."

"We don't always fuck with our guests. Most of the time we are strictly business. But we try to lighten the situation when we can. Wait 'till you see what I have in store for you for tonight's entertainment," Andy said with an impish tone and mischievous look in his eyes.

"Now what, are you going back to your old ways?" David said with an incredulous gasp.

Andy said nothing. The slight smile never left his lips.

After dinner they slowly walked a couple of blocks to Saigon Street and turned into an empty alley. The dark street was ominous. It smelled of urine and vomit. It was then David noticed the small red neon sign hanging into the street beaconing them to enter the Cuntry Club Bar. David was amused.

"Great name."

Andy didn't realize he was getting excited.

"We're going to meet George Zhang Yi here and have some fun too."

The interior wasn't as sleazy as David thought it was going to be. The stage had a couple of very attractive nude girls pole dancing. There were others mingling with the crowd. The smoke hung in the air like a blue curtain. David began to chill out but maintained a sense of vigilance.

"Better than I expected," he said somewhat relieved that the place was in some measure refined.

Andy was familiar with the place, having been here many times before. He loved to take his guests here, never getting a negative review.

"We'll take a booth in the back to give us some security. George will find us there."

Two Chinese beauties wearing skimpy lingerie slid in next to them. Andy ordered a couple of Tsingtao beers. When he saw George, he gave each of them a fifty and dismissed them.

Andy sported a broad grin.

"How are you doing tonight George? Come join us." He motioned with his outstretched hand and looked briefly at the empty space. "This is my friend David."

George acknowledged them both as he nervously pulled up a chair and sat at the head of the table, not comfortable with his back to the room. He wanted a position that could easily be abandoned if trouble came looking. He glanced cautiously toward the front and rear doors making sure no one had followed him in. The air became electrified with his arrival.

"I've got some good information for you. I expect more than the usual, because it was extremely dangerous to get. I had to take the long way around to make sure I wasn't followed."

"Not to worry pal. You know I always take care of you. Now what do you have?"

George leaned in closer, so he wouldn't be overheard.

"After the container is unloaded, the product is taken out and put into a van. The van goes to a private warehouse nearby. I had to climb a mountain of garbage to get a look in the window. I almost broke my leg getting to the top. They opened the large crates filled with the standard one kilo packages of heroin and repacked the contents into smaller wooden crates lined with styrofoam putting what looks like 25 one kilo packs and a radio transmitter inside. They took those and encased them in waterproof boxes labeled Kowloon Shipping and put the 25 kilo boxes into a small van. I got down and waited for it to leave, then followed it to the Kwai Chung Container Terminal past Stonecutters Island. I watched as a couple of guys in the crew took the boxes out of the van and put them in a container for the Lersk *Anne*."

Needing clarification Andy asked, "Where did they put it?"

"They break the seal on a container and load it near the doors. A new seal is then attached. I had to wait several hours to watch the container placed on the stern of the ship, doors facing back."

Wanting to get out of there as quickly as possible, George talked fast.

Andy wondered, "Do you know who's running the operation?"

George was getting increasingly antsy. It was clear he wanted out. Beads of sweat began forming on his forehead. The expanding rings under his arms was telling.

"Not a clue."

Andy slipped him a wad of one hundred-dollar bills.

"Thanks for the info pal."

George grabbed it. As he stuffed the wad into his pocket he bolted for the door.

David was satisfied with the results so far.

"I'll contact Connie back at TOSH and put her on the trail."

Andy motioned for the girls to come back as he ordered a bottle of champagne for the table.

"Now can we have some fun?"

David smiled.

CHAPTER 27

David was the first to get to Headquarters. He wanted to avoid the humiliation suffered last time. He was at his seat, smiling, as he waited to greet each of the Team as they arrived.

Jim was the next to come in. He was shocked to see David, not only because he was there before him, but also because he had a broad grin on his face. He usually slipped in silently and stayed in the shadows.

As the other members arrived, they briefly stood frozen at the sight, before going to the conference table for coffee and morning goodies. As they took their seats they were all waiting for David to start the show and tell.

Godfrey couldn't wait. He was the first to speak. "What gives? This looks like a new you."

"Yeah, I've decided to cast aside my old shell and set myself free. My therapy has taught me a great deal about myself. I no longer have the need to remain in the background. I feel good about myself and my place in the world. I'm going to enjoy each day as it comes no matter what, kinda Zen-like. TJ should understand what I mean. After all his house and yard are like a Shinto Shrine."

TJ broke in, "Hey leave me outta this. I'm just cruising along, trying to mind my own business. That's Zen."

Brad entered the room at the beginning of the dialogue. He listened thoughtfully to the discussion and smiled to himself, recognizing his tactics were working. Pleased with David's transformation, he went to his seat. Jim almost beat him there with his morning coffee.

Brad called the team to order saying, "David, I like the new you, especially the Hawaiian shirt. Give us a rundown on your China visit." David, having already loaded his pictures into the PowerPoint program, turned on the projector and began his travelogue. He described the history of Hong Kong and the tour including the docks.

He wanted to emphasize the discomfort Andy put him through. "We walked down Nathan Avenue through the neon-filled Night Market. All kinds of junky souvenirs are for sale. The merchants attack you hawking their wares. I was taken aback by their aggressiveness and stood frozen. Andy thought this was pretty funny until he finally had to rescue me."

"I'm going to get back at those DEA bastards one way or another." David was almost seething.

TJ broke in, "That is not very Zen-like either, David. You're going to have to learn to live for the day and let things like that slide off your back."

"Well, I guess the journey of self-discovery never really ends does it." David took a moment to reflect on the interchange.

He went on, "Andy, like Ralph made up for it with a great meal." He showed pictures of each dish to make them all envious.

"After dinner we walked a few blocks to our rendezvous with Andy's CI." He put up a picture of the alley and the Cuntry Club sign. He had an impish smile while his head tilted back, eyes closed in a dreamlike state.

Connie smiled at the name, but being the only women in the room she also laughed wanting the guys to know she was one of them.

Coming back to the present, David described the meeting with George and the information imparted. He didn't go into details about the rest of the evening, but everyone guessed what must have happened. Having finished, he returned to his seat, satisfied with how he handled himself. The room remained quiet. All were deep in thought.

Brad got up and approached the corkboard adding to the people caught in their web as the team came back to the present.

"To consolidate what we know. The opium is grown in the Golden Triangle where it's processed into heroin and packaged into bales. Then it's brought down the Mekong River to Ho Chi Minh City, shipped to Hong Kong, and put aboard ships heading past the Outer Banks for ports in Hampton Roads and Baltimore which use the same routes into the Chesapeake Bay. We locate it again when it arrives in the shipping channels about sixty miles east of Virginia Beach and the Outer Banks. The Coast Guard has drones watching the incoming shipping traffic, so from the drones we've been able to ascertain that Tersk and OverSea seem to be the main carriers. It's strange though that neither their central office or ship captains know anything about it."

"The Coast Guard drones have also observed the ship's crew dumping the bales overboard. From David's work we know the bales have locator beacons inside and they've spotted the *Shaft 6* picking up what looks like the same bales from as far as 5 miles away before bringing them into either Rudy Inlet, Lynnhaven Inlet or various locations in the Outer Banks."

"The drones also caught the *Shaft 6* offloading fish at the dock. We think the hillbillies repackage the heroin inside fish on the *Shaft 6* because we never see any bales come off the boat. We see them sell the fish to the public, restaurants, purveyors and distributors. We assume some fish have heroin inside and some don't. We just can't tell the players from the legitimate buyers."

Godfrey added. "We know what's coming off those ships is the same quality China White. We've been able to get a hold of some samples. It matches the samples we've been able to acquire."

Connie was silent for a change, thinking about what might have been going on inside that club. Her curiosity stimulated her vivid imagination.

Brad was playing a chess game in his head moving forward many moves. "David, find out from Andy when the next shipment leaves Hong Kong."

"I'll get Mack to coordinate with the Coast Guard and Navy to see if we can catch them red-handed after a pick-up. If we catch them, we'll try to flip them in the hopes that they'll give up whoever is at the next level."

Talking about a mission involving ships and clandestine operations brought memories of one of the most harrowing assignments with TJ flooding back into his head. If you were getting on a ship you knew it was going to be rough. There were no easy assignments in the SEALs, but the ones that started on a ship were some of the most difficult.

Brad thought of his fellow SEALS who gave their lives for the United States and their memory brought a tear to his eye.

TJ recognized the look on Brad's face and wanted to help him shoulder the emotions by changing the subject.

"Hey Brad, this sort of reminds me of one of our most difficult missions with SEAL Team 6. Why don't you tell that story, I think everyone here will find it interesting."

"OK." Brad paused, his eyes scanned the ceiling to put the sequence of events in order in his mind before he began.

David, Connie, Godfrey and Jim waited with anticipation just like looking forward to an action movie or reading a good book. TJ's diversion took the attention away from Brad's distraught look.

"TJ and I remember this mission well. We boarded the fast attack sub *Amber Jack* in Norfolk. This was one of the first subs to use a detachable six-man minisub designed specifically for the SEALs. We crossed the Atlantic and went into the Mediterranean, heading straight for the Lebanese coast. Three miles from shore, the *Amber Jack* settled to the bottom. Our six-man SEAL team entered the minisub and drove it to within half a mile of a secluded beach near Beirut. We parked it and got out. Our mission was to kill Imad Mughniyen, one of the masterminds behind the October 23rd, 1983 bombing of the Beirut Marine Corps barracks. The papers said Mughniyen died on February 12, 2008 from a car bomb as he walked down a street in Damascus, but that wasn't the truth. It was SEAL Team 6 that took him out. The CIA used a cover story to prevent retaliation."

"The Marine Barracks were near the Beirut airport. 21,000

pounds of TNT was placed on a flatbed truck on a slab of concrete. A marble slab was placed on top of it to direct the blast. It was a gas-enhanced device making it a thermobaric weapon causing a high temperature explosion with a sustained blast wave. This combination makes this type of bomb the most destructive non-nuclear weapon. It lifted the four-story building off the ground causing it to collapse when it came down."

"Ten minutes later a truck with similar but less powerful explosive took out the French compound. 241 US personnel were killed, 58 French, 6 civilians and the 2 suicide bombers. The chain of command started from the government of Tehran via Iran's Ambassador to Syria, Hojatoleslam Ali-Akbar Mohtashemi, one of the founders of Hezbollah. Next in line was the Iranian Red Guard Command headed by Hossein Dehghan. Then to Islamic Jihad, a cover for Hezbollah run by Imad Mughniyen. This took years to unravel."

"George Shultz, Secretary of State wanted a retaliatory strike. Caspar Weinberger, Secretary of Defense was hesitant since there was no clear connection to Iran at the time. President Reagan sided with Weinberger. Six months later a sea assault from the battleship *New Jersey* destroyed the Syrian and Druze positions in the Beqaa Valley. It rained 288 2,000-pound 16-inch shells on the site. They are so big the locals called them flying Volkswagens."

"Still, many people weren't satisfied. It really didn't take out the masterminds who were behind the bombing. Team 6 was sent in years later to settle the score when the perps were found."

"Imad Mughni-yen usually remained in Damascus, but our intel placed him in Beirut wanting to get a first-hand look at the standoff between the Muslims and Christians. He wanted to see if there was a way to better the odds and move on the Christians."

David cut in. "This history is fascinating. I didn't realize how complex the bombing operation and retribution was. You're a pretty good storyteller yourself. Please go on."

Connie was mesmerized by the story told by her knight in shining armor. She was swooning when she asked, "Brad would you continue telling us how you took out the head of Hezbollah."

Brad looked at Connie and noticing her dreamy eyes, he blinked a couple of times to regain his focus. Brad began to notice Connie and how attractive she was. He was becoming aware of his warm feeling toward her. "Sure. The night had a ¼ waxing moon giving us cover. Our infil ran into a snag right away because there were soldiers patrolling the beach both on foot and by truck. We approached stealthily, covered by the sound of the breaking waves. We didn't want to make contact with them but had no choice since the soldiers were between us and the road to town."

"We turned this to our advantage when we realized we could take the men out and wait for the truck to return from rounds. Master Sargent Sweeny ordered us to use head shots only in order to prevent their uniforms from becoming soiled with blood. We put on the dispatched soldier's clothes. When the truck arrived, the men inside had no idea that waiting for them was a SEAL Team instead of the friends they saw only 30 minutes before."

"The Team made fast work of the occupants. We commandeered the truck driving into central Beirut. All was going well until we entered the central business district and approached Martyrs' Square. This was named for the Lebanese nationals who were slaughtered during their unsuccessful revolt against their Ottoman Turk occupiers at the end of World War I. This used to be a beautiful park until the Civil War turned it into a no-man's land between Christians and Muslims."

"We parked the truck on the Muslim side and headed for the building housing our target. Since we didn't have the advantage of surprise, we decided to start a fire fight between the warring camps. Our well-placed shots around the windows on the Christian side brought on a barrage of fire from both sides."

"We thought by wearing the soldier's uniforms we would have an easy approach to traverse the necessary ground and hunt our target. These gave the Team the cover we needed to gain access to the building. We didn't realize that Imad Mughniyen's bodyguards wouldn't let anyone, not even other Lebanese soldiers, into the building."

"Our Team had to battle the way to the top where we finally found Mughniyen and dispatched him with a quick two tap head shot and a third to the heart. Getting back down was easier than going up, but it was still a battle. On the way out, we picked up one of our men who was killed in the initial battle. Two more men had serious wounds, so they required help returning to the truck."

"Getting everyone back in the minisub and finally back on the *Amber Jack* was an ordeal of major proportions."

Brad shook his head sadly, "We took Mughniyen out, but it cost us a good man. The two wounded SEALs recovered enough to resume duty 3 months later."

CHAPTER 28

Naval Station Norfolk, Headquarters of the Atlantic Fleet, is the largest Navy Base in the world. It supports 75 ships including aircraft carriers, attack submarines, Aegis cruisers and destroyers and 134 aircraft along with the Joint Operations Staff College and the NATO Supreme Allied Commander Atlantic (SCALANT). It's located near the site of the battle of the *Monitor* and *Merrimac* during the Civil War.

Brad hadn't been to NSN in a long time but remained familiar with the place from his stint in the SEALs. As he drove west on Shore Drive, he turned left onto East Little Creek Road. He took a right onto Bellinger Boulevard and approached the main gate. Arriving at the gate, he showed his ID to the security guard on duty. He was already punched into the system which made passage easy. As he drove in on Maryland Avenue he turned right on Pocahontas Street, arriving at Headquarters.

Brad had never been in this building before and was directed to the office of Admiral Leonard Burns, XO Naval Station Norfolk. Admiral Mack Davis and Captain Linda Nerf, CO Portsmouth CG Station, were already there. Coffee was brought in as introductions were made.

Both the Navy and Coast Guard would be a part of the mission, so Admiral Mack wanted to fill them in and give them a sense of what they were facing. He told Brad to start from the origin of the heroin and follow the trail as he knew it.

Brad had called ahead to order a PowerPoint projector. He brought his computer stick along, filled with maps and pictures that David put together for him. After putting up a slide of Southeast Asia for his audience to get their bearings, he began. "We'll start at Chang Sean, Thailand."

Brad showed pictures of Chang Sean. "This is the heart of the Golden Triangle and creeps up to the Mekong waterfront."

Brad went on. "These pictures are of the small village of Nam Akhu in Myanmar just across the border. It is one of the places where opium is grown and processed."

The slide of the map of Southeast Asia was put up again.

"Most heroin from the area is usually shipped down rivers to either Bangkok or Yangon, formerly known as Rangoon. Our heroin comes from the same place but is more refined and travels down the Mekong to Ho Chi Minh City and on to Hong Kong, where it is repackaged into 25 one kilo packages with a homing beacon added. It is then placed into a shipping container near its doors. This is placed on the stern of the ship with the doors facing the stern. This makes for easy access when it's time for the drop off the coast. Two crew members pop open the doors, make the drop and put a new duplicate seal on the shipping container. Apparently neither the Captain or shipping company knows anything about it."

Admiral Mack, as he was known to his friends, was tall and muscular. His silver hair and chiseled face gave him a distinguished, patrician persona. He added, "We would like to catch the pick-up crew in the hopes that we can get them to turn on whoever is giving them the orders. It would also be great to find out more about who is responsible for getting it to the ships."

Captain Linda Nerf was in charge of USCG operations and she was pissed that this meeting wasn't taking place in her office at USCG Base Portsmouth as would be proper. The Coast Guard had been part of the Department of Homeland Security since February 2003. They'd been doing operations like this for years and should be coordinating this op too. Their breaking protocol for the meeting made her wonder if there was too much testosterone in the room and the good ol' boy network was in play. She had no choice though, she took her orders from Homeland Security. So, she promised, "The Coast Guard will coordinate with the Navy to set a trap using drones, a Tupperwolf helicopter and a Coast Guard cutter. Just let me know when to put the plan into action."

Brad instinctively knew that Captain Nerf would do a great job. Women had to do more than men in the same job to get the respect they deserved.

Brad almost saluted. He picked up on her resentment and felt bad for her. He always had a soft spot for women. "Will do, ma'am. As soon as we get solid information on the next shipment, I'll contact you."

CHAPTER 29

OPERATION SEA DRIFT

THE GULF STREAM

60 MILES EAST OF VIRGINIA BEACH

EARLY AUGUST

Captain Arnie, 'Raging Bull,' Wallsie, the son of Naval Admiral 'Bull' Wallsie of World War II fame, was in command of Task Force "Pick Up." He went into the Coast Guard instead of the Navy because of the difficult relationship he had with his father while growing up. This was a slap to his father's face. He knew this but also liked the Coast Guard. He thought he would see more action there. He also knew he would never outdo his father's exploits in the Navy and he did not want "second place" hanging on his shoulders.

RB, as Captain Arnie was affectionately called, commanded the Cutter, *USCG James*, for this operation. She was a High Endurance, Legend-Class Cutter, hull number 754, stationed in Charleston, South Carolina. She was one of the newest Cutters of this class commissioned on August 8, 2015. She had a stern notch for a 24.75-foot Over the Horizon rigid-hulled inflatable boat. Although she had a helipad it was determined that it would be better for the Tupperwolf HH-65D Dolphin helicopter they were going to use in the operation to deploy from Oceana Naval Air Station in Virginia Beach.

Oceana, the only Master Jet Base on the East Coast, houses all of the FA-18 air squadrons from the carriers that port in Norfolk. From the base, the ocean was only about 4 miles away, allowing a quick response to the action.

The Dolphin helicopter was affectionately called a Tupperwolf because of its construction from high composite materials. These helicopters were known for their Fenestron circular housing tail rotor at the base of the tail fin and their autopilot capabilities. This allowed her to automatically maintain stable hover 50 feet above the water in any weather. She had an all-black sponson and forward machine gun mount with a M 24 B 7.12 mm general-purpose machine gun locked in place. The Dolphin was part of the HITRON, Helicopter Interdiction Tactical Squadron, stationed in Jacksonville, Florida. It was her job to persuade boat crews to stop, using visual hand signals, sirens, loudspeakers and radio. If they didn't stop she would fire a volley across their bow and use the machine gun to disable their engines if necessary.

Intelligence from TOSH indicated that the Tersk freighter *Anne* had departed Hong Kong and was due to arrive at Portsmouth Marine Terminals in Hampton Roads on Wednesday.

Military satellites tracked *Anne's* position until she reached the coast of South Carolina. At that point a drone from the *USCG James* began tracking her so they could see what was happening on deck.

Meanwhile, the *USCG James* was waiting in ambush. Admiral Mack and Brad knew their plan to use a High Endurance Legend-Class Coast Guard cutter instead of a smaller ship was overkill, but they wanted to send a message to whomever was running this operation that the US Government was serious in protecting its coastline. As the drone from the *James* circled the *Anne*, the Command Center on the *James* saw two crewmen dump 4 packages over the stern. Another drone allowed them to watch the *Shaft 6* trolling nearby. They saw *Shaft 6* pull in the lines and head toward the homing beacons, like a bear to honey.

Captain Wallsie waited for the *Shaft 6* to pick up the packages and then had them close in. The Tupperwolf hovered over the *Shaft 6*, ordering it to stop or have its engines machine-gunned out of commission. The *USCG James* soon pulled alongside the *Shaft 6* and 4 men boarded the boat. To their surprise all they found inside the packages was garbage.

Captain Wallsie immediately contacted Admiral Mack and Brad at TOSH knowing they were watching the operation unfold.

Brad was puzzled, "Our intelligence was good, but somehow they got wind of our operation and put garbage inside the packages instead of heroin. There has to be a leak."

Admiral Mack was disappointed. "Round one goes to them. Hopefully we'll get them in round two, but we need to figure out how they found out about us."

Brad knew this setback was part of the chess game, but he also feared the people they were up against were more sophisticated than first imagined. "The hillbillies aren't going to bring in the heroin themselves again since they know the government is on to them. They must have other means of getting their heroin to shore and we can bet they won't be using this method after today."

"This is a major setback. We have to find a new connection who does business with them and who could tell us what the other line of transport is."

CHAPTER 30

Brad was upset the plan didn't work, but he didn't want this to come across on the speakerphone to the Coast Guard.

"Captain Nerf, Captain Walsey, thanks for your help. We'll need to stand down on seizures for now and let the other intel we are working develop."

Brad began thinking about Moose and his connections to Nick and the pirates on the Outer Banks.

The team was in their chairs and had been watching Operation Sea Drift on the 90-inch screen. They didn't like being blindsided. Brad was really pissed off when he ended the call and let it show to the team. He swiveled around facing the group, his voice menacing.

"Well, our first attempt was clearly a bust. Now we have to sort out how they got wind of our operation and we have to assume it could be anyone. Connie, start checking the bank accounts and credit cards of all personnel that had knowledge of the operation. We've gotta find our mole. Meanwhile, David find out when the next shipment comes in. I want to be on top of it and catch those bastards this time."

Connie felt terrible for Brad. She saw he was hurt and frustrated. She wanted to comfort him, so she followed him out of the building when he left and caught up with him at his car. "Brad, I'm sorry this attempt at catching the smugglers didn't go well." She touched his arm and rubbed it gently. "Is there anything I can do?"

He noticed her perfume for the first time and looked deeply into her blue eyes. "Hop in. Let's get a beer at Dockside Marina and watch the sun set."

Connie was weak kneed as she climbed into his car. She didn't think Brad would ever take her anywhere. "I'll find the mole for you, Brad."

CHAPTER 31

Connie began working magic on her computer. She was more motivated than ever as she pulled up all the people in the Coast Guard and Navy who were involved in Operation Sea Drift. By the afternoon she found one Coastie who had more money in his bank accounts than he should have. He came from the battlefields of the Ukraine and joined the Coast Guard hoping it would lead toward citizenship. He worked himself up to Petty Officer 1st Class quickly because of his advanced computer skills. This allowed him to be intimately involved in the operation from its inception.

She immediately walked up to Brad as he was getting a cup of coffee and put her hand on his back. She unconsciously felt the power of his masculinity. She was becoming aware that this was part of her attraction to him. She was excited as she said, "I found a Coastie that looks like our guy. Go get him."

Brad contacted Commander Buckman, head of Portsmouth CGIS who worked closely with NCIS. He notified him of their discovery. Commander Buckman said the Coast Guard would apprehend the perp and bring him to the NCIS field office at Naval Station Norfolk for questioning. That office had a larger facility and brig than did CGIS.

"See you there."

CHAPTER 32

Connie's investigation turned up a suspicious deposits before the operation. By the next day Petty Officer 1st Class Anton Goyavich was brought into the interrogation room. Commander Buckman, head of CGIS Portsmouth, was there to lead the interrogation while Admiral Mack and Brad would watch from behind a see-through mirror.

"Private Goyavich we noticed you made three $9,500 deposits to your bank account the week before Operation Sea Drift. Where did that money come from?" Commander Buckman said initiating the investigation.

Goyavich looked nervous, he was starting to sweat. "I got lucky with some soccer picks through my bookie. I won $30,000, but I didn't want to deposit all of it to trigger a flag with the bank, so I made three deposits under $10,000. This is the first time I won that big. Luck was with me."

Buckman answered, "You sure learned the banking laws quickly."

"Look, I'm a computer geek and found out how to safely make those deposits under the radar." Goyavich said trying to sound convincing.

Buckman came back zeroing in on the point. "Today your luck has run out. We have reason to believe you passed information about Operation Sea Drift to people involved in shipping heroin. We want to know who you passed the information to and who paid you."

Private Goyavich looked like a deer in the headlights. He quickly put his right index finger in his mouth, swallowing and then instantly falling over foaming at the mouth, convulsing.

Buckman said, "My God he must have had a cyanide capsule inside his tooth. He bit the capsule and died instantly before anyone could react. I haven't seen anything like this since the Cold War."

CHAPTER 33

B rad was angry. "We've lost our mole. They win another round. These guys are more shrewd and dangerous than we thought. The mole killing himself is a new twist on smuggling. No one does that. We have to find a different way into their operation."

Connie again took a deep breath as she stretched her elbows back to release her tight muscles. She was beginning to make a habit of doing this. Her tight shirt showed off her wonderful breasts, nipples hard with arousal. She liked her newfound sexuality.

All couldn't help but notice the pleasant show and each, as if as one smiled approval, breaking the gloom in the room.

She liked the attention and started her report.

"Local cops just found a blonde named Lannie Croft dead in the lady's room at the Cavalier. Looks like she OD'd from a hot shot of heroin."

TJ interrupted, "Brad isn't that the lady you met at the Meet Market?"

Brad nodded his head with raised eyebrows. "Sure is."

Connie continued, "She was there with a shady guy named Lepordaxis who lives in one of the cottages on the grounds of the Cavalier. Turns out this guy is from the Ukraine just like our mole who killed himself. The lab confirmed the heroin she OD'd on is the same kind we've been following. Bit of a coincidence don't you think? I'll see what else I can dig up on Lepordaxis."

David cut in, "My new pals tell me the stuff isn't just coming from Hong Kong anymore. It looks like they're now using multiple ports from Hong Kong to Shanghai. We can't ask the Coast Guard or Navy to follow all ships coming into our ports. They're just too many. I'm not sure how to find the next drop."

CHAPTER 34

BIG DEAL
PIRATE'S COVE MARINA
NAGS HEAD, NORTH CAROLINA
THREE DAYS LATER

B rad and TJ met Moose on his boat, the *Big Deal*. They headed south toward Wanchese. "We're going to pick up lunch from O'Neal's Seafood Harvest and eat at the tables in front." Moose pointed, "Over there is Spencer's Boats and those are other builders around the area."

Satisfied with a good meal and visibility, they got back on the boat. "We'll go back to port and get into my truck. I'll drive to Engelhard to tour Far Creek where a lot of the trawlers dock."

When Brad and TJ saw the beat-up old brown Ford F 150 TJ said to Brad, "Now I know what David must have felt like in Vietnam."

Riding slowly along Hill Road Moose parked at the Big Trout Marina for a beer. "I want us to be seen, hoping it might rattle some of the locals into making a mistake." Brad looked out over the marina then turned to Moose, bringing him up to date with the events and failures.

"We've lost one of our main leads and we're following another. I'm hoping you can pick up another trail down here. We need to know when another shipment comes in and how they get it to market."

Moose thought for a moment, trying to come up with a solution.

"These guys are pretty tight-lipped. They've been through the drill before."

"If Connie can find me a crack in their operation through people they've crossed, I might be able to follow the trail."

CHAPTER 35

B rad loved his houseboat he named *Calm Waters* located on the southeastern end of Bay Island. He owned the small lot but decided not to build. Instead he docked his houseboat and a 30-foot Trojan sport fisher there. It was a relaxing sanctuary away from the hassles of work. He needed it now more than ever. Its 40 by 20-foot dimensions gave him ample room to spread out.

The master bedroom was tastefully decorated with a nautical theme. Hatches separated the rooms. Portholes for windows let in enough light.

He put solar panels on the south part of the roof for hot water and electricity. The wind turbine on the north side also helped generate electricity. He rarely had to pay an electric bill and usually received a monthly check from Dominion Power for the energy he put into the grid.

The living room with sliding glass doors overlooked Broad Bay and First Landing State Park. Facing south he could watch both sunrise and sunset. By looking at the unspoiled trees and dunes of the Park, he could imagine what it must have felt like when the Jamestown explorers first viewed it.

He planted arborvitae trees along the road and the sides of his lot for privacy. While the water in front of the houseboat was shallow and sandy, it provided a good location for oysters. Brad loved them so having the oyster rights with the lot was a definite plus and luckily the world famous Lynnhaven oysters had made a comeback. He could pull up a fresh bushel whenever he wanted. Since sightseers frequently traveled the area to get a peek at the waterfront homes, he put white PVC poles in the water to indicate the shallows as was the custom. He didn't want the boaters to get caught up on the sandbars.

There was a narrow channel he used to come and go by boat when he wanted to go fishing. If he didn't want to take the boat out he could just drop a line in the water and wait, beer in hand. TJ often joined him fishing, but tonight he was solo. He dropped a line and watched the sun set.

Even though he tried to relax, he couldn't help but think about his mission.

Dr. Peterson, his favorite shrink and gifted retired Navy Psychiatrist, now in private practice in Virginia Beach, continued to be a great help to him. He had suffered from mild PTSD during his SEAL stint. Dr. Peterson was an expert at dealing with this. Dr. Peterson put him on meds to help reduce the impact and had him decondition through exposure therapy while taking the meds. He now only need them on rare occasion, but even with the behavioral tools and meds from Dr. Peterson, Brad was still working on quieting his mind.

Dr. Peterson not only worked wonders with the psychiatric meds, he was also a skilled psychotherapist. He helped Brad with his issues of having distant parents. He made him aware that his difficulty in having a meaningful long-term relationship with a woman was due to his mother's lack of consistent nurturing. This made Brad insecure in relationships with women. He loved their attention, but always expected their affection to be withdrawn without cause, keeping him confused and untrusting. He most often picked women who weren't stable enough for a long-term relationship repeating his flawed behavior pattern. He began having feelings for Connie and wasn't sure if this attraction was just repeating his unhealthy behavior patterns or was healthy. He did recognize she was different than any other woman he was ever involved with. He discussed this with Dr. Peterson and was reassured that when he broke through that pathology the relationship would be different. He was hopeful but remained cautious.

He also helped Brad understand that his need to try to right the wrongs and always win was also due to his father's distance. He unconsciously thought that he could win his father's love and affection that way, which didn't work. He incorporated that neurotic behavior pattern into his psyche and was destined to continue to repeat it also. The fact that he was leading his team made him worry that he would push them too hard, making them part of his righting the wrongs of the world. Changing his behavior was the most difficult challenge he ever faced and was told that at the beginning of therapy. Still he had lots to think about himself and the mission. Brad was getting better at recognizing the patterns, first after they happened, and now before they happened. This allowed him to make different healthier choices. That is the way therapy works.

Brad also discussed his team with Dr. Peterson. He was concerned about David's isolation. Dr. Peterson came up with the idea of sending him on special missions to improve his self-esteem which seemed to be working.

Connie was a different story. She seemed to be growing on her own. He and Dr. Peterson were both concerned she might overdo her new-found sexuality and get into trouble. They hoped they could help her safely navigate the change.

Dr. Peterson suggested a different therapist for each team member who would be a match.

Godfrey seemed well adjusted enough. He already overcame his inferiority of growing up in an Oakland ghetto and moving into a white world. Having grown up with loving, nurturing parents, they kept him out of gangs and on an academic path. That, along with his superior intellect, helped him to become accepted into the academic elite. This community didn't see race or background as an obstacle. Smarts were the ticket to assimilation. There were, however, some jealous people who tried to back stab and sabotage those around them to gain position. Godfrey's healthy childhood allowed him to recognize and circumvent them.

TJ was already well known to Dr. Peterson. He helped him with the dilemma of following orders that he didn't agree with, to find solace in his private lifestyle, creating his house and yard as a refuge.

CHAPTER 36

Connie began dressing more stylishly. Her favorite color now was pink. She didn't realize, along with most women, that this color was an unconscious way of subtly projecting their sexuality. Pink was the color of the vagina, no matter the race. This was also the reason women with red lipstick and nail polish look sexier to men. They unconsciously got it. It was like a guy wearing a picture of the Washington Monument on his T-shirt, hanging a pair of dice from his rearview mirror or wearing a tie that is too long. However, as Freud famously said, "Sometimes a cigar is just a cigar" or to apply this to women sometimes pink is just a color.

She didn't have to go far to get the attention of the men in the room. They already respected her for the great job she was doing. She was one of the team. However, aside from Brad, they felt a little uncomfortable about her increasing sexuality, like watching a sister develop.

"Moose found a woman, Janine, married to one of the trawler captains who goes to Mimi's Tiki Bar and gets drunk every night her husband has to stay out all night 'fishing.' Janine complains about it to any man who will listen often picking one of them up for an evening of payback festivities. She has lots of new money to spend according to her credit card bills."

Brad was excited they had another new trail to follow.

"I'll let Moose know. He'll need to start hanging out there and notify

David to let Admiral Mack coordinate with Captain Wallsie when Janine goes out again for a night of fun."

"We already know the trawler, *Rusty Scupper*, is run by Janine's husband. The drone can follow it out and identify the freighter they connect with. We can trace the freighter back to its pick-up port and get a lead on the people behind this expanded setup."

"We can follow the trawler back in and hopefully get Moose to the off-load site before they finish that part of the operation. If we're lucky, maybe we can follow the off-loaded product to its final destination for distribution."

His words were faster, and his excitement increased even more. This would also be another trail to follow.

Godfrey added. "Stan at Task Force Alpha tells me they are finding increasing amounts of the new heroin all around Hampton Roads, Richmond, DC and Baltimore. It's also spreading to smaller towns around those areas. The murder, mayhem and overdoses are an epidemic out of control. We have to put a stop to it."

CHAPTER 37

Moose was used to being up all night. He wasn't a stranger to 2AM. He notified Brad that Janine was at the bar and awaited instructions on where to go. Brad contacted Admiral Mack to notify him that the new lead was in motion. He had been on call awaiting the news.

Admiral Burns was providing support by having his team man a drone to find and follow the trawler. He was now in direct cell phone contact with Moose and would let him know the trawler's location.

After Admiral Burns confirmed the *Rusty Scupper* was home ported at Far Creek and still at the dock Moose, headed down Highway 264 toward Engelhard. While there he would await word when she made the pick-up and follow her to the new local drop-off point. Sure enough, she met a freighter and picked up four packages.

Admiral Burns told him the trawler was heading back and was slowing. She dropped anchor off the entrance to the Great Ditch. He told Moose there was a small box truck with several people waiting on shore for her.

Moose took a left off 264 at Engelhard onto Great Ditch Road. He took a left at the dead end onto Nebraska Road and a right at White Planes Road. He found the small mosquito ditch he was looking for from the GPS map the Coast Guard sent him. This is where the Great Ditch starts and eventually ends as Far Creek in Engelhard.

Having already turned off the headlights on the way in, he pulled off the road and hid his car behind some bushes. He walked slowly up the dirt road, ready to hide if necessary until he got to the drop-off site. There was a quarter moon that provided some visibility, but he also had a pair of Armasight NYX7 nightvision goggles.

He watched as the *Rusty Scupper* stopped 150 yards offshore. A Carolina Skiff was heading for it. There was a truck parked at the end of the road. Two men paced the shoreline smoking cigarettes. He saw the crew of the *Rusty Scupper* quickly move 4 crates from the trawler to the Carolina Skiff named *Heathen*. As he watched, the small boat made for shore and headed to a beat-up dock that had seen better days.

After the *Heathen* docked, he watched the men transfer the crates to the truck. He couldn't understand why the men were struggling with the crates. They appeared heavy. They couldn't contain that much heroin inside. Then he saw the fish in them. *Great way to move the product* he thought to himself.

He wondered why the Highway Patrol and local police who stopped and searched trucks coming from the Inner Banks never found any heroin inside. Just then the smell of rotten fish hit him. He was downwind from the action. He concluded, *they must be packing the heroin under the rotten fish.*

Pretty clever. He thought this was amusing and almost laughed out loud. No officer in his right mind would go rummaging through a crate of rotten fish.

The name on the side of the truck was burned into his mind, "Always Fresh Ocean Seafood." There was a picture of a tuna, clams, oysters and shrimp below the title.

CHAPTER 38

The upbeat mood of the team permeated the air. They were all thrilled by the momentum that was building.

Jim prepared the drinks and made the usual deliveries. He really liked being a part of the Team. There was a bigger bounce in his step.

Even before being called on, Godfrey gave them a rundown of the information he'd been getting.

"The University of Virginia in Charlottesville and the University of Richmond have been reporting an increasing number of heroin deaths. Although they try to keep this from the news like they do campus rapes, it has been leaking out after kids call home. They're upset at what's happening and parents are talking about withdrawing their kids from school. Other universities, colleges, even grade schools and high schools in our target areas are reporting similar problems."

"It's the same heroin we've been following." David was beginning to enjoy the competition with his fellow team members.

"My DEA pal Andy has reported to me that they may have a lead on money originating in Hong Kong. He's trying to find the source."

"He's also getting a handle on the new ships and ports."

Brad looked at Connie and smiled. She would find excuses to get close to him, trying to brush against him whenever she could.

"What have you found out about Lepordaxis?"

Connie loved the attention as all eyes focused on her. She wanted to keep that focus. She was now sporting a new pixie hairdo which brought out her cute features.

She had been looking into perfumes, although she wasn't used to wearing any. She loved antiquing and found an old bottle of New Horizons perfume by Ciro in a Baccarat bottle. This started production in 1941. She thought this fit her new feminine mind-set. This is the one that Brad commented on when they went to the Dockside.

She looked back at Brad with a more than friendly smile.

"I've done a lot of research on him and the area he came from."

"Lepordaxis was born in Luhansk, Eastern Ukraine in 1955. This is one of its top five industrial economic regions. Anthracite coal, produced since the 17th century, and recent natural gas production has made this area an energy and chemical manufacturing powerhouse. This is part of the reason Russia wants it and has stationed troops there. It lies in the most eastern region of Ukraine along the Lugan River where it meets the Olkhovaya River. This was an area where Scythians and Sarmatians lived. The steppe area had rich soil. The grain production here was exceptional. The grassland was also good for grazing."

"In 2004 school children organized by history teacher Vladimir Paramonov discovered the Merheleva Ridge. This setting, used from 4000 BCE to 500 BCE, consisted of four large stone mounds or Kurgans believed to be temples and sacrificial altars. These were the first monuments of their kind found in Eastern Europe. Other Kurgans, later found in the area, contained skeletons in full battle dress. A few contained female skeletons in full battle dress confirming the Amazon myth."

Connie liked the idea women could be as powerful as men especially without having to use sex as a tool.

"Eastern Ukraine and east to the Don River and its connection to the Volga River was known to be Scythian and Sarmatian territory as chronicled by Herodotus. Later Roman history chronicled the defeat of the Scythians. Oral history of the families left behind after that defeat is still passed down today according to information I've found."

Connie put up a map of the area on the 90-inch monitor to orient everybody.

"Lepordaxis was a descendant of the Scythians who were left behind. He comes from a family of great warriors. In fact, there's a lot of information on his family online. They were celebrated for their great conquests before their defeat and partial removal of their cavalry to Britain. His family were among those left behind. There was also an article that said there was a myth that one day a great Scythian King with two gold crowns with rubies would arise and bind the Scythians together again. This man would form an even more powerful Nation and conquer the world according to the author of the article."

The stunned look on everyone's face made it clear they now knew they were up against a really powerful enemy.

David said in a low voice, "Now everything makes more sense. We're dealing with a group comprised of modern day Scythians and they're as brutal as their ancestors. They are removing politicians, bankers and businessmen, anyone who gets in their way. I'll bet more will follow."

The atmosphere in the room remained charged. One could almost see sparks bouncing off the walls. The quiet was deafening as Connie continued.

"Lepordaxis' name means leopard in Scythian. Coming from a long line of military elite gave his family a relatively high standard of living. He joined the Soviet Army out of college. Having served in Afghanistan during the Soviet invasion, he was promoted to Major and led a battalion there. Heavily decorated for his bravery and initiative, he sees himself as a Scythian/Cossack. I have located pictures of him dressed as a Cossack. The Cossacks emerged from the Scythian families left behind. If the Soviets had more like him, they wouldn't have lost."

"Eastern Ukraine, including Crimea and Southern Russia, was home to the Cossacks starting around the 14th century. They trained their children, starting at age 3, to ride horses. Later, tournaments were held to see who had the best fighting skills. These are the same skills the Scythians and Sarmatians held in high esteem before them and they were just as brutal."

"They allied themselves with the Russian Tsars and became more powerful by it. They fought for the Russians during the Napoleonic Wars, then fought for the Soviets during World Wars I and II and Afghanistan."

"The Cossacks were also responsible for a majority of the Pogroms against the Jews in Southwestern Russia during the 19th and early 20th Centuries. The Pogroms were a violent free-for-all toward the rural Jewish population all over Russia and Eastern Europe: Poland, Ukraine, Belarus, Rumania, Hungary. The powers that controlled these countries, especially the Russians and Poles, unleashed their peasant populations to take revenge on the supposed causes of their dire situation. Using Jews as scapegoats allowed the peasants to release their fury on those helpless villagers which should have been more appropriately directed toward the aristocracy."

"Later the peasants wised up and killed the Tsar and his aristocracy during the 1917 revolution. This finally lead to the Communist takeover by Vladimir Lenin."

"The Cossacks were allowed to go into the small farming villages to pillage, burn, rape and kill any Jew they could find. The Broadway musical 'Fiddler on the Roof' was a story about the aftermath of a Pogrom on a Jewish Shtetl (small farming town) in Eastern Europe."

David spoke up. "My father told me a family story, told to him by his grandfather about how we came to America. He came from Simyournifka, a Shtetl, near Kiev and was conscripted by the Tsars' men in 1903 to fight in the Russo-Japanese War. He wasn't going to fight for the Tsar after what he allowed the Cossacks to do to his village, so he threw down his rifle and came back home. Knowing he couldn't stay because he would be killed if found, his family gave him what little money and food they had so he could escape. He walked all the way to Bremen in northern Germany and worked as a baker in the hold of the ship for three weeks to get passage to America. Later he brought his eight brothers, sisters and parents over. One sister stayed behind because she was involved with a Russian boy."

"He tells an interesting story during his journey. While walking through Warsaw two men came running toward him carrying a satchel. They threw it at him. When he looked inside it was full of money. He saw police chasing the men because he concluded they had just robbed a bank. He threw the satchel away and ran in the opposite direction."

"My father asked him why he didn't keep the money?"

"He told him if a young Jewish peasant was found with all that money, they would kill him. Better to live poor than die rich."

Connie found the story interesting and sad, but she was eager to get the spotlight back and didn't realize she snorted while flicking her head at David. She took control of the conversation.

"The current conflict in Ukraine is between the Russian and Ukrainian Scythians and the Europeans. This has been going on since ancient times and is nothing new."

"After the collapse of the Soviet Union in December 1991, Ukraine was thrust into an economic tailspin along with the other former Soviet Satellites. Lepordaxis immigrated to the US in 1995 and settled in Hampton Roads because of its large military presence. He must have felt at home here."

"He moved to Virginia Beach where he developed quite a rap sheet for small-time drug smuggling and loan sharking. He made his real money by importing selected beautiful girls from Eastern Europe to work supposed summer jobs at the oceanfront. Word on the street is that he'd charge for getting them the job and would then threaten to harm their families back home if they didn't cooperate. Getting them hooked on heroin or cocaine, he forced them into prostitution to pay back what they owed and in order to keep their families safe. The authorities haven't been able to nail him for this, but according to our informants a lot of local small-time dealers and pimps are very afraid of him."

"He's said to have the finest stables in the area. His girls entertain the Military Brass of all services and nations. Hampton Roads is the Atlantic Headquarters of NATO. They also entertain the politicians who come down from DC for a 'working vacation.'"

"He keeps himself fit by working out at Inlet Fitness Center on Great Neck Road and frequents hot spots around the Beach."

"He selects his elite as one would select a fine wine, then grooms them to command the high prices he gets from his clients. These girls are class."

Brad interrupted to give Connie a breather. He was very proud of the way she handled herself and was thinking of her as more than a colleague. "Hey Jim, could you bring a refill for everyone and add some of those wonderful chocolate chip cookies from the Fresh Market."

This took some time and allowed small talk between team members' allowing their emotions to settle down.

Once composure was regained he said, "Connie why don't you continue with your information."

It didn't take her long to start up again where she'd been interrupted. She would have taken offense, but after all it was Brad.

"He's currently living in one of the bungalows on the grounds of the new Cavalier and uses it as if it's his personal playground."

"Despite all of this there is no information directly connecting him to our heroin."

Brad seeing Connie had finished, took over the meeting.

"Great context Connie. Even though there is no apparent connection, he is from the Ukraine and so was our mole. Also, Lannie overdosed while she was with him. It looks like TJ and I are going to have to play with the high rollers."

CHAPTER 39

B rad and TJ pulled up to the front of the Cavalier. The hotel and adjoining 18-hole golf course was built in 1927 as a Grand Dame Hotel. It made Virginia Beach famous during the roaring 20s hosting many first-rate big bands and celebrities including F. Scott Fitzgerald, Judy Garland, Will Rogers, Bette Davis, Jean Harlow, Mary Pickford, Betty Grable and Fatty Arbuckle. Adolph Coors mysteriously died after a fall from the 6th floor in 1929. Seven United States Presidents, including Calvin Coolidge, Herbert Hoover, Harry Truman, Dwight D. Eisenhower, John F. Kennedy, Lyndon B. Johnson and Richard Nixon stayed there.

The Cavalier was purchased in 1960 by Gene Dixon Sr., owner of a kyanite mine in central Virginia, after he was refused entrance to the dining room because he didn't have a tie on. The hotel fell on hard times during the 90s to 2013 because of a feud in the family that owned it. But then a major Virginia Beach developer, in conjunction with the City of Virginia Beach, closed a deal to bring it back into its former five-star luxury.

The cities in the area have been forward thinking reinventing themselves as a prime tourist destination. Virginia Beach leads the pack.

Colonial America featuring Williamsburg, Jamestown and Yorktown are forty-five minutes away.

Norfolk's Chrysler Museum is one of the top museums in the country and has the second-best glass collections in the United States after Corning. They now have a glass studio next door for visiting artists. The new renovation speaks highly of the Trustees. Nearby, Nauticus, the Naval Maritime Museum with the battleship *Wisconsin*, is unique. Norfolk Botanical Gardens boasts one hundred seventy-five acres and forty themed gardens. It has one of the best azalea and camellia collections in the country.

Virginia Beach continues to refurbish its oceanfront and boardwalk. It houses the Virginia Aquarium and Military Aviation Museum. First Landing State Park is located at the tip of Virginia Beach where the Atlantic Ocean meets the Chesapeake Bay. It is the site of the first landing of the Jamestown settlers. Oceana Naval Air Station is home to the only Master Jet Base on the East Coast. It houses the Navy's fighter-attack jet fleet made up of F/A-18 Hornets and Super Hornets assigned to the four aircraft carriers based at Naval Station Norfolk.

The weather is perfect: two months winter, three months summer and three and one-half months of spring and autumn.

Brad said, "The old beauty is prettier than ever. It always gives me a warm feeling to be around her elegance."

TJ replied, "I know what you mean."

Brad sighed to TJ, "I never get tired of this place. I'm glad they brought her back to her old glory."

TJ nodded his approval. "Too bad there's slime in there we have to deal with. Hope it doesn't dull her shine," he hissed.

Brad tried to be reassuring.

"Now TJ, we'll suck the slime out and she'll be pretty as ever."

They walked up the small entry staircase to be greeted by the always smiling friendly doorman into the small lobby with its original opulent crystal chandelier that set the stage for what was to come. They could go forward to Becca, the 4-star restaurant, to the Raleigh Room bar and seating area or down the spiral staircases on either side to the lower level which housed the magnificent refurbished indoor pool or to the Hunt Club Bar. They marveled at the retained intimacy and old-world look.

As they entered the Hunt Club through the two black wooden doors with square glass inserts, the dark brown wooden floor contrasted with the white square pillars holding the large black square ceiling inserts. To the left was a white marble bar and tables overlooking the new distillery that made their own high-end brand of bourbon and vodka. Straight ahead were two large soft leather couches facing each other and perpendicular to the original rebuilt fireplace. The six-point buck head tilted so slightly over the mantle looked proud surveying his nightly crowd along with other local mounted animals including ducks. During the 1920's and 30's when Virginia Beach was mostly undeveloped, guests of the hotel would go on hunting or fishing parties. They would bring their prizes back to the Hunt Club, which would prepare them for their dinner. To the right were tables for informal dining.

Brad and TJ were pleased with the remake.

"Man, they really did a nice job on her. The old girl is starting to work her wonders again attracting a number of high fliers and celebrities," Brad said as he scanned the room.

He and TJ slid up to the bar and ordered a round. Brad ordered his Jamison 18 neat. TJ liked his vodka, Grey Goose, of course, chilled. They looked around the room subtly and saw Hampton Roads finest along with a select ration of first class out-of-town upper crust. It wasn't unusual to see a rap star or starlet show up. Oftentimes Wall Street types or politicians would waltz in with their entourage.

TJ saw their prey and nudged Brad.

"He's over there on the couch in front of the fireplace in the blue silk jacket with the brunette."

Lepordaxis' 5'8 height and 220 pounds filled a stocky frame holding a bull neck. His black hair had a slight wave, his face sported a large black bushy mustache. His cheeks were ruddy from too much vodka and this softened his look, but his eyes still had a sinister glint to them.

"Well, let's go over and make friends."

Brad smacked his lips with a determined grin, rubbing his hands in anticipation.

"I'm Brad Johnson and this is my partner TJ Diggs. We're looking to do some business with you."

Brad was cool and smooth.

Lepordaxis was surprised by their brash approach "What kind of bezness?"

Brad continued his cool demeanor not having to try too hard.

"Ditch the lady and we'll talk."

Lepordaxis motioned for his escort to leave.

"OK… talk."

Brad and TJ stood in front of the couch.

"We're looking to score large amounts of China White."

Lepordaxis tried brushing them off as if they were gnats as he brushed the front of his trousers.

"What makes you think I know anything about that?"

TJ cut in.

"A little fly named Roosevelt pointed us your way. He said you're the man to see for the big time."

"Ha! Ha! Ha!"

Lepordaxis was clearly amused.

"What does that black worm know? He can't even tie his shoelaces."

Brad started to get annoyed.

"Regardless, we've got plenty of cash and we're looking to move some heavy weight. If you're not the right guy, we'll take our business elsewhere."

Lepordaxis signaled the waiter to bring another bottle of 2000 Veuve Clicquot "La Grande Dame."

"Have a seat my friends."

All watched as the glasses were poured, bubbling up to the top without spillover then refilled to the ¾ mark as only an expert sommelier can. Lepordaxis smiled, amused by their boldness.

"If you got it, what would you do with it?"

Brad was serious and convincing.

"My partner has good connections from here to Charleston. We'll start with 30 kilos a week and increase as business expands. We don't want to compete with you. We just want to expand our market."

Lepordaxis was intrigued. He already knew about TJ's rescue of Roosevelt along with his description which was why he allowed them to sit down. He wanted to check them out more fully.

"I'll get back with you."

He dismissed them with a hand gesture before they even got a taste of the bubbly.

CHAPTER 40

B rad was again at the corkboard filling in the blanks as he addressed the team.

"We have a pretty good idea that the majority of heroin goes to Lepordaxis and we think the hillbillies report to him. After our attempted bust, they aren't going to use their boat for pick-ups anymore. We know they connect with Nick Hollaran in Manteo for pick-ups."

The team felt good about this new connection.

"We also know the heroin gets put into "Always Fresh Ocean Seafood" trucks. We know they head for Richmond and Baltimore to deliver the goods. We still don't know how the distribution takes place from there and we still don't know the brains and financing behind the operation. It appears some of the money is coming out of Hong Kong."

Brad looked at Connie. He continued noticing how attractive and sexy she was. He wasn't quite aware that her womanly scent tweaked his deep-seated sexual unconscious any time he was near her. His voice was softer than usual.

"Connie, we need to know where the financing comes from. See what you can dig up."

As he moved his eyes to David, Brad's voice returned to its usual business tone. Connie noticed the difference, wondering if the others picked up on it. "David, find out where they are getting their weapons from, not only the modern ones, but also the ancient ones."

Godfrey cut in. "Boss, my labs have found where the spears, bows and arrows are coming from."

Brad raised his eyebrows and with a nose point urged him to go on.

"I've traced the metal in the spear tips and arrowheads in addition to the wood in the spear shafts, bows and arrows to the Altai Mountains in Southern Siberia and Northwestern China. This is the homeland of the Scythians. They could have these weapons made anywhere. Manufacturing in their place of origin seems a bit much."

TJ broke the silence. "This leaves no doubt that we have ancient Scythians galloping across the eastern American piedmont and seaboard, delivering their poisonous trade goods now in modern times. These guys are real fanatics. Sounds crazy to me." He shook his head from side to side.

Brad brought the team focus back together.

"No matter how crazy it sounds, we have to follow where the trail leads."

"Godfrey, call Stan at Task Force Alpha. Connect with Evan Stahl and find out what you can about 'Always Fresh.' As FBI liaison to the DEA, he should have the knowledge and resources to uncover who they are and how they fit in to this operation."

CHAPTER 41

G odfrey was glad Brad gave him a chance to get out in the field. He pulled into the parking lot of the Circuit Court building in downtown Richmond in his silver ice metallic Chevy Volt and waited for Evan to arrive. He was impatient, got out of his car and started pacing even though the sky was overcast and held a light drizzle.

Evan finally pulled up in his gray Ford Taurus. Godfrey got in and slammed the door a little harder than necessary. Evan noticed that Godfrey was antsy and asked, "What gives?"

"I guess I want to catch these bastards already. I hate the wait." Godfrey was used to solving problems quickly. He didn't like slowing down because everyone else wasn't as smart or quick as he was. He learned to do this grudgingly. He occasionally allowed others to catch up when it was necessary. This had its good points in that he solved problems fast which brought out his best. It also had its bad points because some of those who were left behind resented it. It sometimes made him enemies, but he didn't care.

Evan took the hint and began giving Godfrey background on the area.

"We're going to South Side Richmond, the other side of the James River, to take a tour of Manchester and the Port of Richmond. The fall line ports of Richmond, Fredericksburg, Washington, DC and Baltimore are located on the eastern edge of the fall line of the Coastal Plane. This was the farthest inland ships could travel in Colonial days."

"The Port site was originally the site of Falling Creek Ironworks established in 1619 and destroyed in the Indian Massacre of 1622. The port was later rebuilt. Virginia Governor Thomas Jefferson said ships of 220 tons could get there. The main export was tobacco. The main import was sugar and slaves. The British burned it to the ground in 1781. It was rebuilt again in 1940."

"It is now a multimodal Domestic and International distribution gateway by water, rail and truck. Adjacent to I-95 for north and south destinations, easy access to I-85, I-64 and I-81 for southwest destinations and I-70 for northwest destinations makes it an ideal location."

Evan drove around the modern facility which complies with all Homeland Security regulations. After which they went to the adjacent Manchester neighborhood.

Godfrey turned up his nose at the rundown buildings and trash strewn streets. It reminded him of where he grew up and his memories were not at all pleasant.

"This looks more like an area where heroin smuggling would take place," he sounded distant, his voice trailing off. The rhythmic whooshing sound of the wipers broke the silence.

Evan was also lost in thought about his younger years. "Yeah, I know. I grew up in a mixed low-rent neighborhood." As they drove through the area, they took solace knowing that each had similar feelings.

He finally parked several buildings down and across the street from "Always Fresh."

Godfrey was surprised by the building's appearance, "It really doesn't look like much. I don't know if I'd be willing to eat fish from that company."

Evan complained, "I've had staff watching the place since we found the trucks carrying heroin from the Inner Banks coming here. They arrive full, unload and leave empty. We know the heroin goes in, but we haven't been able to figure out how it goes out."

Godfrey looked stumped.

"That is a puzzle. They have to be getting it to the streets somehow. I sure wouldn't want to eat anything from the 'European Bread and Pastry' bakery next door either. It looks pretty dirty too".

CHAPTER 42

B rad looked around the room, pleased to see his team busy at work. He took pride in the fact that they were melding into a cohesive unit. "Godfrey has some new information. Let's get to the conference table. Jim, refresh everyone's drinks and put some of your famous snacks on the table."

Godfrey was excited that he was able to report different information. He was glad he was picked to do more than just chemical analysis, although he wasn't too fired up about what he was about to report.

"Evan and I went to take a look at the 'Always Fresh' warehouse. It's in an old rundown warehouse district on the South side of Richmond, next to the modern Port of Richmond. He's had it under surveillance since we traced their trucks from the Inner Banks to that location. He reports full trucks going in and leaving empty. He doesn't see any heroin distribution, just fish."

His excitement dulled, "We're stuck."

Connie as always jumped in. She was beginning to learn how to apply makeup subtly highlighting her facial features. She switched from New Horizons and now started wearing a new perfume, Danger. This was another antique Ciro product first manufactured in 1938. She found it on the internet in her hunt for feminine products. She couldn't wait to find the third in this line of perfumes, Surrender, first manufactured in

1932. The last in the line of the four Ciro "Remember Me" perfumes was Reflections produced in 1933. She found the ad with pictures of all four to frame and put in her condo next to her dressing table. Its slogan was "Four Ways to Say Remember Me." She decided this was a subtle way of moving along her budding relationship with Brad.

The team was intrigued as they watched her transformation continue and noticed David also becoming more well-rounded. The camaraderie and support of each other made the team more cohesive and effective. They didn't realize this was Brad's intent.

Connie went on, "After learning both Lepordaxis and the mole were Ukrainian I started checking out the employees of 'Always Fresh' and it looks like everyone who works there is from Eastern Ukraine. You know, where the Scythians come from. This can't be a coincidence. The ownership is through a number of shell companies and stops in the Cayman Islands, I guess for tax purposes and laundering profits."

"For curiosity I looked up 'European Bread and Pastry.' They also only have Eastern Ukrainian employees, a few men, but a much larger number of women. They have retail outlets all over Richmond and Baltimore. It also appears they have opened up other retail stores in our target areas. The ownership is similar to 'Always Fresh.'"

TJ couldn't contain himself. "I'll bet somehow 'Always Fresh' gets the heroin to the bakery which then distributes the heroin. But how?"

Godfrey blurted out, "We didn't see any connection between them except they were next door to each other."

Jim spoke up wanting to be more involved. "I wonder if there is a connecting door toward the back of the room or adjoining basements that allows them to make the transfer without being seen?"

Everyone already felt Jim was a part of the team and appreciated his input. He was after all a skilled leader and combat veteran. His insight seemed to nail it.

Brad played devil's advocate hoping his team could expand the connection. "OK, let's say they transfer the heroin to the bakery. We haven't seen how the bakery distributes it. We do know they make regular deliveries to their retail stores, but no heroin is ever seen going in or coming out." Godfrey was looking at the ceiling deep in thought as the light bulb in his head went off.

"Those...clever...bastards," he almost shouted. "I'll bet they hollow out loaves of bread and stuff them with heroin that they package for street use in the fish house or bakery. No one would see any deliveries. They could have their distributers pick up a loaf of bread at the retail store with their order inside. I bet they enjoy the bread while giving out the packs to their corner boys."

"By the way we picked up a loaf of bread at one of the retail stores. It's pretty good."

Connie added.

"Women mostly run the 'European Bread and Pastry' warehouse and retail stores. They're also from Eastern Ukraine and many are married to the Ukrainian men running the other parts of the operation." She suddenly wondered out loud, "Are they Amazons?" She hoped so. That thought only made her bolder in her new feminine identity.

Brad took back control to summarize.

"Eastern Ukraine is part of the ancient home of Scythians. We know they are fierce fighters, letting nothing stand in their way. We know they run the operations of the fish and bread companies. We know Lepordaxis is also from Eastern Ukraine and has samples of new heroin. He has to be connected to the hillbillies and is probably running the operation."

TJ pushed everyone to consider the possibilities.

"I doubt he has the money and connections to be the one behind the whole operation. There has to be somebody above him."

Brad complimented his team for their great work and their deductive reasoning, which only came from a team that had solidified. He loved watching them bounce ideas off each other, leading them further along the road to solve the problem they were facing.

Brad then changed focus.

"I've kept this information for last."

He had a sheepish grin that turned into a broad smile.

"Lepordaxis finally got back to me and set up a dinner meeting at the Cavalier. TJ, we're going back to the Grand Old Lady."

CHAPTER 43

Brad smiled to himself. "She seems to be smiling at us knowingly." He and TJ walked casually up to the front doors of the Cavalier on the Hill. The doorman greeted them with a toothy smile and welcomed them as was his custom. The crystal chandelier set the stage for the grace that she exuded. As they walked up the curved stairway to the main floor her ambience enveloped them. Dressed in their high-end clothing, they headed toward Becca, the main dining room, where they were to meet Lepordaxis for dinner at his invitation.

He was sitting at table 27, the booth in the back center, the command table, the one with the best view of the restaurant and the most privacy. He had two stunning women with him, one with jet-black hair wearing a low-cut dark red silk dress, the other a strawberry blonde in a backless green silk cocktail dress.

As Brad and TJ sat, he dismissed the women. The sommelier immediately brought over a bottle of 1990 Tattinger Compte de Champagne. All watched as he poured a glass for each of them.

"Gentlemen, I'm going to enjoy doing bezness with you."

Lepordaxis raised his glass of champagne in a toast.

"I'll supply 20 kilos per week at a price you can't beat as long as you only distribute from the North Carolina border and further south."

Brad smiled sealing the deal and TJ nodded in agreement. "That's what we're looking for."

Lepordaxis extended his hand to shake with Brad and TJ. "Good, then we have a deal."

Brad ignored the hand. "We'll have to meet your boss first." He wanted to continue moving up the ladder to get the bigger fish. "And we want to make sure you can supply the weight before we commit."

Irritated, Lepordaxis became cautious and scowled. His voice turned harsh. It seemed as though the air around them froze. "The weight is no problem, but my boss is a very private man. I don't think he'll meet with you."

Brad was defiant. "If we don't meet with him, no deal."

Lepordaxis mulled this request over. He thought this was a good business move but meeting his boss, that was another thing altogether.

"I'll see what I can do. Now, let's enjoy dinner in the company of beautiful women."

Lepordaxis motioned for the ladies to return and for dinner service to start.

CHAPTER 44

ALAIN MANSION
ALANTON
VIRGINIA BEACH, VIRGINIA
SUNDAY—NEXT DAY

"I've checked these guys out, boss. They've been mid-level importers of MJ and cocaine from Colombia and Mexico with distribution from Hampton Roads to South Carolina." Lepordaxis tried to reassure Lance along with himself.

Lance was excited at the new potential. "If this is the way they want to play it, we'll go along. If we make the deal they would have to stop all distribution in Hampton Roads. We want them to continue to distribute their MJ and cocaine from the North Carolina line as far south as they want to take it. We'll let them add our heroin to their pipeline, build their distribution network and take out the competition for us. Then when we're ready, we'll take over their operation and take them out. This couldn't be more perfect if we had planned it ourselves. Set up the meeting at my house."

Lance was as cocky as ever, not realizing this might be a mistake.

Lepordaxis beamed with pride. "I'm going to bring in more Scythian Cossacks from Eastern Ukraine for muscle. They are already battle hardened from the war there. The first ones did a great job in Baltimore, Richmond, DC and the smaller towns."

"I'll continue to have the hillbillies get the fishermen in the Outer Banks to pick up the packages from the ships. Our Scythian Cossacks will get it from them and bring it to the distribution sites."

Lance was ecstatic at how his plan was coming together. He couldn't wait to tell his father who he knew would be pleased. "We'll continue to house and train our new recruits at Altai Stables. I want you to set up safe houses and warehouses with legitimate business fronts of fish and bread along the I-95 corridor. I want to continue our retail businesses as fish stores and bakeries, so the wives aren't left out. We are, of course Scythians, and our women will add muscle when necessary."

Lepordaxis let out one of his contagious belly laughs. "Hah, hah, hah. This is easier than fighting the Europeans in Ukraine and more lucrative."

He was proud to have lost most of his accent.

"I'll buy buildings in the rundown warehouse districts in DC and Hampton Roads like the ones I bought in Baltimore and Richmond. These can supply the smaller cities and towns with the heroin they need."

"Starting a turf war among the gangs by pretending we were Russian Mafia out of Brighton Beach worked out better than expected. They shot each other, doing most of our work. We of course helped out. With the leader, his second in command and his 7 to 8 lieutenants gone, it was easy to establish a new leadership under our control."

"The new warehouses I buy will continue to be set up as a fish distribution center with our bakery center next door. We'll continue to bring in our product from Hampton Roads but mainly the Outer and Inner Banks in fish trucks. I love the idea of placing the product in the middle of iced fish with a few well-placed smelly fish. Just as predicted, the cops are too lazy to search the trucks completely so the product will be safe, especially with the stench."

Lepordaxis let out another of his belly laughs. "Our system is working perfectly, but our need is growing. I have a next-level plan. All auto manufacturers fill the front and rear bumpers of cars with styrofoam. We'll replace it with 7 kilos of heroin in each bumper. The back seat will have a hydraulic system which can only open when the radio is turned on, the right turn signal is engaged, a foot is on the brake and then a toggle switch under the dash is thrown. Just like the smelly fish and the bread, no cop will figure this out. The backseat compartment will hold 26 kilos. The full load will be 40 kilos."

Getting more and more excited, he finished outlining his plan.

"One pure, fentanyl-laced kilo increased by 60% here with mannitol becomes 1.6 kilos equals 1,600 grams equals 16,000 packs. At $12 per pack we get $192,000 per kilo of finished product. We will need 25 kilos per week for Hampton Roads and Richmond, 35-40 kilos per week for Baltimore and 50 kilos per week for DC. Add 20 kilos per week for our new partners. We project our needs to be 135 kilos of finished product per week or 54 uncut kilos per week and can easily bring in 75 kilos of uncut heroin per drop at 25 kilos per bale and 3 bales per drop. So, we will need one drop a week. For the finished product that comes to about $26 million per week or about $1.35 billion per year minus cost of $50 million equals about $1.3 billion per year for starters."

"We'll have some excess after cutting but we'll need this in the beginning to build an inventory at each of our processing plants in case some gets stolen, confiscated, lost through any number of unforeseen circumstances such as weather or problems at the source."

He didn't want to bring up the most obvious unforeseen circumstance. What if one of the flock turns rogue? He knew this was unlikely. If they did their entire family would be killed and his bloodline wiped out.

Lance worked through the numbers also making sure Lepordaxis was correct. He was thrilled things were coming together so smoothly.

Lepordaxis' concern never crossed his mind knowing the consequences were too dire to even consider the thought.

"As we ramp up and get our choreography synchronized and running smoothly, we'll spread our reach further up and down the East Coast."

"Our intelligence network is also working beautifully. I would love to have seen the look on the pursuer's faces when they opened the bales of garbage. They have no idea who they're up against."

"My father's ability to put our organization together is masterful. The loyalty of our Scythian brothers and sisters is better than any other group in the world. Their excitement at the renewal of our nation brings a commitment like no other."

"Hail King Colaxais!"

Lance finished with a sense of accomplishment. He was high on success knowing his father would approve. If he didn't that was too bad.

The atmosphere in the room was full of celebration as Lance brought out a bottle of 1989 Domaine Lartigue Armagnac and a couple of well-vintaged Padron Familia Reservas 80th cigars. Lance and Lepordaxis loved the high life and the amenities it brought.

CHAPTER 45

Brad was hopeful as he addressed his team.

"Lepordaxis has set up a meeting with Lance Alain, his boss. TJ and I are going to his house in Alanton. Let's see where this takes us."

Standing at the corkboard, he smiled at Connie, consciously appreciating her sexuality. He uncharacteristically became a little weak in the knees. He brushed these thoughts aside as he said, "We're filling in more of the puzzle. Lance Alain is next in line after Lepordaxis. Connie, what have you found out about him?"

She was pleased that his look was more than just business, as a spark of electricity flashed between them.

"He was schooled at Lawrenceville Preparatory School in New Jersey, then went to Oxford undergraduate and then on to Harvard Law. A pretty smart guy, he was always at the top of his class. His father is Arthur Alain from one of the First Families of Virginia who came over in the first wave of colonists. He is a majority shareholder of the Gold Crowns Tobacco Company. The family goes all the way back to Northumberland, England. They own Castle Arthur there. Arthur claims to be a descendent of King Arthur. That myth comes from the Scythians' forced migration to northern England after their defeat by Rome in 168 CE. This looks like the connection to the arrows, scalping and mutilations we've been finding."

"Arthur has many powerful connections worldwide in banking, politics and business."

Connie went on, "Lance is in the family business. I wonder if and how he uses these connections?"

Godfrey pondered out loud, "Why would his son become involved in heroin? Doesn't the family have enough money and influence?"

David sounded like he knew people like that, "Some people can never have enough money and power."

TJ jumped in, "Maybe he's trying to outdo his father? I wonder if he has Oedipal issues? You know, kill the father and marry the mother."

Brad wanted to bring the team back to their primary focus. "OK we're starting to go way off field. Speculation and conjecture are fun but won't get us to our goal."

Connie was amused and looked at Brad. In a sing-song voice she asked, "Don't you like having fun, Brad?" She hoped he caught the double meaning. "You're just too serious and push us too hard."

She was almost begging as she gave him a sexy look, eyes dreamy.

"You ought to be a fly on the wall and watch us when you aren't here."

She was trying to make him jealous, learning that men can't avoid being trapped by the wily ways of a woman.

All smiled, as Brad dropped his head in defeat, slowly shaking it. He was a good sport and took the ribbing in stride. He also realized she was a smart, beautiful, sexy woman who he might want to get to know better.

CHAPTER 46

ALAIN MANSION
ALANTON
VIRGINIA BEACH, VIRGINIA
THREE DAYS LATER

B rad and TJ headed to Alanton. Brad pulled his car up to the gate at the given address. They couldn't see over the 8-foot-high stone walls with spear points on top. A voice told both Brad and TJ to look into the cameras on the stone walls on either side of the gate. As the gate opened, they pulled into the driveway.

"Nice fortress on the water." The house was out on a point in Alanton jutting into Linkhorn Bay near the narrows.

Alanton was one of the original King's Land Grants to be given to the early settlers. It had been a plantation. Some of the old 18th century plantation houses remain and are scattered around Virginia Beach. In Alanton, there was an original 19th century house now in private hands. It is said that Robert E. Lee attended a wedding there just before the Civil War broke out.

The stone house was well-built, and the property was bristling with surveillance cameras. Brad and TJ were sure there were also infrared and sound detectors. The stone wall with spear points on top covered not only the front but also the sides. The house was separated from the water by what appeared to be a moat. There was a large dock and boathouse with a forty-foot red Cigarette moored next to it.

Brad was mesmerized. "Virginia Beach sure looks different from the water. It's like a different city altogether."

"Yeah, the split personality never ceases to amaze me." TJ continued his appreciation of the area.

They approached the front door but before they could ring the bell it opened. A beautiful auburn beauty with hazel eyes wearing a light orchid yellow dress greeted them.

"Mr. Alain is expecting you." Her voice was soft and sultry.

They followed her past the large entryway decorated with Greek and Roman battle gear along with eastern European suits of armor and weapons.

TJ clicked his tongue as they continued further in. "He wants to leave no doubt who's in charge."

The hallway had openings on either side at the far end. A wall between them housed a life-sized, odd-looking stuffed horse. It was shorter and more muscular than horses Brad and TJ were used to seeing. It was built for speed and duration. It was in a full gallop. On its back was a warrior with leather armor, a bow and quiver over his shoulder and a lance to his side. Further down, on the back side of the saddle, was a leather shield. He wore a conical hat and shoes with toes curled up and facing back. There were what appeared to be scalps hanging down from the reins. A large fierce dog with a spiked collar was next to them, also at full stride. The look in the horse's, dog's and warrior's eyes was concentrated and fierce.

"You wouldn't want to tangle with that guy." Brad whispered to TJ with raised eyebrows.

The moment was broken by Lepordaxis. "Gentlemen, welcome." Lepordaxis was his usual jovial self but had a slight sneer at the corners of his mouth. "Come sit with me while we wait for Mr. Alain." He motioned for them to follow him with his broad muscular arm.

He led them to the large door that opened into an expansive living room with a wall of windows facing the water. There were alcoves in the opposite wall with books and weapons of all types from different ancient and medieval cultures. As they looked at the artifacts, Lance Alain entered the room. His stride and manor looked like a King leading a procession.

"I hope you enjoy my collection, all museum quality." Lance puffed out his chest as he boasted. "It took me quite a while to amass it. All objects are rare; some are one of a kind."

"Quite impressive." Brad couldn't contain his appreciation of the objects. "The workmanship on the weapons is exquisite."

TJ nodded his head up and down expressing his appreciation. "What do the horse, dog and rider in the entry hall represent?"

"That is a Scythian warrior on his steppe horse with his battle dog." Lance proceeded to give a bit of history of Scythians, steppe horses and battle dogs.

"They all look quite fierce." TJ's astonishment was genuine.

"Fiercest fighters ever," Lance bragged.

The auburn haired beauty brought out the drinks. Brad's drink was served first. She said, "Jamison 18 neat," as she placed the glass on a napkin in front of him. She then went over to TJ and said, "Grey Goose on the rocks." The glass was again placed on a napkin in front of TJ. She served Lepordaxis his Grey Goose straight, the same way. Finally, she went to Lance, "Middleton Barry Crockett 30-year-old Scotch." Her sultry voice softened the tense atmosphere.

Lance was smug, knowing he was in control of the situation. "I understand you gentlemen would like to partner with me." His tone was arrogant. His head was cocked to one side and slightly lowered while he looked through his eyebrows.

Brad looked over the edge of his glass at Lance, "How do we go about doing that?"

Lance rattled off the terms. "There will be a strict separation of territory. You will not be allowed to sell anything in Hampton Roads north or west. You can only sell in North Carolina south and west. If you stray from this, you will be killed. We will provide all the heroin you can sell and all the muscle you require. You can sell anything else you wish. But if you get too close to others in the drug trade who might want to expand to heroin or are already into heroin, I will see this as an affront to our deal. They, as well as you, will be taken out. This is non-negotiable and there is no compromise."

The air was thick with tension. Brad looked at TJ and they both nodded slowly in agreement. "I believe we can live with those terms." Brad's shoulder blades tightened. "How soon can we expect delivery?"

The words slid out of his mouth with a viper's wrath. He hated people like Lance, the privileged who only arrived at the top by chance of birth.

"We will start you with 20 kilos a week at 60 thousand dollars per kilo, beginning three weeks from now. I want to make sure you can move the weight." Lance was skeptical they could do that.

"We can do a lot more than that, but we want to be long-term partners, so we won't push." Brad wanted to be accommodating. The faster they got this deal going, the faster they'd see things from the inside.

"Good, Lepordaxis will contact you when he is sure you can fulfill your end." Lance's tone didn't hide the finality in it. He stood and left the room icy cold. Lepordaxis showed them to the door.

When he returned to the living room, Lance was already pouring each of them a 1957 Domaine de Pugay Armagnac into 1920s Lalique Art Deco snifters. He also pulled out a couple of Cuban Cohiba Behikes.

Almost laughing with delight, Lance was on a high. "We must celebrate this good fortune. After they secure the Southeast with our help, we'll take over their operation, expanding our business down the coast. In the meantime, having a new set of players in the field using different techniques will confuse the authorities further."

"Ha...ha...ha...," Lepordaxis produced one of his famous belly laughs, overjoyed at his good fortune.

Lance loved his Armagnac. He particularly liked it because most people in the US have never heard of or tasted good Armagnac. He was always sure to serve it at the end of the meal as the climax of extravagance, just as it was served at the finest restaurants in France.

"On a recent trip to Bordeaux to taste and purchase rare vintage wine, I decided to visit the nearby Labistide d' Armagnac. This is a charming small village in the heart of the Bas Armagnac area. Surrounding this town lie the small farm producers."

Lance continued to explain, "In addition to the Domaine de Pugay, I love the Domaine Lartigue 89, Ferme de Labouc 66, and Chateau de Ravgnan 71. I've had the vintners put away a barrique of each for me. Brandy continues to age in the barrel and stops once it is bottled. I have them send me 4 bottles each per year. I'm hoping this lasts my lifetime."

"Most people drink Cognac from Condom 100 miles north of

Armagnac. Even the finest Cognacs come from an easy-to-grow nondescript grape and are harsh and burn the throat because they are double distilled."

"Armagnac actually pre-dates Cognac by 150 years. It comes from five different varieties of grapes that I compare to instruments in an orchestra. It is single distilled and blended to make its taste, texture and aroma superior. Tasting it is like experiencing a magnificent symphony."

Lance liked to use analogies to the symphony which he loved. He was a patron of the Virginia Symphony, housed in the beautiful Chrysler Hall in downtown Norfolk, which put on first-class productions.

CHAPTER 47

Brad grabbed a cup of coffee and pulled a chair next to Connie at her workstation. He was drawn to her. Before he sat he instinctively put his hand on her shoulder. He didn't want to lead her on and knew it wouldn't be appropriate to have a relationship with a subordinate, but he couldn't help himself. "We've confirmed what we think is the top to Arthur Alain. I know that you have already been working on that." Brad continued to look deep into her eyes as he sat down in his chair wondering if what he sensed was correct. "Tell me what you've found out about him."

Connie fluttered her eyes and blushed as she looked at Brad. "Arthur Alain is a megalomaniac and a recluse. He seems to fashion himself after King Arthur, even named his sons Lancelot and Richard. Remember the Knights of the Round Table? Richard died in childbirth. His wife died soon thereafter, hit by a drunk driver. It's interesting that the driver's headless body showed up two days later in the Chesapeake Bay near Deltaville. This is a short drive from Richmond. The head was never found."

"He has a one-thousand-acre estate he calls Altai Stables in Loudoun County near Middleburg. He raises horses; thoroughbreds and steppe horses, and a rare breed of hunting dog. He used to first race his thoroughbreds at Colonial Downs just south of Richmond until it closed down. He now races at Laurel Race Track in Laurel, Maryland just north of DC and at Pimlico Race Track outside

Baltimore. If they won first place, he took them up the racing circuit. If they came in second or worse, they were never seen again. Rumor has it, he feeds the losers to his hunting dogs."

"His house and stables are built fortress-like. In fact, it looks like a castle." Connie brought up a satellite photo of the estate land and buildings. "Besides the main house, there are stables, kennels and what looks like barracks that can house up to one hundred men."

"We've caught some satellite footage of his troops practicing on steppe horses wearing the battle dress you described at Lance's house in Virginia Beach. The dogs follow closely astride. No modern weapons are used, only weapons of ancient Scythian design: bows, arrows, swords, lances."

"There is a white horse fence surrounding the property with a 50-foot grassy buffer, followed by at least 75-feet of forest. At the edge of the trees, is a 12-foot high double-wire fence with concertina wire at the top. Inside that, there is another fifty-foot-wide grassy buffer with a paved road next to it."

"DEA sent some recon out as hunters, and it appears the place is wired with infrared and sound detectors. They're not sure but think some areas might have land mines."

Brad was impressed. "This guy likes his privacy and is willing to enforce it."

Connie didn't let Brad go any further. She continued. "There are reports of hunters and hikers disappearing around the area, but nothing solid. The police can't make anything stick."

"The house has one hundred yards of open ground around it. There is a twenty-foot moat next to the house with only one road in. There is a drawbridge over the moat. The house is surrounded by a twenty-five-foot high wall with parapets. The turrets on the top of the wall at the corners are covered. DEA thinks they may house machine guns and rocket launchers strategically placed. This guy rarely leaves his fortress except to race his horses or to travel to his other houses and penthouse apartments."

"He often hangs out at the track, racing the horses he raises. There is an upcoming race of 1-year olds next weekend at Laurel Park. He has a horse named Prairie Fire in it."

"Great!" TJ was standing nearby and overheard this last bit of info and was excited at the prospect. "Let's go see the ponies run."

CHAPTER 48

"What a fine day for a horserace, right Boss?" TJ's enthusiasm was almost contagious. The air was warm with high humidity, standard for the beginning of the month.

"Too much horse shit for me." Brad turned his nose up, pinching it with his thumb and forefinger, while closing his eyes.

"Well, someone's got to be here to meet the old man, so let's have some fun."

TJ's excitement couldn't be lessened. He loved horse racing. His father used to take him to the track when he could and taught him all about the horses, but he rarely had a chance to go anymore and he missed it.

"Now, TJ, remember we're here to meet Arthur Alain not to bet on the horses. Keep focused." Brad, chided trying to bring TJ back to business.

"OK Boss, I'll try."

TJ was a little annoyed that Brad wanted to rain on his parade.

They went to the stables to look over the horses, hoping to bump into Arthur Alain.

As they came to Prairie Fire's stall the groomsman was doing his final brushing before fitting the saddle. Arthur and Lance were there supervising.

TJ was explaining loud enough for anyone within earshot to hear, "Brad hand simply means the height of a horse at the shoulders. Look at the haunches for speed. Look into his eyes. You can tell how alert the horse is and how seriously he takes race day."

"Brad, TJ is that you?" Lance was surprised to see them, taking a step back.

"Lance?" Brad feigned surprise as he raised his eyebrows, head back, arms down, palms open. "What are you doing here?"

"Prairie Fire is my father's horse. I try to accompany him when he races one of his stock for the first time. The competition and battle for first place is always exhilarating." Lance's face shone with pride. He squared his shoulders as he looked first at Brad and TJ and then at his father.

"Let me introduce you to my father, Arthur Alain." Lance had already discussed them with his father. "Father, these are the gentlemen I was telling you about, Brad Johnson and TJ Diggs, our new business partners."

Arthur looked a little surprised at his son's openness and introduction. "Pleased to meet you." Arthur was uncomfortable meeting them. His face and voice were not friendly.

"Let's invite them to the box for the race." Lance pushed his father's discomfort level to greater heights.

"Of course. We must get to know our new friends better." Arthur was seething and would deal with Lance later.

They walked to the clubhouse and took the elevator to the top floor. There was a short walk to the Alain Box in the center.

"This is a beautiful view of the track and in such comfort." TJ always admired what wealth could buy but also resented it.

"It appears you know something about horses TJ." Arthur flattered TJ trying to catch him off guard.

TJ impressed Arthur with his knowledge of horses and horse racing. This broke the ice, allowing the conversation to drift to business, but only for a moment. Then all followed Arthur's lead to watch the track.

Prairie Fire was loaded into the gate, the bell sounded. He was first out of the gate and around the track until the last stretch. "He's slowing and won't make it first to the finish. His lungs aren't big enough." Arthur was disappointed in his assessment.

"Second isn't bad." TJ tried to cajole Arthur as the race finished.

"First is the only way." Arthur was annoyed as he rose and left the box. Lance followed.

CHAPTER 49

After Brad called the meeting to order, Godfrey spoke first. "There is a small factory in the Alti Mountains producing Scythian armaments. Connie traced the financing back to Arthur Alain. I guess he didn't think he needed to cover his tracks there too carefully. Hopefully his arrogance will be his downfall."

As quickly as she could, Connie broke into the conversation, "I've traced all the financing for the Asian part of the operation to a shady character named Wu Jan." She didn't want to be bettered by anyone. Her breathing was shallow and rapid. "DEA there has confirmed it."

Her emotional excitement was palpable to all in the room.

She took in a deep breath trying to steady herself. "He's into many unlawful and quasi-lawful businesses. He runs prostitutes and drugs along with the manufacture and smuggling of knockoffs. He has legitimate restaurants where he launders his money. His vast wealth allows him to be connected to the highest echelons of government. Bribery, blackmail, kidnapping and murder help keep his businesses running smoothly. He is said to have museum quality Chinese antiques in his extensive collection."

Brad exhaled slowly. Raising his eyebrows then furrowing them while scrunching up his face. As he thought about this new information, he finally spoke. "It looks like we're not only going to take down Arthur

Alain and his son but also Wu Jan. The coordinated attack needed to destroy their operation will be complex. Looks like we'll have to make a two-pronged assault to get them all."

"We'll need to take Arthur and Lance alive to find out who in government, banking and business is on their payroll. This is clearly a very organized and far-reaching operation."

BOOK IV

THE TAKEDOWN

CHAPTER 1

Aside from Connie and Godfrey everyone in the crowded room was ex-military. Brad asked Admiral Mack to temporarily assign Task Force Alpha to Virginia Beach to help with the complex task of planning and executing the next mission. TDY in Virginia Beach is a plum assignment, so they were thrilled.

Although his team had been working with Task Force Alpha for the past 6 months, this was their first face-to-face meeting. Brad decided to introduce them to his team, including Jim Walters. Jim had become an integral part of the team, giving advice and consolation wherever needed. He made sure morale was always at the highest levels. The necessary chairs had already been added to the conference table and computer spaces around the room. Brad introduced himself and asked his team to do the same. When they were done, he turned to Stan who followed Brad's lead.

Brad kept seated after all introductions were made. He looked at each team with a smile. He could tell everyone in the room took their mission seriously and a bond between the two teams was cemented with this first face-to-face contact. They would continue to work well together.

"I've served with many teams and this one is one of the best I've had the honor to serve with. You've all done a magnificent job pinpointing the source of this blight upon us. And you've done it in record time!"

"Task Force Alpha, I had you temporarily stationed here so we can better work together to take out this scourge before it becomes any bigger. As you know, the murders of Congressmen, CEO's, lobbyists and powerful lawyers occurred before our heroin began showing up and have continued. We've discovered the connection. The Scythians, a 2,000-year-old brutal dynastic empire, have remerged and have built a well-funded, sophisticated network. We've found their tentacles attaching to politicians, bankers, businesses, the Ukraine and even further afield pulling them all into one cohesive mass. Doing this so rapidly is a testament to their agility and commitment." Admiral Mack lingered in the background. Now he stood and introduced himself after Brad gave him a nod.

"I'm Admiral Mack Davis. I've handpicked all of you because each of you are the top experts in your fields. As Brad said, you've done a spectacular job getting this far this fast. You've coalesced into an amazing, well-oiled machine. We now have one final task to accomplish. We have to destroy this empire."

"We could wait until the principles are in their castle and threaten to destroy it if they didn't surrender. If they refuse we could bomb it into rubble. That wouldn't guarantee their demise. In fact, we need to take Arthur and Lance alive and all their electronic information in order to untangle their web of power and destroy it completely."

"As always, I will be available to smooth out any obstacles in your path with any agency, military or civilian."

The room was charged with excitement. They were ready for this next phase.

CHAPTER 2

"Glad to see everyone is ready to move on after your week of well-deserved leave." Brad's tone was firm and confident. He stood tall, muscles tense and began to bark orders as a seasoned General would. His TOSH Team had never seen this side of him. Although he gave orders in the past, they seemed more like suggestions. His whole character was more relaxed then.

All recognized that this new direction was deadly serious. Men would die. Fewer if their information helped plug gaps and find weaknesses.

"Connie, I need you to track down the architectural plans for the Alain compound and how many fighters we'll face in addition to the kind of equipment they have."

"As for the rest of you, the Alains have a sophisticated intelligence network and it's up to you to track down all of the members. It is imperative you communicate only with the people you trust. This is classified Top Secret."

"Stan, I need the DEA to start surveillance on our targets and I'm putting you in charge. We need to know everything about their patterns, where they go and who they see."

"We're only going to have one chance at this folks so leave no stone unturned. We need all the intel we can get."

CHAPTER 3

HEADQUARTERS TOSH
JOINT EXPEDITIONARY FORCE LITTLE CREEK
VIRGINIA BEACH, VIRGINIA
FIVE DAYS LATER

Brad called a Team meeting. "I want to go over information about the Castle first. We need to have that in place before we try an easier snatch and grab of our targets." He felt it necessary for the Team to learn from Connie what she had so far.

"Thank you Brad." Her voice was becoming sultry. Jim noticed and decided he would talk to her about that. Connie found new excuses to interact with Brad because she felt the connection growing. She changed her perfume to Danger, the next Ciro perfume toward her goal. Surrender and Reflections were next in line.

Connie stood as she delivered her information. Her voice returned to normal.

"I was able to hack into the architect's office and find the plans for the Castle. I've also found the major contractors and hacked them too. I tried to hack the Alain's computers. They have private servers. Their firewalls are the most sophisticated I've ever encountered. I couldn't get in and neither could my friends over at NSA."

She motioned to Jim. "Will you please turn on the computer and the PowerPoint projector." The first slide showed the architectural renderings of the Castle. Each subsequent slide contained a satellite photo of what she was describing.

"It's laid out on the points of a compass with the entrance facing east.

It has been placed on the highest hill on the property. A 100-yard grass buffer surrounds the castle. There is a 20-foot-wide 10-foot-deep moat surrounding the Castle with 1 drawbridge allowing entry. There is a 15-foot rising slope from the moat to the walls. The walls are made of stone, 5-feet thick and 20-feet high. They're filled with concrete and rebar. A walkway, goes all the way around the top of the walls. This parapet has 4 square turrets, one at each corner. There are several round indentations on the parapet floor between turrets. It's not clear what these indentations hide. They drop down into the wall, but I can't find what's in them. The back has a large patio facing west. It lies 15-feet above the ground, which falls off. All the windows are bulletproof and have automatic electric metal shutters. It has 2 doors to the outside that have a larger metal door in front that can slide closed automatically. There are satellite dishes and a radar dome on the second highest hill on the property. Others are located on top of the Castle."

At each description Connie paused, looking around the room to make sure all were following her description. Hearing no question, she went on.

"There's also a barracks that can house up to 100 men. The stables allow 25 horses to be housed. There is also a kennel. Satellite pictures show Scythian cavalry riding steppe horses accompanied by Scythian battle dogs. The dress is what Brad and TJ described at Lance Alain's house in Alanton."

She put up a slide showing this from a website she found about Scythians.

"Some of the dirt from the moat was placed in a line as a backstop to the firing range. The rest of the dirt was used to raise the land from the moat to the walls to the 15-foot level."

"There is only one road in. It starts on State Road, SR 626. A large metal gate opens when known people come or go. It heads west through the woods and curves every 100-feet."

"A white horse fence with a 50-foot grassy buffer surrounds the property. This is followed at least 75-feet of woods. At the inner edge of the forest is a 12-foot-high electrified double-metal fence with concertina wire on top. This also surrounds the estate. Next is another 50-foot grassy buffer followed by a single-lane asphalt road. From there the forest resumes to the grass surrounding the Castle."

Connie was almost out of breath when she finished. She looked around the room ready to field questions. Since there were none she sat down.

The excitement in the room was subdued but perceptible. The aroma of sweat from tension percolated through the air.

David took in a deep breath and exhaled loudly. He didn't feel the need to stand. He decided not to, even though he now felt confident enough to be the focus of attention without problem. He was aware that Connie liked being in the limelight and surmised that was her reason for standing. He would give her that.

"I started doing research on the Scythians when it first became clear that they were involved in the gang deaths. The Scythian warriors were extremely fierce and fearless. Death in battle was their most heroic way to die. Their large battle dogs were also fierce and bred to fight lions and bears and of course, trained to attack the enemy. All mastiff breeds today come from them."

"Their women were also trained warriors, as fierce as the men. Don't let their gender fool you. When we storm the Castle be prepared to take them on as well."

"They used Israeli Tavors for the 'gang wars' but satellites show them using AR-15s at their firing range. They are probably using these because of their 30 round 5.56 mm magazines."

Ryan Thompson, sensing David was finished, started. He had pertinent ATF information to share.

"Yeah, the Tavors are great for close-quarters combat. They might use those inside the Castle but the AR-15s make more sense for field operations."

"I've checked with my connection at ATF. I'm concerned with what might be lurking in those circles on the walkways on top of the wall. The Norfolk Naval Shipyard in Portsmouth is the oldest and largest industrial facility owned by the Navy. It is one of the largest in the world. It specializes in overhauling, repairing and modernizing both ships and subs. As farfetched as this might seem, my buddy's come up with a possibility. Two Phalanx guns had been stolen from the Norfolk Naval shipyard in Portsmouth when an Aegis cruiser was in for overhaul about 9 years ago. There is no proof they're in the Castle but rumor points to them being there."

"The Phalanx is a radar-guided 20 mm M61 Vulcan Gatling gun and fires 50 rounds per second. It is used for close in surface and air threats. That is one awesome piece of firepower." Ryan paused having nothing else to add.

Evan Stahl felt it his turn to report. "The FBI has heard rumors of what sounds like small missiles, SAMs, being delivered to the Castle. Could these weapons be in the other circles?"

The silence in the room was deafening. You could hear a pin drop when Fred Sierles spoke. "Boy is this guy well-protected. The DEA has gone up against some powerful drug lords, but this is like taking out the Kingpin on his own turf. We've never tried anything like this. If we had to, we'd just blow the whole place up. Since we can't because we have to capture the 2 main principles alive, this is going to be a costly venture."

Brad stood shaking his head. "If they have all those armaments, we're going up against an unbelievably powerful opponent. We'll have to plan very carefully."

He, as well as everyone in the room, sat in silence in deep thought as they each contemplated the problems they faced.

TJ spoke up. "Remember we also have to take out Wu Jan and his organization at the same time."

Offering some relief, Lou Reynolds decided to make his point.

"I was in the Coast Guard before going to Customs. I'm now Customs liaison to DEA. The Coast Guard, DEA and Customs are allowed to operate internationally. We have limits in country, in that we're only able to act as consultants to a sovereign nation. They have to invite us in. They use their own crew for the action. We can advise and actively help if necessary."

Godfrey wasn't too happy about this.

"I've worked with the DEA in Hong Kong. They're first rate. But how can we be sure the agents in Vietnam, Hong Kong and China won't sell us out and warn Wu of our plans? He would be sure to warn the Alains and our element of surprise will be blown. Surprise is one of the few assets we have on our side."

Stan Ferguson, ASAC Baltimore DEA responded.

"Just as we carefully vet our agents, they also carefully vet theirs. Everyone in this business knows how dangerous it is. One leak can get agents killed. No one anywhere wants that hanging over his head. We can trust them to be discreet."

Brad took the floor to summarize.

"All right. We have to attack the Castle at Altai Stables with surprise. We need to capture Arthur and Lance Alain alive in order to take down their entire network, so we can't bomb it. Finding their computers is a must. Alain Stables is set on 1000 acres with fencing surrounding it. There are probably sound sensors in the woods near the fence to alert them of intrusion from the road or anywhere else on the property. Rumor has it, there might be mine fields. The Castle is probably protected by as many as 100 well-trained troops. Most are battle hardened, coming from Eastern Ukraine. They could use horses as cavalry with battle dogs in the woods. If they are as well-trained as Scythians, they would be excellent shots on horseback. They would enter battle with a taste for it and would be willing to die fighting, seeing this as a hero's death."

"It is possible they have 1 or 2 Phalanx guns and SAM missiles. It wouldn't surprise me if they had RPGs and shoulder-fired missiles. They probably have machine guns in the turrets. Their soldiers will be armed with AR-15's with 30 round magazines."

"We will have to breach the moat after crossing 100 yards of open field and blow open the Castle at the front and back patio doors, so we can enter. Close-quarter combat will ensue. They will have an advantage there by having Israeli Tavors. Hand-to-hand combat will most likely follow."

"At the same time, we will have to coordinate with the Coast Guard, Customs and DEA to take out Wu and his Asian network."

"Since we anticipate 100 enemy soldiers we will need 300 of our own men. A 3:1 advantage is standard for this type of operation. See how many you might be able to deliver from your respective agencies. This is no ordinary operation. We're going to need helicopter firepower and Bradley Fighting vehicles."

"Stan, I'm putting you in charge of Logistics—acquisition, storage and distribution of resources. TJ and I will be in charge of Tactics—arrangement of troops and equipment to gain an advantage." He defined these term for the benefit of those in the room without military training.

"I'll give you a week to make plans. Everyone here is available for consultation. I advise you to talk with each other to get full input. Since an assault on the Castle will be a very difficult task, see if you can come up with an easier way to get our targets."

Brad explained things very carefully. Some on the Team were not familiar with creating a battle plan. He found that people who don't fully understand are hesitant to ask questions. They think this would make them look inadequate. He wanted to make sure that everyone grasped all the information being discussed. This made him a good teacher and great leader.

CHAPTER 4

The combined Team were all seated at the conference table with their morning Joe, bagels and breakfast pastries lovingly supplied by Jim. As Brad took his seat at the head of the table, Jim brought him his usual, coffee with cream and a croissant. The room became silent. The anticipation of moving forward on their objective had some almost salivating even before breakfast.

Brad stretched out his arms and arched his back, exhaling slowly relieving some of his muscle tension. "Now let's see where we are."

"Stan, what has the DEA come up with?"

Eager to present his information, he shuffled some papers in front of him. He picked up the top sheet. "We have been able to track both Arthur and Lance. Arthur stays mostly at the Castle but does make forays to the outside periodically. There is no pattern except when he goes to his Richmond house twice a week. He usually starts at 10AM and returns at 4PM. He likes to drive himself in his Diamond White Metallic Mercedes S 550 convertible coup with Silk Beige/Espresso Brown leather interior. The license plate says, 'ALTI.'"

Even though the car's details weren't necessary Stan wished he could afford to drive a car like that. He paused and looked up from the papers. He had an impish smile curling his lips. "With the top down, it must make him feel like he is riding one of his steppe horses."

All in the room smiled recognizing Arthur was as eccentric as they come.

Brad said, "No doubt. Go on."

Stan picked up the next paper in front of him. "Lance will be easier to grab. He leaves his house every Monday through Friday at 9AM sharp to go to the Inlet Gym on West Great Neck Road near Shore Drive. He drives a Rosso Settantanni Red Ferrari 812 Superfast. It is a V12 with 800hp. This is the highest performance, most powerful Ferrari ever built." Envy showed on his face.

TJ let out a soft whistle and raised an eyebrow. "That will be a hard car to catch if we have to chase him."

There was silence in the room until Brad brought everyone out of their fantasies about the car.

"We ought to focus on setting up a snatch and grab on Arthur after he leaves the Castle and before he hits the first intersection. We should do the same for Lance."

Stan followed up, "We'll keep satellite surveillance on both men. DEA will get two drones in the air the morning of the snatch. One will observe each car as they leave their houses. We can have agents in a car come in behind them and one stopped blocking the road in front of them. This should be easy."

Ryan questioned, "As a Marine for 16 years and having served in both Afghanistan and Iraq on the front lines, I wonder about the radar at the Castle. Won't it pick up the drone and provide a warning to Arthur?"

"We'll have them high enough and far enough away from the house so even if radar sees them they won't think it's focused on either of them," Stan said assuredly.

Brad was pleased that his Team was efficient and always thinking ahead. "Great, lets follow them for the rest of the week. If they continue to follow their patterns, we can set up the takedown for a Tuesday after we're set. It should be relatively easy to nab Lance. I don't see any way for him to warn Arthur. If we don't get Arthur, we'll have a problem. He'll retreat into his Castle fortress."

"TJ, take Evan, Charlie and Fred with you to get Lance. I want you to lead that Team." Brad knew TJ loved cars and getting close to the Ferrari would be a bonus for him.

"Evan, I don't want to use anyone we can't vet. Since you have been with the FBI for a long time pick two agents you trust to accompany you and TJ. Have them meet you here at TOSH at 7AM the Tuesday of Operation day. Don't give them any other information until then."

"Stan, I want you, Ryan and Lou to accompany me to get Arthur. We'll go up to Quantico on the Monday night before we put Plan A into effect. Pick two of your agents you trust. We'll have them stay overnight and meet us at 6AM to go over the plan."

"Don't you think we should add couple of agents to each Team?" Stan had been part of many operations like this. He knew that even the best operations don't always go as planned.

"No," Brad answered. "I realize there is a risk to any operation. I want to keep our Team numbers, our conferences and transit times to a minimum. We want to reduce any potential leak warning our targets of the operation. I only want to use three cars for the same reason. One in front and two in back of the targets."

Connie felt left out, having nothing to add, but she did like being a part of this exciting adventure. "Now, let's work on Plan B," Brad said as he concluded the meeting.

CHAPTER 5

TOSH Headquarters was a mess. Jim did all he could to keep some semblance of order. Blackboards and corkboards were brought in for each phase of the operation.

For logistics, one corkboard summarized the areas split into procurement, transport and storage of equipment. Another listed what was needed in both men and equipment. Housing 300 men from different disciplines and training them at the same site to become a cohesive unit was paramount.

Flip charts were filled out and tacked to the corkboards. All had the chance of viewing the latest information and commenting on it before they were updated. Adjustments were made to refine what they had. The old charts were discarded and burned along with all the paper used in the office. When all agreed with the final version, the information was entered onto the blackboard.

All appreciated Jim keeping them supplied with coffee and food that never became boring. They usually worked late into the night and started early in the morning. Brad wanted his Team to quit at 10PM but that rarely happened. He wanted his people to be rested and clearheaded, knowing fatigue caused mistakes. Sometimes he had to kick his people out and insist they leave to refresh themselves. Even though they to a person griped, they were secretly grateful for it.

Brad requisitioned an empty building near TOSH. He had it fitted with beds, showers and a lounge with a TV. He wanted his people to be close and comfortable. He didn't want anyone on his Team, both TOSH and Task Force Alpha, leaving the Base. He was concerned that someone might slip-up and accidentally provide information to a spy.

TJ and Brad had the task of formulating the Tactics necessary to complete their assignment. As with Logistics there were several flip charts listing the necessary equipment and how it would be deployed. The Team was also able to continually view and comment on it.

Brad called a meeting to consolidate and share what they had so far.

"We're going to need 4 M2 BFVs, Bradley Fighting Vehicles. These require 3 personnel: a commander, a gunner and a driver. These will fit a 6 man fully equipped infantry squad inside and bring them past the fence, through the woods, across the 100-yards of grass and hopefully to the moat. They are armor protected to withstand small arms fire, artillery and small mines. They have six firing ports on each side for the infantry, which are rarely used during battles. These will be essential for our purposes. They also house TOW—**T**ube-launched, **O**ptically tracked, **W**ire guided missiles and Stinger missiles."

"In addition, we'll need 4 HUMVEEs, High Mobility Multipurpose Wheeled Vehicles, which carry the TOW BGM-71H Bunker Buster. They will be faster and more agile than the Bradleys. We're going to need those to break through the doors in order to gain entrance to the Castle."

Stan said, "We need a company, about 300 men, if they have 100. The DEA has 5 Rapid Response Teams (RRTs). One is stationed in Afghanistan, so we can't include it. The other four are stationed in Stafford, Virginia. We'll be able to tap 3. These each consist of a 6-man squad. That's 18 men. They are supported by 21 part-time Special Support Teams (SSTs). Each has a 6-man squad. We can only count on 14. All are trained to handle the weaponry we'll use. That's 84 men who have all trained together. The DEA Academy is located at Quantico."

Evan Stahl was next to speak. "The FBI has 8 tactical operators on the Hostage Rescue Team (HRT). We will be able to tap 6. They are also located at the FBI Academy in Quantico."

Ryan Thompson didn't want to be left out. "ATF has 5 Special Response Teams (SRT) located across the US. We can count on the one from Washington, DC. The ATF Academy is located in North Las Vegas. They each have 130 full-and part-time members. These consist of field operators, a canine division, tactical medics and negotiators. We can count on 28 field operators. Do you think we'll need the medics or dogs?"

TJ replied, "I don't think so. We currently have 136 men. Let's go through the plan first and then see what we're lacking."

Brad waited for all the reports to be delivered. He had an impish smile on his face that no one on the Team had seen before. He unconsciously looked over at Connie with a gleam in his eye, while trying to contain himself with the news he was about to deliver.

"I'm going to have to give a little history lesson before I solve the problem of topping off our men and equipment."

"The Federal Jurisdiction Act of 1789 allowed military support to civilian authorities. This is a common law or state law allowing a sheriff or other law enforcement offices to draft any able-bodied men to assist him to keep the peace and to pursue and arrest a felon. This allowed the summoning of a militia for military purposes and was used later for the North to fight the South."

"Rutherford B. Hayes (R) oversaw the end of reconstruction in the South. He lost the presidential election in popular votes to Samuel J. Tilden (D). 20 disputed Southern votes in the Electoral College gave Hayes the presidency in the Compromise of 1877. The Democrats would agree to the assignment of those votes to Hayes if he would end the military occupation of the South and end the North's meddling in Southern politics. This became the Posse Comitatus Act of 1878. The military could no longer act in civilian matters."

"Statutory exceptions have been made to this since. Ten USC 371-380 Congressional laws and Annual DOD Authorization Acts allow the military to support Law Enforcement Agencies. The National Guard can help states and remain under state control in a number of situations like riots and disasters. The President has the power to put down domestic violence. The Drug Exemption allows the Secretary of Defense to make equipment and troops who operate them available in drug enforcement."

"The Coast Guard is exempt from the Posse Comitatus Act in peacetime and the Navy may assist in the seizure of drug vessels."

Brad paused for effect and looked around the room to make sure everyone was following him. He was chomping at the bit to get to the next piece of information.

"To add to our shortfall of men and equipment we are going to borrow 20 SEALs from active duty units here in Virginia Beach. We are also going to bring onboard half a dozen former SEALs that TJ and I have worked with in the past. They should all be helpful in any situation that arises."

"That gives us 162 troops. We can also count on 150 Marines and their equipment from Quantico. We'll include their medics and a MASH unit. We won't need the ATF Medics. We may face dogs, but I don't think ATF dogs would be right for this operation."

TJ had an ear-to-ear grin on his face when Brad finished. He spoke up, "Now that we have the manpower and equipment we need a place to house and train our troops. We also need a call sign."

Stan cut in thinking out loud, "I thought SEALs and Marines weren't allowed to work on domestic soil? You've opened my eyes to that change. We've worked with the military before and most of our Special Teams are former military, so they'll fit in just fine." He seemed to be answering his own question and just sat back realizing this was a remarkable twist. He originally had some doubts about the success of the operation, especially if they had to assault the Castle. After hearing the manpower roster, those doubts disappeared.

He went on, "Since the FBI, DEA and Marines are already trained or housed at Quantico we'll go there to muster and train for this operation. ATF and SEALs can join us there."

"Great." Brad enjoyed working with top-notch people and these were as good as they get. "I want to have this plan in place and ready to go in case we don't get our targets out in the open."

Before sitting down Brad again looked over at Connie, who noticed and smiled seductively, rolling her tongue across her lips. She offered, "How about Roman for a call sign. They defeated the Scythians once. Why not again?"

CHAPTER 6

TJ and Brad had been going over tactics. When they put up a new page from the flip chart on the corkboard, all gathered around. Brad began, "As you can see we have a number of obstacles to overcome. The horse fence and forest are no problem. The first problem is the electrified double fence that circumvents the property. We've had some of our SEALs run intel on the target. There's a 50' interior buffer between it and the next set of trees. This contains a road. Two security patrols each in a HUMVEE run the loop varying their intervals between 30 to 60 minutes in opposite directions. We are going to muster our troops on SR 626 out of sight and sound of the objective."

"We will make a three-pronged assault. One will be up the Castle entrance road. The other two will be at the four and the eight positions from them. When we hit zero hour, our forward team will take out the patrols. They will notify the side positions to begin the assault with infantry. They will cut through each fence but keep the electricity flowing. If it stops their security will be warned of trouble. Once through they will proceed forward still as a single column, fanning out once they are discovered. A Bradley and HUMVEE will follow the column and take the lead after contact. The center position will hold at the entrance until the sides start to receive fire. This position with 2 Bradleys and 2

HUMVEEs will then blow the heavy metal gate and proceed forward."

"Each Bradley will house 6 marine infantry, plus a commander, a gunner and a driver and the HUMVEE's 2 marines. These will proceed forward of our infantry. They will use their TOWs to knock out the towers, Phalanx guns if they have them and whatever else is in the circles on the parapet. As they gain ground they will have to use their Bunker Busters to blow a couple of holes in the wall at the Castle entrance and patio entrance. We don't think the Alains will be located there."

"I want our infantry to proceed to the edge of the woods. They will stay there and use them for cover. When we have sufficiently suppressed enemy fire, they can proceed to the Castle. The Bradleys in the center will pull narrow pontoon bridges behind them. These will be available to cross the moat if needed."

"I am going to add 2 UH-1Y HUEY-VENOM helicopters to transport 6 SEALs each with TJ in one and me in the other. Once inside both SEAL teams will converge and locate the Alains and their computers. The rest of the assault teams will mop up any remaining resistance and provide backup if necessary."

"Once fire is sufficiently suppressed, we will bring my HUEY to the Castle entrance. We will fast rope down. TJ's Team will go to the patio after a HUMVEE blows open the steel door with a Bunker Buster in order to get inside. The front door will be opened during the main assault by a Bunker Buster allowing access to the Castle."

"If either helicopter is taken out before depositing their Teams, we'll have to rely on the pontoons and their soldiers to get across the moat."

"Connie provided us with plans of the Castle. It shows housing for 25 attendants and what appears to be a subterranean command bunker below the center of the Castle. That will be our target. The Alains will most likely be located there."

TJ added another bit of information. "I went on recon with an old buddy. We found a couple of locals who worked on that bunker. The 3-foot-thick walls are reinforced concrete with a 2-inch-thick steel outer layer. It is self-contained and has enough supplies to last 9 men for a month."

Brad continued. "Unreal. These guys are really prepared. They are the quintessential survivalists. It is going to be tough. I want our assault Teams to get their supplies and train at Quantico until we're ready to go. I don't want them to know our objective until we're ready to launch."

Brad asked if there were any questions or comments. No one came forward with any. All were inside their heads going over the plans. He slowly walked over to the blackboard and drew out the plans as discussed.

CHAPTER 7

The aroma of coffee perfumed the air. Jim was already there and helped serve his usual breakfast goodies. He liked being needed and was pleased to be a part of the action. This was way better than any retirement he could imagine. Evan milled around with his FBI buddies making small talk.

TJ found his place at the head of the table. "OK guys, let's get this started." With outstretched hands he motioned for everyone to sit. Evan took his place beside him. "Jim please turn on the PowerPoint projector."

The first slide showed a road map of Virginia Beach from Independence Boulevard east to the oceanfront and south to Laskin Road.

TJ shined a red laser pointer on the map. "We're here," as he pointed to TOSH HQ in the Joint Expeditionary Force Little Creek Base. "Here's our route east on Shore Drive to North Great Neck Road, where we turn south. We'll turn east on Mill Dam Road and follow the curve as it heads south, then turn east onto Woodhouse Road. I'll enlarge the map now."

Jim put on the next slide showing all the streets in Alanton.

"We're going to turn north on Alanton Drive and go to the end. Evan in the lead car will turn left onto North Alanton Drive and turn 180 degrees and pull off to the side. I will take one of you, pointing to the agent with the bushy orange handlebar mustache, and stop 100 yards before the turnoff. When Lance comes out of Alfred Circle and turns onto Alanton Drive, I want Evan's cars to pull up behind him at opposite 45-degree angles. Yosemite Sam and I will block the road in front of him and take him down."

The agent said sarcastically, "Gee, I haven't been called that before. How did you know?"

TJ responded, "Your nickname preceded you," as he turned to Evan and winked.

All in the room broke out in laughter breaking the solemn mood.

Yosemite Sam asked, "Will he be able to drive around us?"

"No," TJ answered. "There are trees and large bushes, as well as drainage ditches, on both sides of the road. He has nowhere to go but into our waiting arms."

Another agent asked, "How will we know when he leaves the house?"

TJ also had that covered. "DEA has a drone in the air. They'll let us know when they see red."

"OK guys, we leave at 0800 and will be in place by 0820. Relax until then."

CHAPTER 8

The small conference room seemed crowded, even though there were only six people in it. Stan introduced Brad to his people.

Brad started off. "Thanks for agreeing to be a part of this operation. It should be relatively easy. We have been trying to take down the organization behind this new heroin hitting the streets that you've been chasing. We've traced it to the two principals at the top of the chain. We have a Team in Virginia Beach that will get the second in command this morning."

"Our Team is going after the leader, Arthur Alain. He has two houses. He visits the one in Richmond every Tuesday and Thursday, leaving around 1000 hours, from his more permanent residence in Loudoun County. That one is a Castle fortress. We're trying to avoid going after him there. We'll hopefully get him as he drives to Richmond this morning."

"The Castle is north of Middleburg on SR 626. This is a small country road. I want Stan and his two cars and three agents to be just north of the Castle. I'll be with Ryan in a car, south of the Castle at a turn that has large trees and drainage ditches on both sides. I don't want him to be able to go off road. As soon as he leaves the Castle, Stan, I want you to follow. I'll block the road at the stop site. You pull in from behind. When he is cornered, we'll pull him from his car and place him in mine."

CHAPTER 9

"Is everyone in place?" TJ called over the com.

"Affirmative Chief, sitting and waiting to pounce," Evan answered.

One car passed TJ just before 0900. It wasn't the mark.

The Drone operator came on at 0900 sharp. "Red Riding Hood is in the woods."

TJ moved his car across Alanton Drive, blocking it.

Evan replied, "The wolf is in pursuit of Red Riding Hood," as his cars roared to life. They quickly pulled in behind the Ferrari as it came to a stop in front of TJ.

TJ ran over to the driver's side and trained his gun on the driver. Evan took the other side. And with all guns now aimed at the driver, the driver opened the door and put his hands up. TJ grabbed him by the jacket and pulled him from the car.

"Who are you?" TJ asked in surprise letting him go.

"Hey, don't shoot," answered the driver with a smile the Cheshire cat would be proud of. "I'm Ivan Chernovski."

"Where's Lance?" TJ shouted, anger in his voice.

"Oh, he had to go out of town for a couple of days. He wanted me to take his car in for service."

TJ found the cell phone in Ivan's pocket and pushed him toward the officers, so they could take him into custody before he had a chance to alert Arthur or Lance and quickly contacted Brad.

CHAPTER 10

"Brad," TJ yelled into the radio. "We didn't get him! The guy in the car was a plant. I have a bad feeling they're on to us. I hope you have better luck."

"Shit!" Brad replied, then called over the com to his team, "I just got word from TJ there was a substitute in the car. It's up to us guys!"

"Is everyone in place?"

"Roger," Stan's voice was determined. "I wonder how they got a heads-up? We were so careful."

"We don't know that yet. It could have been a coincidence." Brad was hopeful. "Now we have to wait."

At 1001 the drone operator reported in, "The horse has left the barn."

Brad's eyes narrowed to slits with conviction. All were ready.

Stan reported, "We see him and we're closing in." He pulled his car behind the white Mercedes and trapped him in front of Brad.

Everyone jumped out of their cars and ran toward the Mercedes. The driver got out of the car casually. It wasn't Arthur.

CHAPTER 11

TJ took his Team to an awaiting Navy flight from Oceana to Quantico for the next and more dangerous phase.

Seated at the conference table were the 3 SEALs who would lead each prong of the three-pronged assault as well as the two UH-1Y HUEY—VENOM pilots along with Brad and TJ. The 7 men in the room were all business and the air almost vibrated with adrenalin.

"We have a difficult task in front of us," Brad began.

On the board was an outline of the plan and TJ remained at the screen with the satellite image and pointed to each item as Brad ran through the plan in great detail. When he got to the end he looked over his men, "Let's go get 'em!"

"We will muster on SR 626 after State Police block it off to all traffic from north and south. Our left flank will be designated Remus, our right flank Romulus, the center column She Wolf. Romulus and She Wolf will advance to a forward position north of the front gate. Remus will come in from the South to their forward position south of the front gate. When our advance scouts take out their perimeter guards, Romulus, Remus and She Wolf will advance to their entry points. The infantry of Romulus and Remus will cut through the fence and maintain electrical integrity by attaching a wire to each side of the fence. They will advance as a single column in case there are any land mines or IEDs. Once the first shots are fired, they will fan out. Their Bradley and HUMVEE will start in their rear and then advance forward."

"At the same time, She Wolf will blow the main gate and proceed up the road. The Bradleys will lead the column, followed by the HUMVEEs and the infantry. I want to get these HUMVEEs to the open field so they can use a Bunker Buster to open the main entry and patio door."

Romulus Team Leader "Rat" Jones said, "The forest looks pretty dense and probably contains some large trees. The Bradleys can knock down small ones but might get blocked by larger ones."

TJ had already thought through this problem and said, "The gunners can take out any small trees that block their way. The Infantry will carry HMX and use it to blast out the bigger trees if necessary."

Brad went on, grateful that his men were already thinking through unforeseen problems. "Using the woods as cover, the infantry will remain in the woods at their junction with the open field. The Bradleys will use their TOWs to take out the corner towers and whatever might be hidden in the circles on the parapets between them. The infantry can advance once we control the firefight."

"As things subside we'll bring in the HUEYs. They will be designated Legion I and II. I'll be in Legion I with a 6-man SEAL Team. We'll fast rope down to the front entry and go inside once a HUMVEE blows open the front door with a Bunker Buster. TJ will be in Legion II with his 6-man SEAL Team. His HUEY will have to wait for a HUMVEE to launch a TOW to blow open the steel door and gain entry. They'll fast rope down to the patio and go inside."

"All teams will converge on the Castle and mop up any resistance. No one except Legions I and II will enter the Castle unless we call for it."

As he finished, Brad took in a deep breath and exhaled slowly. The focus of the group was intense.

"Any questions or comments?"

"Juice" Davis, Remus Team Leader asked, "Why don't we blow holes in the Castle sides to acquire more entry points?"

Brad was quick to respond. "We believe the Alains will be in their command bunker in the center of the Castle. In case they aren't we don't want to increase the risk of their death if we have multiple entry points."

'Juice' questioned, concern in his voice, "How are we going to destroy the two towers on the far corners of the Castle? They might continue to be a problem, especially for TJ and Legion II trying to go through the back patio."

TJ handled this question. "We want Romulus and Remus to flank the Castle sides once the front towers are put out of commission. They can use their remaining TOWs to do the job."

All nodded their heads in agreement with the plan. Brad concluded the meeting, glad a mock Castle site had been constructed at Quantico. The Teams had been training there for the past week.

"It's fortunate that we will get there before the leaves fall. That will give us some cover. We need to get into position before sunrise. Make sure everyone has night-vision goggles."

Brad didn't want Plan B personnel to know about Plan A the prior morning. For security sake he wanted to keep it compartmentalized. If it went well he could always call off Plan B. If it didn't he wanted to be ready to go with it. That was now a moot point.

CHAPTER 12

At 0500 hours Brad and TJ surveyed their Teams from a HUMVEE as they rode up and down SR 626.

When they were sure all were in place, they moved to their helicopter staging area. The forward scouts had gone in 90 minutes earlier to take out the Castle HUMVEE security patrols and open the fences.

Brad said over his com at 0600 hours, "Commence Operation Roman, Plan B."

All units moved from their staging areas to their attack positions and reported in.

"Romulus in position and moving in."

"Remus in position and moving in."

"She Wolf in position and awaiting fire to move in."

As planned, the infantry moved forward in a single column to minimize injury from potential land mines. About 50 yards in they began receiving mortar fire from the Castle. The Bradleys and HUMVEEs made their entrance, moving to the front of the columns and proceeded forward. She Wolf blew the main gate and advanced up the road. Brad and TJ launched their HUEYs and watched the battle unfold.

The infantry fanned out in the woods, thankful there were no mines. She Wolf was not so lucky. Their lead Bradley hit a large land mine 50 yards in, which blew a hole in it through its thick armor killing all on board.

'Warf' Taggert, She Wolf's second in command, took control in the remaining Bradley. He reported in. He was convinced there were more road mines. "How did they know when to arm the mine? It couldn't always be active."

TJ came back, "We ran across radio armed IEDs in Afghanistan switched on when needed. They were set in series with infrared detonators. When the beam was broken it went off. Send a squad up the road to check for them. It will be quicker to go up the road if you can."

"Wilco," Warf replied, "What a bunch of clever bastards."

Remus was making good headway until machine guns, heavy mortar fire and RPGs from the Castle towers and parapets made them dig in.

'Juice' said, "We're going to have to bring up the HUMVEE to take out our tower. Until then we can't move."

At that moment a hole in the floor of the Castle parapet opened. A small missile emerged and fired at the HUMVEE destroying it. Two Phalanx guns were next to appear on both sides of the front wall. Each took aim at Romulus, Remus, and She Wolf. They were no match for the high-tech weapon which took aim at the remaining Bradleys and HUMVEEs. As their ammunition ran out, the doors to the barn on the right of the battlefield opened. 20 cavalry in Scythian battle dress came galloping out along with their battle dogs and headed for the woods where Romulus was dug in.

'Rat' was astonished at the sight. "What the hell? We never had to deal with anything like this in battle."

Brad had considered this but thought it too unlikely to occur. "Remember we have them outnumbered. Keep picking them off. Use pistols and knives on the dogs."

The air was thick with the smell of cordite, blood and growling. The sound of bullets whizzing, gunpowder exploding, rockets flying filled the battle zone.

Remus was doing better, not having to deal with cavalry and dogs. 'Juice' reported, "Our HUMVEE has been destroyed and our Bradley is hit, but capable of moving." Shouting orders, he said, "Move the Bradley to the edge of the woods and fire a TOW at that front tower."

As the tower exploded in a fireball, stone rained down on the field and into the moat. A sigh of relief was audible rising from the forest.

"Great! Now go around the side and take out the back tower. Don't go too far. I don't want anymore missiles to take you out. Once that's done bring your Bradley to the front wall and offload your infantry. They will provide cover as the rest of the infantry comes out of the woods."

Romulus had taken heavy casualties but was able to prevail against the horsemen and dogs. Their HUMVEE and Bradley were destroyed. 'Rat' had disappointment and solace in his voice as he reported, "We can't take out the tower on our side. Our equipment has been destroyed."

Brad ordered, "Join up with She Wolf. Help them get their remaining Bradley into position to take out that tower with their TOW. Then go after that last tower. We've been in the air watching the action. We nearly got taken out by a SAM. Luckily our countermeasures worked. We're going to have to destroy their radar and the rest of their missiles. We'll monitor via our drone circling above. Our Team back at TOSH HQ has also been monitoring. Your Team was heroic."

'Warf' reported in. "She Wolf will move our remaining Bradley to the right flank and team up with Romulus to take out the towers on our side. We still have one functional HUMVEE. We're moving it into position to blow the main entry."

With a whoosh the Bunker Buster left its launch vehicle heading straight for the drawbridge. A very loud explosion erupted upon impact. Wood splinters and stone were strewn about the gaping hole half filling the moat.

"Nice work!" Brad's voice was optimistic. He knew the operation wasn't going to be easy. He already lost too many men and welcomed that sight. "Now get around the right flank and take out that last tower. They're taking too heavy a toll on us."

"Roger boss." Warf snapped back.

Legion I and II both had 50 cal machine guns. Brad ordered, "TJ come in low over the trees and pop up. Get those radar domes on the back side of the property. We'll do the same for the radar domes on the Castle. We don't want any more SAMs shooting up."

Both radar sites were gone in a flash.

Brad was a Boy Scout and always wanted to come to the rescue. He signaled to all he was coming in. He told TJ to hang back until the last tower was destroyed. As Legion I came in over the trees the right tower exploded with a sharp crack, smoke billowing up.

"Cover us, we're going to the front gate." TOSH HQ watched as Legion I fast roped down to the ground, picking off stragglers as they presented themselves.

Romulus, accompanied by She Wolf, couldn't get to the last parapet before their Bradley was put out of action. Fortunately, the occupants were able to exit the vehicle before it was destroyed.

TJ and Legion II came in over the trees in the back of the Castle. "We are going to have to use our Bunker Buster to take out that last tower. That leaves us no way to get through the patio door." His voice reflected his disappointment and deep concern about not being able to accomplish his mission. They fired their Bunker Buster at the tower and watched it explode into rubble.

Brad's attitude changed, "I have a surprise for you TJ, the drone watching our mission is a Predator. I didn't want to use it earlier because of the close combat conditions."

He switched focus, "Predator Team, use your Bunker Buster and blow that patio door."

"Roger, Legion I." That sweet voice from the Predator was a gift from Heaven. It was as though the gods were watching and could be called on when needed.

The steel patio door shattered into pieces along with stone.

TJ responded excited and greatly relieved. "We're heading in, Boss!" His Team fast roped down to what was left of the back wall and patio and entered the Castle. "We'll mop up here and meet you at the rendezvous point in the center of the Castle. It never ceases to amaze me that you always pull a trick out of your ass!"

"Roger that. Always pays to think 3 steps ahead and then go one step further. Be careful. I don't want us to get caught in a crossfire." Brad came back, urgency in his voice.

TJ alerted Brad. "Hey, there are women here with Tavors. Watch your step."

"Remember, Scythian women are also trained to fight. They can be as deadly as the men." Brad warned as he pointed his weapon at a beautiful petite woman in a short black skirt and matching shirt with a white apron holding a Tavor. He squeezed the trigger before she could get off a shot.

The Teams met in the center. "I want two from each Team to accompany me and TJ down the stairs. The rest of you stay up here and take out anything that threatens."

Brad picked the 4 SEALs that he and TJ had the most interaction with in the past. They all thought as one.

Brad led the Team down the spiral staircase pausing at the bottom. He was relieved there was no resistance. "Tex, bring the HMX and place it around the hinges and lock. The rest of you go back up and brace yourselves." Tex was one of the best breachers the SEALs ever had. Too little explosive and the door would be untouched. Too much explosive and the entire Team could be taken out.

He followed Tex up the staircase making sure all were set and said, "Tex, blow it."

A loud blast echoed within the Castle as the walls shook. Even with fingers in their ears, the ringing within their heads ensued. Allowing the dust to settle and for the Team to regain their equilibrium, he proceeded back down the stairs to the open maw of the control room. The six occupants put up a valiant fight wounding two SEALs. Brad was nicked in the arm.

"Where are the Alains? Surely this is where they would hide." Brad was perplexed. "Tex, you and Murph grab the computers and any info you can find. We'll get a team in here to go over the place with a fine-tooth comb later. The rest of you go back up and search the Castle for the Alains, dead or alive. I hope we didn't take them out during the assault."

They searched the castle over the rest of that day and the following day. All the computers and files were rounded up, but they discovered the computers were wiped clean, their hard drives destroyed.

CHAPTER 13

Brad and TJ entered the room. Their Team was already there, standing and clapping in a hero's welcome. All stared at the bandage on Brad's left arm with concern about his wound.

Noticing, Brad said, "It's only a scratch. Please sit. Operation Roman cost us more than we anticipated. We lost 38 good men with another 92 wounded. We were able to take down the heroin smuggling enterprise. DEA and State police raided the bakeries and fish markets closing them down. The Inner and Outer Banks have been cleaned up. At the same time the Coast Guard and DEA in conjunction with local authorities raided the production, packaging and transport sites."

"Unfortunately, Wu Jan has enough money and connections to wiggle out of any jail time."

"The computers were wiped clean and destroyed. We got nothing out of them."

"Our biggest failure was not capturing the Alains. We have no idea where they are. They were not in the Castle nor were they at their respective homes in Richmond and Virginia Beach."

"The DEA will be able to confiscate all of their property including the Gold Crowns Tobacco Company. The haul will be substantial."

"I congratulate you all for a job well done. Now go home and take a two-week vacation. You've earned it."

With that the Team members got up and milled around talking about their victory and speculating about what had happened to the Alains.

Connie came over to Brad and began stroking his injured arm in a way only a woman could do. She was wearing her coveted perfume Surrender in anticipation of what she hoped would happen.

Brad looked deeply into her sky-blue eyes and said, "Let's get out of here."

He put her into his car with a gleam in his eye and raced to his houseboat. Upon entering they clawed off one another's clothing and collapsed onto the bed where they made passionate love for the next three hours. When the hormones subsided, they grabbed a couple of beers and watched the sun set over Broad Bay.

Brad thought, "This is as good as it gets." As Connie cuddled up against him.

EPILOGUE

Hidden to everybody, the Alains had a small chamber below their Operation's Room. As the Castle was attacked with no hope of repelling the assault, they moved a secret slab in the floor out of sight of the people in the room. It led down to a small bullet-shaped rail car. They climbed in and rapidly traveled the mile to the end. Climbing out and up a staircase, they moved another slab hidden in the ceiling. This concealed the exit which when closed, looked like the rest of the floor of an old barn.

They climbed into a waiting Mercedes and drove out. Traveling to West Virginia, they hopped aboard their Lear Jet and headed out of the country.

They didn't forget to take the two gold crowns and skull cap wine cup with them.

Arthur was already beginning to formulate plans for their next attempt to bring the Scythians to world conquest.

AUTHOR'S NOTE

This novel is historical fiction based, in part, on fact. Any resemblance to actual persons living or dead or places is purely coincidental. The history of the Scythians from their origins to King Arthur is fact. They are the basis of the Amazon legend and possibly dragons from the early Middle Ages. Their brutality was legendary. Scalping, skinning hands and backs and using gilded skull caps of their enemies for wine cups is fact. From that point on it becomes fiction emanating from my wild imagination. The original Scythian battle, the siege of Prax, is based on fact but is my fictional account of how it would have happened.

I became fascinated by the Scythians after I saw their gold artifacts, which included the two garnet-laced gold crowns and their symbolic plaque. These are unique and are 2,000 years old. Their ancestors were the first people to domesticate the horse 5,000 years ago, first to breed and train Mastiff dogs to fight lions and bears, in addition to going into battle with them, the first to use cavalry in battle and the first people to start and continue the Silk Road for 1,000 years. Because of these and other accomplishments, they became not only powerful but also wealthy.

Scythian gold can be seen at the Museum of Archeology and the Museum of Historical Treasures of Ukraine in Kiev, Ukraine. They can also be seen at the Hermitage Museum in St. Petersburg, Russia.

The Silk Road exists even today, although it travels through different routes. The Mongol hoard from the 13th century led by Genghis Khan followed the tradition of the Scythians and conquered even more territory than they did. The Cossacks followed similar traditions although their connection to the Scythians is probably fiction. The Chinese are currently building a modern Navy to protect their trade routes calling it the Belt Road Initiative.

The Scythian Myth of return to power after the return of the two gold crowns with rubies to their rightful heirs is fiction. I wondered what it would be like to have modern Scythians trying to take over the world today. They would certainly be much more powerful and organized than the modern scourge of Islamic terrorism.

The colonial history of Virginia and Hampton Roads is fact. Since I grew up in Miami Beach, I had no idea that Virginia had such an important role in Colonial America. It all seemed to blend together with the other colonies. Virginia is the birthplace of English America starting with the first landing of the Jamestown colonists at the northern tip of Virginia Beach. This area is now First Landing State Park. It is a jewel in the city. Hampton Roads at the entrance of the Chesapeake Bay is one of the world's largest natural harbors. The huge military presence and shipbuilding and repair industry is fact, as well as the location of most SEAL teams. The Virginia Beach oceanfront has been a draw since the Roaring Twenties and continues to this day. The resurrection of the Cavalier Hotel and upgrade of the oceanfront tourist area is on the way to propelling Virginia Beach to again be a top tourist destination.

All of the descriptions of the attractions and history of the surrounding cities of Hampton Roads: Norfolk, Chesapeake, Portsmouth, Hampton, Newport News, including Williamsburg, Jamestown and Yorktown is fact, as is its ideal weather.

There are four distinct seasons. Each a mirror of life with its temperature peaks and valleys. A crescendo from the prior and decrescendo to the next. It allows one to experience the spiral in the life of all things. This gives one a perspective of one's place in the Universe. Both humbling and expansive at the same time.

Stephen Holder's character is loosely based on Michael Teller of TK Asian Antiquities with his permission. Missie, the waitress at Pirate's Cove Marina, is loosely based on Missie Smith of Nags Head with her permission. All other characters are fictional and any resemblance to people living or dead is a coincidence. All places are real except the Meet Market, Ebony Bar, Castle, Lance's house in Alanton and Brad and TJ's houses. Any resemblance to real places is a coincidence. The action that takes at the real establishments is fantasy.

Maps of the Hampton Roads area and Virginia can be seen at Google Maps to give a perspective to the geography of this special area and where the action takes place.

The history of pirates and smuggling to Hampton Roads and to the Outer Banks of North Carolina is fact. Heroin is the up and coming current drug of choice. The history of opium growth, production, refinement and transport is fact. The discovery of morphine and heroin is fact, as well as big pharma's role of its spread.

The addition of fentanyl makes it even more deadly. According to the Virginia Board of Medicine 54.6% of heroin deaths in Virginia in 2016 were due to Fentanyl.

The Opium Museum in the Golden Triangle is real and should be reproduced around the United States and the world to educate our youth of its dangers. All other dangerous illegal drugs should be added to it.

David's entire story about his grandfather leaving the small farming village in Ukraine, walking to Bremen and baking bread for passage to America is true. It is my paternal grandfather's story of how we got here. I asked him about where we came from before that. Oral family history traces us back to the Spanish Inquisition. We left there for Turkey, went to Poland and ended up in the Ukraine with I'm sure many stops in between.

As you can see from the descriptions of meals, I am a foodie. The restaurants and menus are real as are the descriptions of the food. They represent some of the wonderful varied dining in this area as well as other areas.

My wife and I have lived in Virginia Beach for the past 40 plus years and raised our two daughters here. We saw the potential and watched it grow from an outdated place to one of growing sophistication.

I am a private practice psychiatrist who loves travel, cooking and woodworking. My appreciation for Japanese culture, as well as Shintoism has led me to the art of bonsai and collection of suisecki stones and scholar rocks. This has also led me to landscaping my yard as an informal Asian garden.

I have always been attracted to aboriginal cultures and nature. Perhaps this is why as an Army psychiatrist at Fort Sill, OK 1972 to 1974 I was adopted by the Kiowa. I still visit and connect to my Indian family and the uniqueness of their culture.

The Hampton Roads area is often overlooked because most people aren't aware of its historic significance and what it currently has to offer. I hope this fictional tale of Scythian rebirth and heroin smuggling expands the awareness of this fantastic area.